Everybody But Us
by Ben Rose

Published By
Breaking Rules Publishing

Soft Cover – 10680
Published by Breaking Rules Publishing
St Petersburg, Florida
www.breakingrulespublishing.com

DEDICATION:

PALS

Author's Note:

I have traveled extensively through our nation over my lifetime, which has afforded me a chance meet a great many people of all types—both in my travels and in the rooms of recovery. That said, there are aspects of my own person in certain characters. I am a cis-gendered ally, and I have experience with certain topics, including addiction, recovery, abuse, and homelessness.

I heard several great stories over a few evenings and asked to include them as part of a novel.

As usual, the stipulation was that I change the names and never reveal who the people are. The characters in this novel are based on amalgamations of various people. The novel is inspired by their stories.

Ben R.

Chapter 1

"Let's get one thing straight. I'm not."—Anonymous

I have to face the events of my early life. I don't have a choice. There's not much else to do, except drink coffee and write, while I wait for my girlfriend. Kenzie's finishing her intake forms for law school. My Al-Anon sponsor, Branca, suggested that I write my story. Branca knows the score, a fact that irks me. Lately, any little irritation flips my bitch switch. Both Branca and Kenzie have noticed.

Branca cares. She wouldn't help me so much if she didn't.

"That shit's been eating you up like a cancer. Best to write it down, get it out."

It's been six years since I was kicked out of my home for being bisexual. There were plenty of times I never expected to make it this far; most of the first year, in fact. I wasn't supposed to make it. I was supposed to realize how dangerous the outside world was for unmarried girls and crawl back home like a whipped puppy, accepting male domination and denouncing my sexual identity. I came close a few times.

If this dude on the raised platform would end his amateurish cover of Green Day's "Good Riddance," I could get on with my story. I admit, the lyrics fit my mood; but, his cover sucks!

The last six years have been rough, not the time of my life. I didn't start out in a good place, and only recently has life gotten any better. Maybe Branca's right. Maybe writing about it will help.

* * *

My story started in Central Florida, between 2010 and 2011, when I was fifteen years old. I was subjected to traumas meant to erase my existence as a bisexual. My parents raised me and my four siblings in a Baptist sect that believed conversion therapy could "cure" my deviant sexuality. For months, I sat on a hard, wooden pew and endured painful sessions with the elders and a pastor. I was told: the world rejected my sexuality; I was the abomination we had heard about in Sunday school; I was the only gay person in the church; and, I'd contract HIV and AIDS.

But, it didn't stop with those hurtful talk-therapy sessions. The elders ordered me held down while they lashed my butt with their rods of correction. They forced me to watch clips on a screen of girls holding hands, hugging, and having sex. While I watched, the elders hit me, slapped me, and screamed in my ears. I was supposed to associate those images with the pain. I was supposed to—once and for all—turn into a submissive, straight woman.

Before you get to thinking that I'm exaggerating, or that this sort of abuse would never be allowed, let me set you straight. I was raised in a home where, from an early age, I was placed on a blanket and left there. By an early age, I mean six-months-old. Every so often, my mother would move my hand or foot off the blanket and hit the offending limb with a light stick or a wooden spoon. Not hard, but enough to draw tears. In this way, she taught me to stay put unless she permitted me to move.

Some of my earliest visual memories are the colorful samplers my mother stitched and hung on the wall. "Perfect Obedience Leads To Perfect Faith", "Pray and Obey", "Stay Sweet", and "His Judgement Cometh And That Right Soon."

Once my blonde mane of hair was long enough, they taught me how to braid it into a severe up-do. I never wore pants, as that was deemed inappropriate for females. Skirts and dresses were ankle-length, sleeves were long, and necklines were high. The possibility of tempting males was too great, and any temptation was the fault of the female.

My life consisted of chores, homeschooling, more chores,

and church. I played guitar and sang in the choir, but that was the single enjoyment life offered. By eighteen, I was expected to meet a boy; he'd court me, we'd get married, and I'd squeeze out a quiver full of children. Being bisexual didn't fit into that plan.

The conversion therapy didn't work. Not that the elders and my parents didn't give it their best shot.

One day, on the cusp of my fifteenth year, my mother came into the kitchen where I was washing the dishes. "Come to the table. I need to talk with you."

I dried my hands and sat. My heartbeat increased, and my throat constricted. I feared that my internet searches had been discovered, although I was careful to erase the search history.

"You have been attending camps for a number of years now." She referenced the quarterly gatherings where children from our church took placement tests for homeschooling. "Has The Holy Spirit led you to feel anything for a certain boy? Your father said a number of boys asked about courting you, but we hoped you may be drawn toward one in particular."

I lowered my eyes, blushed, and shook my head.

"It's alright, Destiny. You may speak freely. You are almost a woman. Is there no boy?"

"No, Mother. I struggle, though. I know that the elders, and Pastor Ruby, believe that it is wrong for boys to like boys and girls to like girls...I mean, in that way."

"It is an abomination. I should hope no child of mine would sin so."

I blushed harder. I couldn't find the words to explain, and she didn't give me a chance.

My mother's face looked as if someone held a small turd under her nose. "You are vile and disgusting. Better that you had never been born. Your father will hear of this and put an end to it."

She stormed out of the kitchen. My stomach knotted into a ball, and I mustered all of my strength to hold back the tears.

That evening, I was called into my father's den. I realized, by the look in his eyes and the strap on his desk, that he and my mother had spoken.

"Destiny, is this true what I hear?"

I looked down, silent and ashamed.

"Look at me, you filthy rag!" He forced my face up with his left hand. "No child of mine will bring such shame on my household." His right hand raised and cocked. "Tell me you are not a lesbian. Say it, damn you!"

I convulsed with sobs. His back hand across my face was followed by a forceful, forward slap. My head rocked and blood trickled from my lower lip, which began to swell.

"The church has ways of purging the sin of homosexuality. You leave me with no choice. Now, bend over my desk. I will rebuke that sin here and now."

I froze, and my father forced me over his mahogany desk. He held me with his left hand and undid my skirt with the right. The air conditioner chilled my skin, followed by flames licking at my exposed cheeks and thighs as he whipped me with his heavy strap. My howls of agony urged him onward.

"Confess your sins, you disgusting spawn of demons. How dare you behave this way. You bring shame on your mother and me. Better that you had never born." The words were punctuated with full-force licks from the strap.

The following day, while my siblings were homeschooled, I was marched into the church. They forced me to sit on a hard plastic chair despite my bruised flesh. Pastor Ruby turned on a TV screen.

"Young lady, you are not to move from that chair. If you do, you will receive the rod of correction and be tied there."

My eyes widened when an image appeared on the screen of two naked models kissing. The taller and bustier of the two lifted her partner, who wrapped her legs around the taller model's hips. My nether region warmed, growing moist; I tried to breathe normal so as to appear unaffected. Without warning, two elders dumped a cooler of ice water over my head and drenched me.

I shrieked. "Why did you..."

Pastor Ruby slapped my face. "Look at this mess! Get down

on your knees and clean it up!" He shoved me onto the floor.

As I dried the floor, Elder Barlow started reading from a book. The text involved a female engaging in cunnilingus. I stopped cleaning and looked up in shock. Elder Hale pulled me back by my hair and kicked me in my bruised bottom.

The torture continued for three hours before they sent me home. My mother made me sit in the broom closet with the door closed while my siblings enjoyed lunch.

That night, my father again asked me if I had any interest in one of the boys from the church. I couldn't answer him, and he whipped me with the belt again.

The punishments would've been worse than what I received at church and home if the adults knew what I secretly watched on the Internet. My parents frequently left for the whole day, or entire weekends, to attend conferences. As the eldest female child, I was required to babysit.

Once I knew my parents weren't returning for a while, I'd sneak into my father's study and look up the word "lesbian" on the computer. The images I found aroused me. Afterward, I would rush to have a shower before bedtime. That was the sole place I could release my urges. Had I been caught, as stated, the tortures would have been more severe.

My brother, Derek, had once been caught looking at a magazine in bed and touching himself. Father duct taped Derek's hands together for two days, denied him food, and forced him to drink from a garden hose. Derek was eleven at the time.

The sessions had an effect. I began to doubt myself. Could I go to Heaven, despite being gay? The question haunted me. In church, in my home-school lessons, and in my family, being gay was rarely discussed; when it was mentioned, it was described with contempt as being the worst sin—comparable to murder, rape, and child molestation. I didn't want to experience the pain of eternity in Hell. I didn't want to be despised by everyone around me.

However, my feelings never changed. I listened as the girls in Sunday school giggled about boys. Meanwhile, I pictured the girls without clothes on, kissing me. After a few months of torture, my father gave up on me.

I was sent to church early one morning. When I arrived, the pastor and two elders were waiting in the worship hall. Pastor Ruby called me to the altar.

"Destiny Marie Wilbury," he shouted, his oily and hypnotic voice full of accentuated syllables and drawn-out vowels, "you are nothing more than a vile sinner. This church, with all its love and care for your soul, has tried to drive the demons of homosexuality from you. Now, I realize that the most drastic measures are required to cast out these demons."

He pushed me over the altar and pulled up my skirt, tucking the hem over the waistband. I tried wrenching away, but he held me there as I sobbed. "Homosexuality is an abomination before The Lord. Before this morning is over, we will cast your perversion out in The Holy Name of Jesus."

Elder Barlow and Elder Hale stood beside me, one on either side, and removed their belts. They took turns lashing my butt and thighs. I screamed and begged, but they kept hitting me.

"I...I'm sorry. I try not to think about things, but I can't help it. I can't help who I am attracted to. Please! No more, sirs. Please, no. I'll marry who you say."

Pastor Ruby threw me to the floor. "You evil girl. The darkness is in you, and you refuse to repent. Be gone, filthy sinner. You will not make the house of The Lord unclean with the noxious odor of your sins any longer. Go! Get you hence and pray that you are not consumed by hellfire on this very day."

I fixed my skirt and hobbled out of the church. My lower body was on fire, and I could barely breathe. As if that was not enough, I returned home to find a backpack on the porch filled with my clothes. My father stood on the porch with his arms crossed. He kicked the backpack toward me.

"This family knows you not. If you can ever see the grave error of your ways and obey the ways of The Lord with full subservience, you might be allowed to return. If not, you are a filthy rag. Now get away from my home!" my father roared.

I grabbed the pack and ran as best I could. A quarter-mile later, I entered the parking lot of a local convenience store. I didn't know where to go. I had no friends outside of church. Instead, I leaned against a concrete staircase and prayed.

I had been leaning on the steps of the store for a half hour, rubbing my bruised and welted legs, when four men approached. My heart started up a speed-metal, percussion solo. I tried walking away, but the men surrounded me; the stench of sweat, malt liquor, and tobacco filled my nostrils.

Fear sent me soaring toward flight. Fight wasn't an option for females in my home or my church. I was no mind reader, but the men's intentions were clear. My chest constricted. Sweat soaked my blouse. Breathing grew difficult and thinking was impossible. Backing up to escape landed me in the arms of one of the men. He pushed me forward while cuffing my butt. My head lightened, as if I might pass out.

I'd been warned, as had all the girls in my Sunday school classes, what happened in the secular world if one chose to disobey the edicts of the church elders and one's father. I hadn't obeyed, and here I was. As I willed myself to pray for divine intervention, fate took me by the hand.

Three older teenagers appeared, two girls and a boy. They leaned against a gunmetal-gray Chevy van, waiting for their gas tank to fill. The boy, his left hand resting on the roof, pushed off from the van and approached the men who surrounded me.

"Time to shove off, guys. She doesn't look happy with your attention." His bass voice was even, matter of fact, but with the slightest edge of ice.

One of the men stepped forward. "Piss off, dirt bag!" The growled insult hung in the air.

The lanky boy gave a slight toss of his braided, red mane and looked down at the man. "Wrong answer, Jack. I said blow!"

"And I said fu—"

The man's words were cut short as the sole of a Nike

connected with his crotch. He fell to his knees, grunting. The tall teen tapped the man across the rear of the head with his foot, stepping back to take an open stance.

The other three men turned, their mottled faces becoming ashen. My ears filled with the sound of boots retreating across pavement. I bolted in the opposite direction, searching for somewhere to hide.

The man on the ground rose, clutched himself, and scrambled away. The teenaged male stood with arms akimbo, observing the hasty retreat. He turned in my direction. I backed up, cowering against the steps to the mini-mart. My stomach knotted, and I fought the urge to pee.

"Hey. You OK? Sorry I had to do that, but you can't reason with their kind. Name's Rory." The rich, bass voice was soothing and pleasant, not like my father's. "You need a ride somewhere?"

One of two girls remained against the van, watching the action while rubbing her distended belly. The other focused on filling the gas tank. I stood, my chest tightening; I willed myself not to cry. With another silent prayer came a sense of calm. I approached the threesome with my eyes lowered.

"Th...thank you for your help, sir," I sniffled, rubbing my eyes with my sleeve. "My name's Destiny Wilbury."

Rory's head snapped toward me, eyes registering shock. He recovered quickly and helped the girl finish pumping gas.

The older girl waddled over, holding her back. She was carrying low. "Where you heading? We'll give you a lift."

"I...I'm not sure. I...I can't go home. Could...could you give me five dollars for the bus?"

"We can give you a ride to a friend's house or something."

"I don't have any friends to stay with. I just...I need to go away."

The corners of her mouth turned downward. Rory walked over to join her. "Um, baby, hold up a sec." He held up a hand, gazing at me with gentle eyes. I started backing away, and he squatted down to even our heights. "Are you related to Donald James Wilbury? Like in Wilbury Properties and

Wilbury Used Cars?"

My breath caught, and I turned to run. Before I got to the store, I bent over and threw up. Something wet spread below, and I realized I had peed myself.

Rory loped over, and the pregnant girl waddled behind him. He put a hand on my back, waving away a few concerned bystanders.

"It's OK. My sister just has the flu." He informed them before whispering, "You're safe, Destiny. I'm not one of them. I swear it."

I tried catching my breath as tears blinded me. The pregnant girl looked at us, confused and concerned. "Her father's a name in this area. He's part of the church run by Ruby. You know, like the book we read in Fam-Soc last year," Rory explained, pronouncing it fam sōsh.

"Jesus Christ! That just says it all!" The girl helped me stand. Her dulcet, twangy voice was soothing. "Pleased to meet'cha, Destiny. My name's Sheila. You should go in and clean up. We'll wait for ya."

Sheila backed off and stood next to Rory, her curly, auburn hair cascading in every direction. She wore jeans with rips at the knees and a green maternity blouse. They seemed kind and helpful so I did what they said, hoping for the best.

Chapter 2

In the ladies' room, I locked the door and tried to collect myself. I washed at the sink as best I could, putting on a fresh pair of underpants from my backpack. I threw my vomit-covered blouse in the trash and changed into a clean one. My skirt was fine, except for a few splatters which I washed away. I returned ten minutes later, ready to face my saviors.

Sheila and Rory waited, as they'd promised. The girl who had been pumping gas joined them. Sheila smiled at me and waved.

"That's a really pretty blouse. I like the pastels and the open, airy cut of the sleeves. Did you sew this?" Sheila reached out to touch my sleeve, but I drew back.

"My mother sewed it for me last year." I twisted the toe of my right shoe into the ground, fighting back fresh tears.

Rory walked toward the van, looking back over his shoulder. "We'll take you wherever you want. As far as New Jersey, anyway, which is where we're heading."

I followed, figuring that I had no choice. I couldn't stay put, but maybe these three would let me stay with them. "You know my parents? And Pastor Ruby?"

Sheila nodded. "I've read one of Ruby's books. So has Rory."

"Can we hold up a minute? I need a drink. Anyone else?" The third girl piped up before dashing back to the store.

Rory shook his head, laughing. "She's such a flight case."

Sheila also laughed. "That's why we love her." She turned back to me. "So having read that douche canoe's book, and his belief in women as baby machines, there are a lot of things you could've done to piss off your family. What happened?"

I stood by the van, staring holes into the asphalt. "I can't expect you to understand, ma'am. They say I'm the worst kind of sinner."

Sheila gave me a steady gaze that I couldn't meet. "Try me. I'm pretty sharp."

Taking a deep breath, I forced myself to speak. "I'm attracted to girls. I've met a few boys I like, but not like-like. I mean, not in that way...not yet." I blushed.

Sheila's eyebrows traveled up her forehead. Her mouth opened, then snapped shut. She shook her head and backed up a step, tilting to look at Rory from across the van. She returned her gaze toward me, and the sweet voice turned razor sharp. "Run that by me again? Did you just say you were kicked out of your home because you're bisexual?"

"Yes, ma'am. I don't have any friends outside of the church, either. The church members want nothing to do with me anymore. I'm a sinner of the worst kind." Staring a hole in my shoes, I continued. "My father won't have that sort of sin in his home. I've tried praying, tried changing."

"Your father's an asshole! So was mine. To Hell with 'em." She glared, and I backed away. Better to avoid people when they were angry. After a moment, the gentleness returned to Sheila's voice. "Like Rory said, we're heading back to college. Rory's the daddy of my baby. And that blue-haired minx heading back here is my girlfriend, Jeanie. Trust me, honey, we totally understand."

I studied Jeanie as she approached. Her sky-blue hair was level with her jaw-line and styled into spikes on top. A notch over five feet tall, she wore red shorts and a purple t-shirt that accentuated her perky breasts and slender hips. She flitted toward us and wrapped her thin arms around Rory's side; so petite, her head only reached his stomach. Jeanie reached up and stroked the end of Rory's thick, red braid. His full beard and mustache twitched, his eyes exuding compassion. All the smiling unsettled me, especially from Rory. I feared that I might vomit again.

"I need a ride, sir, ma'am. I'll go wherever you're going." I gave in and started sobbing again. "I can't give you money for gas or anything, sir. I don't have any." One part of my mind sent signals not to take the ride, but another part reasoned that I had no other options.

Jeanie opened a plastic bag and extracted three bottles of Pepsi for us and an Aquafina for Sheila. We climbed into the van, and they made a space for my backpack. While Rory pulled off, Sheila reclined in the passenger seat, and Jeanie sat beside me on the leather-covered bench behind them. The other seats were folded into the floor to make room for a sleeping space behind the luggage.

"Next stop, South Carolina," Rory said.

Jeanie turned to face me, cross-legged. "Not that I care who you love, but why not just tell your folks you liked one of the boys? I mean, that'd hold them off until you're eighteen and free. At least they'd allow you to stay at home until then."

I shook my head. "It wouldn't work, ma'am. If I mentioned a boy, we couldn't be together unless we were courting. Even if my father allowed that now, once we got married I'd have to obey my husband."

Jeanie rolled her eyes. "Get the hell out! Do people still behave that way? That shit is positively Middle Ages!"

I took a sip of Pepsi, the icy liquid soothing my stomach. "You have to understand my church, ma'am. That's how I was raised."

Jeanie frowned. "Why? They sound loony tunes."

My heart raced from fear of saying the wrong thing. The irritation radiating from the girls was palpable. "I'm the oldest of five kids, and mother's pregnant with twins. You've read Pastor Ruby's teachings." Cars whizzed by as I stared out the window.

Sheila said, "Rory and I have, not sure Jeanie has. Her church bastardizes the teachings of Christ and promotes child abuse, like mine did. I told you about that one time."

Jeanie reached over to pat my hand. I flinched and said, "I'm sorry. I'm making you mad. I'll get out and walk."

Sheila shook her head, causing her hair to fly around. "I'm

not pissed at you, honey. The church you got kicked out of is full of shit! I understand them just fine. Don't agree with them, though. I study child psychology."

I winced, shrinking down in my seat. My eyes stung as I blinked back tears. "I'm sorry, ma'am. I didn't mean to upset you."

"It's Sheila. Calling me ma'am is like putting an elevator in an outhouse. It don't belong." She relaxed, sipping her water. "The crap your pastor teaches just gets in my craw. It's abusive—and, girl, I've seen enough abuse for one lifetime."

"I'm sorry. I've been getting in trouble with my family and the church forever." I shifted in my seat, uncomfortable with my sore butt and legs. "I'm weird. Other girls at church get to giggling about boys while I'm thinking about how pretty some of the girls in my Sunday school class are. But, I never told anyone. Mother brought up boys, and I couldn't tell her the whole truth."

"Nothing weird about liking girls. I do." Jeanie shrugged.

"The Bible teaches that sexual desire is sinful outside of marriage, and marriage is strictly between a male and female." I jolted when Jeanie cut loose with a boisterous laugh.

"Give me a damned break, chick! Sexual desire is natural at any age. Once hormones kick in, the desire is constant. You can fight it, but it'll happen anyway. And why should love be limited? We're not actually male or female, you know? We're all both—or we start out that way." Jeanie shook her head, amused.

Confusion clouded my mind. "What do you mean that we're all both male and female? The Lord created a male named Adam. And then he created a female named Eve from Adam's rib. There's a difference in how the sexes look."

"Jeanie's right, honey. I studied it in first year biology. After the sperm meets the egg, we're neither male nor female. The testis cords or cortical cords are undeciphered for a time. Who's to say that a female can't have romantic feelings for another female?" Sheila explained with patience, adding, "If it's acceptable for males and females to fall in love, why can't one girl love another?"

My temples throbbed. Sheila might have been speaking in tongues for all I understood. She continued with, "At our essence, we're all females and males. The romantic attachments of our souls could form prior to our gender determination."

I pondered things for a few minutes. "My homeschooling texts don't say that. Adam was created with male parts. Eve was created with female parts. I know that much."

Sheila raised her eyebrows and tilted her head. "I gather your education began and ended with The Bible. That sucks. Even if we only go by Genesis, I'm still not wrong." She spread her hands apart, palms upturned. "Let's say that Adam and Eve were created as already mature adults. I won't argue that point, either way. But when they had Cain, Abel, and Seth—among others—their children still had a point where they were neither male nor female. That's a biological fact. Even if The Lord predetermined the outcome, there was a short duration where biological laws took place. That being so, my argument is valid that humans might develop a love instinct at the moment of conception."

My eyes ached as I tried not to cry again. "Th...that's really confusing."

"Still isn't wrong." Sheila turned back to put in another CD.

Jeanie's eyes softened, and she reached out to pat my shoulder. I let her inch closer and stroke my cheek. It had been years since anyone had comforted me in that way, but this was different. Jeanie's touch set off an odd sensation in my lower belly which I had experienced a few times while sneaking onto the Internet.

She reached into a cooler and handed me a bottle of apple juice. Rory cleared his throat. "I couldn't imagine having to hide who I am. My parents were both conceived at Woodstock. They raised me to be full of love for everyone. Hell, I even feel bad for that guy I beat up—even though he didn't leave me much choice."

Hot tears splashed down my cheeks as I watched the

broken lines on the highway blur into one solid form. "What's Woodstock?"

"Woodstock's a hamlet in upstate New York. There was a famous music festival near there that was named after the town."

We rode in silence for a while as Bob Dylan sang through the speakers. I was scared, but my eyes drooped. I snapped back to consciousness every few minutes and drifted again. My slumber and thoughts were interrupted by the succulent smell of barbecuing meat as Rory pulled into a gravel parking lot. Saliva wetted my mouth and my nostrils twitched as my stomach growled and gurgled.

"I need food and a bathroom. Anyone else hungry?" Rory leaned over to kiss Sheila. "I bet they have plain rolls here and can probably make some meat without the sauce." Rory turned and winked at Jeanie before climbing out of the van, grabbing his bag, and having a good stretch. "Destiny, order whatever you want. My treat."

The bathrooms were crude, pine outhouses set back about three hundred feet from the tables. The narrow space buzzed with fat, black flies. The decaying stench of excrement caused me to gag until I choked up acidic bile. I conquered the ordeal and washed my hands in the icy flow from a nearby water pump.

I rejoined the others by a dark, stained picnic table. The restaurant was located outside, amongst trees and dirt. A central building was made of bricks, scrap wood, and discarded tin with a chimney that belched smoke and delicious smells of cooking meat and sauces.

As the four of us sat down, a girl—no more than twelve years old—scampered over. She had bare feet and wore a dress made of patches. Her skin was reddish brown and her hair was done up in dozens of tiny cornrows shooting out in every direction. She smiled, revealing bright white teeth.

"Can I get y'all a cold drink? We has pork, ribs, or hot links. You get bread or beans with that." She pronounced pork as poke in her lilting voice.

Rory placed the orders. "I'd like the ribs with beans and a

Coke. The lady with blue hair will have the same. The other lady would like some pork with no sauce and some dry bread. If you have a bottle of water, she prefers that. If not, a Sprite will do. What are you having, Destiny?"

"The same as you, please, sir." I watched the girl skitter away after I ordered.

"I'm not a knight. Call me Rory, or bro, or dude—anything but sir." He chuckled. "You were homeschooled? Did you ever question what you were told?"

Jeanie's eyes caught mine, and a sense of exhilaration tensed my insides. I blushed and looked down at the table. "I started reading at five. Sure, I asked a few times about differences between the Bible and science. I'd read such things in the newspaper. I'm not dumb. I got my lessons quicker than other kids. Elder Barlow told me that a lot of scientists were put here by The Devil to keep us separated from The Divine One. That applies to people who support homosexuality and women's rights, as well."

Sheila's eyes narrowed once more, as did Jeanie's. I stared at my shoes, waiting to be rebuked for my words.

"Honey," Sheila reached out and lifted my chin, "you will not get beaten, ok? I was raised in rural Kentucky. My maternal grandparents were Jesus Freaks and my parents were Holy Rollers. Hearing you raises a lot of issues. Where procreation was concerned, my home church encouraged treating the female congregants as a rancher might treat his prized cattle. Breed 'em young and often. That isn't to suggest that they promoted marriage before the age of eighteen. Gotta say, though, once a girl was betrothed, there was negligible difference between her vagina and a clown car."

I laughed so hard that my belly hurt. I tried to stop, and couldn't. "Tha...that's exactly what I was taught. Only they never compared us to clown cars. And women should have long hair and keep it braided like mine. Women don't wear pants. Only skirts or dresses to the ankle."

Sheila laughed and shook her head. "Don't get me started, honey child. Have mercy!"

I grew braver and said, "At the store, I would see girls in pants or shorts. Their hair was cut with bangs and barely touching the collar. I asked about that."

Our food came, and we dug in. It beat having a scoop of tater-tot casserole and a single hot dog. I had rarely seen so much food on my plate.

"And?" Rory's mouth was half-full of rib meat.

"Father called me a harlot for daring to ask. I got the paddling of my life on my bare behind in front of everyone. I had to stand in the corner with my pants down while my siblings and I got a biblical lecture about original sin and Eve being a temptress. I was eight."

Rory's eyes softened, and his face registered sadness. I wanted to trust that he cared. We ate in silence for a while. Sheila finished her food and sat back with her hands on her belly.

Hot tears splashed down my cheeks once more. "I tried fitting in. I prayed all day and night. I even fasted. I tried, sir."

Rory and Sheila shook their heads sympathetically. Jeanie held a napkin to my nose and told me to blow.

Sheila gave me a smile. "We'll be in South Carolina in a couple hours, honey. There's a church store we know about that offers free clothing. To Hell with your creepy church elders and your family. My advice is ditch all but one of the skirts and a blouse. You might need one fancy outfit some time or another. You can exchange your clothes for jeans and t-shirts."

I thought about Sheila's advice for a while. She was right. My church didn't want me, so why should I care what they thought? She was right about the church store, too. I traded my dresses for jeans, shorts, and six t-shirts. I also claimed a pair of brown, cushioned, canvas hiking boots. The weight of the boots contrasted the heavy load lifted off of my heart.

An hour later, the emotional load eased further when Rory pulled off beside a lake. The wind blew over the water and cooled the air; the sound of crickets and bullfrogs pierced the silence.

"I assume you've never smoked before. You mind if we do?" Rory smiled at me and opened his arms, inviting me to hug.

I wasn't sure how to react on either count. Something inside wanted to trust him, but experience cried out not to. I settled for giving him a side hug. He didn't press the matter.

"No, I've never smoked. I don't have a death wish. But, I don't care if you do." I wanted to trust these people and, after some prayer, I decided that I would. It couldn't hurt any worse than I already hurt.

"I got green bud. Sure you won't try? Might relax you." Rory's eyes took on their concerned look. Jeanie and Sheila nodded their agreement.

I sat with them beside the lake, and they taught me how to inhale from the short, fat glass pipe they passed back and forth. Sheila abstained because of her pregnancy. At first, nothing happened; but, about fifteen minutes later, my senses numbed to everything. A warm cocoon surrounded me, and I giggled as my previous tension melted.

I was enjoying the sensation when Jeanie stood up and shed her clothes. My eyebrows raised, and my heartbeat increased. I swallowed several times as a warm sensation spread through me. I tried not to stare. Jeanie stepped into the lake and waded up to her chest. Sheila stripped as well, and my breath caught short.

They waded around in the lake, kissing and hugging. Other than on the Internet and during church interventions, I had never seen naked girls kissing. My inclination was to touch myself as I did in the shower; but, being in public made that impossible.

I wanted to swim, too, but my insides were a jumble of emotions and my skin still hurt from the beating I'd endured. I could tell myself that I didn't care what my family thought, but getting naked in front of strangers was several steps too far. Instead, I sat watching them swim while Rory napped against a tree.

An hour later, we smoked some more and climbed into the van. Rory passed around pears and trail mix. From the cooler, Sheila took out more bottles of water. After we ate, Rory and Sheila fell asleep in the back of the van. Jeanie sat on the bench behind the drivers' seat. She carefully took the bobby-pins and clips from my hair and let it tumble down. It fell to my mid-back. She ran her hands through my thick, blonde mane like my mother used to do on rare occasions. My heart thumped. A strange sensation surged through my belly.

"I have scissors and a razor if you'd like me to give you a new style tomorrow."

I leaned my head against her shoulder. "I'd like that. You guys are so great. You just...don't even know."

Jeanie stroked my face with a finger. Having someone love me as a woman was everything I had thought about for years. No matter what I had been told, it was my deepest desire. And yet, just being held was sensational. I wanted more, and Jeanie's affection made my heart skip; but, I was unsure how or what to ask her to do.

I fell asleep leaning on her. The warmth of the rising sun brought me to consciousness. I cuddled closer. My cuddle elicited a murmur. Jeanie drew me toward her and gave me a gentle hug. We looked behind us to where Rory and Sheila still slept.

Jeanie and I slid out of the van and found a spot to relieve ourselves. After that, I took a swim in the lake while Jeanie read a textbook. As I climbed out of the water, still wearing shorts and a t-shirt, Jeanie examined the bruises on my legs. There were tears in her eyes, and she rubbed my shoulders. As she held me, a renewed longing deep in the pit of my stomach brought forth a sigh.

"I'm scared. I don't know anyone away from the church. I mean, I have you guys now. I've never been allowed to know anyone not in the church."

"We'll hit Edison by tonight. That's where we go to college. You should stay at our apartment. In the morning, I'll ride you to Weehawken and show you where to catch the ferry to Manhattan. The city is huge. You'll find all kinds of help there. You should finish school. See how much you need to catch up on for college. In a way, you're lucky. At fifteen, you got a jump on the scene. You really should find help, too. Like counseling and a safe place to live."

"I could live with you."

"That's not a good idea. We have a nice relationship, but we're probably the first people to ever treat you with kindness. I like you. They do, too. But, Destiny, it isn't what you need. We've spent a couple of years bonding. You only just met us."

I swallowed the lump in my throat and blinked back tears. "How do you guys know so much?"

"I study psychology and social work. I'm gonna work with rainbow teenagers."

I cocked my head at her. "You know, like Gay, Bisexual, Trans—all of it, really. They're studying the same stuff."

I stepped behind some bushes and changed as Rory and Sheila started coming to. Jeanie reached into a suitcase and took out a leather container that held barber's scissors and an electric razor. I gasped as she cut eight inches off of my hair. The lightness from my shorn head was delicious. I enjoyed the sound of the scissors snipping and trimming, here and there. A few minutes later, Jeanie had me lean forward; she shaved my neck and the next layer of hair. I was shocked when I checked in a hand mirror. I looked pretty, and yet my father and the church leaders would have had a fit.

"I love it! Thank you, thank you!" I squealed and hugged Jeanie. "But we're leaving it blonde. Blue isn't me."

"Sweetie, you'd look good in any color. You've got style!" Jeanie kissed me on the tip of my nose and put away her hair supplies.

Rory and Sheila finally climbed out of the van to take care of their morning needs. I side-hugged them both and rubbed Sheila's round tummy. "Good morning, little boy."

"Ah, welladay! And 'tis for sure a wee lassie has shorn her locks." The corners of Rory's mustache twitched.

"Don't mind the overgrown leprechaun. You look fabulous." Sheila giggled.

I blushed. "If I'd ever worn my hair this way, I wouldn't have sat for a month." Tears formed, but I choked them back.

"Honey, show me one place where Jesus spoke any of that crap about long hair or ankle-length skirts? That was Paul. You mention the Old Testament, and we'll be discussing blended cloths and dietary habits until way past bedtime." Sheila winked at me. "My grandparents were Jesus Freaks, remember. I know my shit."

After Rory and Sheila washed up, the four of us got situated in the van and found a diner for breakfast. Rory smiled, passing me a menu. "Order what you like. We got our expense money a couple days ago. Part of our student loans. We got you."

The waitress—a vivacious, buxom brunette—flitted over with coffee and glasses of ice water. I ordered a breakfast platter. Rory and Jeanie ordered pancakes and sausages. Sheila had toast and orange juice.

Sheila patted my hand when I inquired about her eating so little. "If I eat too much in the morning, it makes me sick. Can't even drink or smoke out. I can't wait for the baby to arrive so I can enjoy food again."

The food arrived, and we ate with gusto. I listened while the others talked about professors and classes. I was growing comfortable around my new friends, yet the fluttering in my belly and the tightness in my chest remained. I was as nervous as a cat about to kitten. So much had happened, and my life was changing faster than ever before.

Chapter 3

At seven in the evening, we arrived at an apartment building. The place was down at heel but respectable enough. There was a well-tended flower garden in the front, its fragrance carried in on the breeze. I helped load all the luggage onto a cart, and Rory took it to the fifth floor on a service elevator.

I spent the first part of the ten hour ride asleep on the bench seat with my head in Jeanie's lap. Stress, plus a huge meal, left me exhausted. I woke up twice and had a bottle of water. There were vague discussions about linear formulas and someone named Castaneda. I didn't try to follow the conversations as my mind eased back into a calming abyss.

The nap left me refreshed, if still nervous about my situation. Sheila handed me a small case full of CDs. "Pick something you'd like to hear, honey. We have eclectic tastes. Rory was raised on folk music and the oldies. I prefer country and bluegrass. My minx likes jazz."

I looked through the collections and found a CD of an Appalachian gospel group. "This one looks like the only stuff I know. My parents say that modern music is evil."

Rory laughed. "I'd mostly agree, but not for the same reasons, I suspect."

Jeanie chimed in. "Some modern stuff is out of sight, but nothing compares to Miles or Bird."

Sheila put in the CD I had chosen, and a banjo started playing "Are You Washed In The Blood." A fiddle and an accordion joined in. My blood stirred as the familiar hymns played. My nerves subsided, and I sang along.

"Lord, honey!" Sheila gasped. "You sing like a bird! You

could go pro."

The unexpected compliment made me blush. "I was in the choir. I play guitar, too."

Later, after everything was squared away at the apartment, Jeanie sorted mail while Sheila dusted some counters. I sat on the couch and had a glass of orange juice. The living room appeared smaller than it was, due to three desks—complete with laptops—a wrap-around sofa, an old coffee table, and a stereo system connected to a television. The fluorescent bulbs overhead had been replaced with black lights, giving the room a calm glow which made every individual dust particle dance.

Jeanie finished with the mail and showed me her room. She had a queen-sized futon that she offered to let me use. I said the couch was fine. The sound of running water vibrated through the walls along with Rory singing a song about seeing rain on a sunny day. His bass voice lightened my heart. Music often did.

After Rory emerged from the shower dressed in shorts and a tank top, which showed off his rippling muscles, we all sat in the living room. Jeanie demonstrated the use of a gravity bong to smoke pot. The effects were quicker than the pipe and I melted into the couch, half-aware of my surroundings. I wasn't asleep, but the surrounding air pressed in like a comforting hug. I could move, yet had no inclination to do so.

Behind me I heard Rory's deep, rich voice ordering dinner. He hung up, walked to the kitchen, and returned with three bottles of ice-cold Heineken and a bottle of water. I had never tasted beer, but the immediate effects were pleasant. The yeasty smell reminded me of fresh bread.

I sat on the couch next to Jeanie; resting my head on her shoulder provided a comfort I craved. When my mother had a baby, she gave it the attention a girl gives her favorite doll. That attention was taken away when a newer dolly appeared. I dozed off until Jeanie shook me awake.

I finished my beer with an egg roll, steamed dumplings, beef and broccoli, and orange chicken over fried rice. The food did me in. I curled up on the couch.

The next morning, I woke up late. It was almost ten. A sense of urgency engulfed me; I prepared to face the music because I hadn't helped with the morning chores. It took a moment to realize that I wasn't home. Rory and Sheila sat at the kitchen table, drinking juice. Sheila showed me the bathroom, and I cleaned up.

"Whatever you find to eat in the fridge, help yourself." Rory yawned.

I found some milk and cereal, fixed a bowl, and sat down. "You guys are incredible. I've never known anyone like you."

Sheila sipped her juice. "Sounds like you've never met much of anyone who wasn't goose stepping to the dogma of your church. Now you're free. You got big world out there. You get lost or scared, give us a call."

I took a bite of cereal. "I don't have a phone."

"Just stop in any store that sells them, Sprint, Verizon, T-Mobile, whatever. They always have test phones. Just use one and call us." Rory handed me a piece of paper with his number.

I put the paper in the front pocket of my backpack. "I'll do that. Thank you."

"I'm glad we met you." Rory gave me a tender look. "We do our best to help others. We have our own reasons. In my case, it's how I was raised. My parents were born in New Jersey in May of 1970. My grandparents were hippies and knew each other. They raised my parents on the beliefs of equality and freedom. My parents passed that on to me. And whatever you might think about me, I'm only four years older than you. So is Sheila. Jeanie's seventeen, but she started college early. I guess what I'm saying is that we don't necessarily have it all together, but together we have it all."

My emotions took over. "Thank you. I'm glad I met you."

"Stay in touch, honey. Stay safe." Sheila kissed me on the cheek, and I blushed.

An hour later, I was saying my goodbyes. A sense of fear and panic gripped me anew, but I realized that staying with these people forever wasn't possible. The sensible part of my brain told me that I was free and needed to move on. The rest of me knotted up. Except for using the bathroom, I had never been entirely alone in my life.

"Thank you again. A blessing on your home." I stood by the door looking at my three new friends. Gentle tears filled my eyes.

Rory gave me a kiss on the top of my head. Sheila hugged me and gave me a kiss on the cheek, as well. "Our pleasure, Destiny. Pay it forward."

Jeanie looked up at me. "I'll take you to the ferry. Here's twenty bucks. That'll pay your fare and get you a Coke. Stay in Manhattan, and you'll be real close by. We can come see you sometimes, and you can come here." I leaned down to give her a kiss, and she side-hugged me. "Remember what I said about finding a support group or some counseling."

The ferry ride across the Hudson was smooth, the air a mixture of diesel fuel and salty, sulfuric fumes. The sight calmed me, the vast city approaching from across the water. I decided that instead of being abandoned and alone, I was taking a vacation. Perhaps this was part of a greater mission, much like people in The Bible were sent on. The thought released even more tension.

After docking in Manhattan, I disembarked and looked around. I had a few dollars left, so I bought a Coke. As I walked along, my mind spun in amazement at the tall buildings. My ears and nose began adjusting to the noise and smells. The city was unlike anything I had ever experienced. At once, a jungle of chaos juxtaposed an inner tranquility. The crowded sprawl of varying architectural designs was breathtaking.

A beautiful girl sat on a bench. Something stirred inside of me, similar to when I first met Jeanie. The term poets use is kismet. The girl was five feet tall, could not have been more than one hundred pounds—only if she jumped in the East River fully clothed. She wore a t-shirt, dirty jeans, and scuffed blue sneakers. Her chest was slight enough that she didn't wear a bra beneath the t-shirt which read "Mike Hunt for President in 2012." She had aqua eyes and her chestnut-brown hair was shaved short on the sides but left thick on top, falling in curls down her neck to her shoulders. The look she gave me could have melted an iceberg.

I sat and returned her smile. "Hi. You from around here?"

She shrugged. "Jersey City. I've been hanging out in the city about a month."

"I was looking for an art museum. Someone on the ferry said it's cheap to get in."

"Lots of those around. The Metropolitan Museum, that's the cheap one. Still one of the best, though." She shrugged again. "You can get in for a nickel, if you want, but that's a real dick move. We can walk it. Might take a half hour. I can show you, if you want."

My brain buzzed, and my heart raced from her offer. I averted my eyes briefly until my heartbeat slowed; but, it quickened when I looked up again at her radiant smile.

"My name's Mackenzie. Mackenzie Guevara."

"Destiny Wilbury. You can show me...I mean, if you really want to." I blushed as my guts began a gymnastic floor routine. "I've never been to New York."

"Wouldn't have guessed." She giggled, and we started walking. "Come on, let's bounce. You hungry? I'm buying."

I looked down at Mackenzie, who was six inches shorter than me. "Thank you. I don't even know where I'm staying tonight."

She glanced up at me with a frown. "You're in the city alone? Figured your mom and dad had a hotel or something. So you're not a tourist? You got any money on you?"

"Yes, I'm here alone. No, I have like fifty cents. I thought you were paying for the food."

"I am. Just...never mind. I misunderstood."

"Do your parents live near here?"

She stopped, looking away at some distant spot. She put her hands in her back pockets and her shoulders trembled. "Parent. Just my mom. She's in Jersey City. I ran away.

It's...complicated. Home was a mess. She doesn't want me back."

Mackenzie shook her head as if to clear it, and we walked to a vendor cart. She bought us a giant pretzel with mustard, four hot dogs with everything, and cans of Pepsi. I noted the thick wad of bills that she pulled from her backpack. We sat on a bench and talked while we ate. She had a lot in common with me, but there were plenty of differences.

I chewed on a piece of pretzel. "Why'd you run away?"

Mackenzie was quiet for a few minutes. She bit into the hot dog, savoring the taste as she chewed, then belched softly. She delicately licked her lips before looking at me again. "You wouldn't understand."

"Let me guess, you're mother doesn't accept that you like girls?"

"I doubt she'd give a shit, even if she knew. Why would she?" Mackenzie's eyes narrowed as she tilted her head. "Hold up. Is that why you ran away?"

It was my turn to stare into space. "I didn't run away."

"Shit. Where you from, girl? You got ash-canned?"

"Ash-canned?"

"Thrown out with the trash. Your mom and dad hate queers?"

I nodded. "Yes. So does my church. The Bible says it's a sin."

"Bigger sin to toss your kid to the curb, if you ask me."

"Why'd you run away?"

She paused a moment before replying, "I'm the third of eight kids. Four sisters and three brothers. Same nag, eight different jockeys. Two of my sisters are half-black and one brother is half-Asian. Not that I give a rat's ass. She needs money, and the Feds give money and food to poor families with kids. Works out better if the mother's single. So mom finds a guy and brings him home. They screw and, once she's pregnant, she kicks him out."

I gasped. "How can she manage a family without a man around?"

"What the hell does that mean? Women can take care of themselves just fine, chick! But, yeah, there was usually a man around. Just he wasn't around for long," Mackenzie said with a stiff shrug.

When she spoke again, her voice grew softer from the strain. "From the time I was four, Mom would come through the apartment at all hours and make us leave. We'd have to go play in the area behind the projects. There's a dump back there with old furniture and ripped mattresses. I used to jump on the mattresses like a trampoline. It got old, though. I'd be woken up at three in the morning and told to get dressed and get out of the apartment. I was always tired at school, if I even went. Last month, I finally left home for good. I called from a pay phone to tell mommy dearest, and she told me to stay the hell out. I guess I'm just an ungrateful little bitch for not liking how things are."

I finished my food and drew her closer to my side. I placed her head near my heart, and then brushed her tears away with a finger. That had always worked when calming my younger sisters. MacKenzie kept crying, letting out the hurt she'd trapped inside. Her tears soaked my t-shirt throughout her emotional onslaught. I kissed her cheek, and she looked up at me. Her right hand brushed my breasts. We kissed on the lips. It was my first romantic kiss. The sensation in my lower belly made me wish we weren't in a public park.

We sat for a few more minutes, and I told her about my life. She looked shocked at certain points. "Two days ago, Pastor Ruby told me to get out of the church and never return. My father kicked me out of the house that afternoon."

"Fuck Pastor Ruby. Fuck your parents. Stay with me. I got your back."

My own emotions gave way. Sobs and hyperventilation escaped my throat while MacKenzie held my hand. "So your parents tried to pray away the gay? They tried to force you to be straight?"

"Yes. But then, I met these people who are in college. They gave me a ride to New Jersey. The guy saved me from these men who were about to hurt me. One of the girls is beautiful and sweet. Her name's Jeanie. She has hair the color of a blueberry, but on her it looks good. I stayed in their apartment last night, then came to New York and found you. Maybe that was The Lord's plan all along." I slowed my crying and tried to breathe. Mackenzie held me in a tight embrace.

"Wouldn't know. Church is Christmas and Easter. If it was the plan, then I'm glad." She sneaked a glance at me, smiling shyly. "You're pretty."

Chapter 4

We stood up and found a water fountain to wash our faces. Mackenzie readjusted her pack, and I shifted mine. We kept walking toward Central Park, holding hands, until we reached the museum. It was closing soon.

"I don't even know where I'm going to sleep tonight." I sat on the steps with my new friend. "I'm scared."

"We can get in here for fifty cents. But, tomorrow might be better. We'll spend the day. Stick by me tonight. Mostly, I've been sleeping on the subways and asking for spare change. I got almost three hundred dollars left from the past week." She smiled, adding, "We can try asking someone to get us a room tonight."

"Is it OK if I call you Kenzie? You look cute, like a Kenzie."

"You can call me Kenzie. I like that." She giggled as we sat on the museum steps.

We kissed again, and I put my head on Kenzie's shoulder as she wrapped her arms around my waist. We sat there until late into the night, her arms enveloping me in a warm comfort that had eluded me for most of my life.

After a couple of hours, we walked to the subway station. The surrounding buildings soared, and the sound of steel drums and trumpets rang from a distance. As we entered the stairwell to the station, and the air turned sour and thick. The smell of urine mixed with a smell of rotten eggs. I tried holding my breath but could only do so for a minute.

Kenzie gave me a sympathetic smile. "You'll get used to the smell. It's the stink of the city."

She bought us each a card for the subway. We rode to Union Station and changed over to an F Train. There were just enough people in the car to cause cramping. My chest tightened, and I clung to Kenzie. She appeared oblivious to any danger.

After changing trains, we rode to Brooklyn. The street we emerged on was less crowded and the buildings weren't quite as tall. The openness of the area left me feeling exposed; I scanned in every direction, sensing danger in every alley.

Kenzie approached a man on a bench. He smelled like a skunk's spray and needed a bath in bleach. His suit was wrinkled, his hair unkempt, and a shave was in order. She kept her voice was even and conversational, eyes locking on the man's face.

"Hey. We need some help. I'll get you back if you help us."

The man looked us over and shrugged, smiling in a way that made my skin crawl. "What you need?" He slurred, the question sounding like "washer need?"

I backed away, but Kenzie gripped my shoulder hard enough to numb my legs. "Get us a room at that hotel across the street. We can't get it ourselves. Too young. If we go in with you and give you eighty dollars, you can get a room. We leave, you give us the key, and I give you fifteen dollars to buy your next bottle."

The man stood and tottered. "I know something you could give me, sweetie. How about we get a room together?"

I broke free from Kenzie's grip and looked for a police officer or someone who might help. The surrounding people didn't look promising.

"Wrong answer, dude. It happens like I said, or no deal. We'll ask that guy down the block." She forced me to turn, and we walked away.

The man stopped us and agreed to her proposition. The entire process worked as Kenzie had said. Once we were outside again, the man handed her a plastic key card. She handed him a ten and a five.

He reached over and stroked her hair. "Sure I can't join you girls?"

Kenzie's elbow flew like a spear toward the

man's crotch. It connected hard and he doubled over, clutching himself.

"Back off, asshole! I'll cut your balls off!" She stepped back, reaching towards her back pocket.

The man turned and ran down the block. Kenzie and I used a side entrance and took the elevator to the tenth floor. The elevator had graffiti on the walls and smelled of stale beer.

I had the urge to pee. "Do you really have a weapon?"

"Not in my pocket. I got a blackjack and a taped-up pipe in my backpack. Don't need it with dudes like that. From my height, a quick and dirty uppercut to the dick works. So did the elbow shot. You'd be better off with a palm heel to his nose, and then a knee to his balls." Kenzie looked irked. "And what's with the running away shit? Don't ever abandon me in a fight!"

"I've never had a fight in my life. I'd pee myself, or run away, before I could hit an adult." I continued to shake as more tears welled up. "I'm sorry. If you want me to leave, I will."

"No. You and I are a team. But you best learn how to fight back, chick. I'll teach you some moves tomorrow. You can't survive in this city if you don't fight."

We exited the elevator, sneaked into our room, and locked the door. The room had an old double bed with a musty comforter, a small dusty TV, and a desk with a chair that was more duct tape than seat cushion. The bathroom looked nice though. It had pink tile on the walls with a somewhat new bathtub.

Alone in the room, we stared at each other. Then something happened that I still have trouble describing. It was as if Kenzie psychically pulled me towards her. I gazed into her beautiful eyes, stretched out my hands, and traveled to another time and place—somewhere distant and primal.

For a moment, I clasped her fingertips—a fragile, light touch. As I dipped my head, my hand pressed against her side; she moved, as if to step back. I tightened my grip on her wrist, a reflex, but loosened it a moment later. I had never experienced raw, carnal energy to that degree, but it was exquisite. In my mind, a stunning tapestry unfurled—green fields, warm winds, and the subtle perfume of flowers. No matter that I and Kenzie were walking on clouds, we would never fall.

She murmured something, sharing a soft smile. We stared into each other's souls. I realized that in this mental land we'd entered, circumstance demanded we act. Couples who entered this realm remained together.

"When I saw you sitting there, I felt something." I tilted her head up with a finger under her chin.

"Felt what?" She asked with longing.

Thinking it was one thing, expressing the thought was another. I wet my lips then murmured, "I don't know. My whole life, I've been scared. I used to sneak on the computer, trying to find what I wanted on the screen. I never thought I'd find it. I know it's wrong; and yet, I know it's right for me. I tried to stop my feelings and couldn't. I longed for validation. Sometimes I got so sad wondering if I was kidding myself about ever being free. Do you understand?"

"I think so." Kenzie appeared to lose herself, anchored by my eyes. "I totally understand. Getting away seemed so impossible late at night on the streets in Jersey City, and I never wanted anything more desperately."

I took Kenzie's hands in mine. "Your hands are freezing."

"Yours too." She reached up to stroke my cheek. Her touch jolted me as if I'd touched a live wire.

"When you touched me I saw fireworks. Great pinwheels of blue and green lights. Exploding radiance of red and purple and white." I traced a parabola in the air. "See them?"

"Yes. They're beautiful." Kenzie cooed.

"You're not just saying that?" I leaned closer, my lips ready and on fire.

"I see the fireworks." Her lips looked moist, almost dripping wet. She angled her head up to receive the kiss.

The rockets rose, joining together in an explosion of hearts and stars before they descended into a cascade of falling light.

My lips brushed against hers. She trembled in my embrace. The boundaries of magic were about to be breached. We kissed deeply, holding each other for a few minutes as our bodies vibrated in unison. After a while, we calmed down.

"I was scared down there," Kenzie admitted. "But you can't show anyone in this city your fear. They feed on that and use it against you."

"I don't know how not to."

"I'll teach you. If you stay with me."

"I'm staying. I'm exhausted." I yawned until my jaws ached.

"What are we going to do tomorrow?" Kenzie relaxed beside me after our kissing session.

"We can figure it out. I promise I'm staying with you. We need money, though. Don't we? I still want to see the art museum. Sunday's a good day to find food at churches after the services, but I don't know where we can stay. I just don't know what churches are around here." I yawned again. "Baptist is what I was raised on."

We climbed into bed in our clothes. Kenzie plugged in her phone, and I turned on the TV to some news program. We fell asleep in each other's arms. The frequent sirens awoke me, but each time Kenzie cuddled closer.

Chapter 5

The next morning, I awoke to the sun shining on my face through the window blinds, and a small hand lifted my t-shirt to stroke my belly. I smiled and looked at Kenzie. "Good morning. You're tickling me."

"You're still here?" Kenzie lifted my shirt more. She stroked my ribs.

I squirmed. "Where would I go? I don't even know where we are. I mean, in this room, obviously. But, this is your city, not mine."

"I figured you'd sneak out and leave me."

"I said I'd stay."

"Yeah, but...never mind. As long as we have the room, I need a bath. That's one thing about living on the streets."

"What?"

"A lot of kids never change their clothes or wash themselves. It's gross. Adults, too. Any time I can take a bath, I do it. You get lice and shit otherwise."

I stood and walked into the bathroom to fill the tub. Kenzie started undressing.

"Plus, you get better money from people if you don't stink." She unbuttoned her shorts and unzipped them. I traced a finger over her breasts. She wrapped her arms around me and buried her face in my chest, purring.

I had undressed in front of my sisters without a thought, but undressing now made me blush. I pulled everything off and climbed into the hot water to soak. Kenzie sat between my legs, her head resting on my chest.

She closed her eyes and inhaled steam. "Yesterday, I was thinking I wanted to die. My life was a wreck. I had nothing to keep me going."

I ran a small bar of soap over her neck and back. "You're a runaway. I got thrown out of my home. For whatever The Lord's reasons, we were both forsaken by Him and put through a time of testing. But, right here and now, we have each other and The Lord has us both." I held her and sighed as we soaked together.

"What about church?" Kenzie sounded relaxed, as well.

"I'll call a few. The services are usually scary, but the music is nice. At least where I attended. The food is the best part. You don't have to worry about how much you take."

"I'm starving. You can use my phone later."

We soaked until our fingers and toes shriveled. We drained the tub and dried each other with the thin towels. I put on fresh jeans and a blouse. Kenzie had a clean t-shirt but wore the same jeans.

I made some calls to a few Baptist churches on the surrounding blocks and in nearby neighborhoods. The third church I called said that they were having services in two hours and that there was a potluck lunch every week. They invited us to attend. Jackpot!

Kenzie and I grabbed our backpacks, sneaking out through the hotel's side entrance. Sweat dripped from my forehead into my eyes as we walked fifteen blocks in the boiling sun. The day was shaping up to be a scorcher.

"I know this sort of people. You're my baby sister when we get there. Our parents aren't big on church, but they don't care if we attend. Stick to that story and don't offer more details unless we have to. If you don't, people will ask questions and we'll end up in a church-run group home. I've seen it happen before. After the services, we can eat as much as we want and probably get food to take with us."

"No problem, sissy. You don't have to be so bossy, though. You always boss me around. I'll tell Daddy on you." Kenzie's eyes crinkled in the corners as she put her hands on her hips. I stuck out my tongue at her.

We pulled brushes from our backpacks and fixed our

sweat-plastered hair before entering the building. The church was lovely, filled with stained glass windows and an interior far more elegant than my parents' church in Florida. Even so, my heart raced and my guts knotted.

Kenzie grabbed my arms. "We don't have to do this. If you can't handle being here, I totally get it. We'll figure out something else."

"I'm fine, baby sister. I can do this. These aren't the same people who hurt me." I took a few deep breaths and let them out slowly. "Let's sign in."

I took the pen and wrote Loretta Webb and Crystal Webb. We accepted programs and greetings from an usher before taking seats in the last row. The building was older with ornate designs, gold filigree in the ceiling, an elaborate wooden cross at the front, and chandeliers which lit the chapel.

As the choir band started playing a slow number, Kenzie turned to whisper in my ear. "What's with those names you signed?"

I giggled. "Maiden names of Loretta Lynn and her baby sister, Crystal Gayle."

Her laughter turned several heads and brought stern looks. In response to the glares, I raised my hands and shouted, "A-MEN!"

The ushers turned toward us with pleasure written on their faces. As if I had toppled the first domino, several other congregants in the pews raised their hands and waved. The band broke into a raucous cover of "Shine, Jesus, Shine." I stood with Kenzie and side hugged her.

After several fast numbers, the mood settled down. My body vibrated from the adrenaline rush that many mistook for a spiritual experience. Announcements were read and a prayer recited. The pastor spoke and, inside of three minutes, my eyes were open wide and my mouth agape. Pastor Affenhoden's text was from Luke. He spoke of how Jesus helped those in need and how we all should do likewise. The idea was that the poor were not to blame for their poverty. The rich had an obligation, having been blessed, to provide for those in need on a personal level instead of simply expecting the government to handle everything. It was a far more liberal interpretation than I had ever known a pastor to preach.

When the sermon ended, the congregation was dismissed. Kenzie and I freshened up in the ladies' room before following the crowd to the basement for lunch. The food offerings were incredible, the scents tantalizing. I ate fried chicken, greens with fat chunks of ham, melt-in-your-mouth buttermilk biscuits, pasta salad, potato and cheese casserole, and lasagna.

Afterward, I devoured three plates of assorted desserts. I ate until I could hold no more. Kenzie ate as much as I did, refilling our cups from a pitcher of lemonade.

"We gotta come here every week, sissy." Kenzie wiped her mouth with a paper towel. "This rocks. And it's free."

"I'm sure mother and father won't mind. Pastor Affenhoden said they have Bible study on Wednesday nights. There's coffee and cake afterward," I said with a wink.

After we finished eating, we bagged up some fried chicken legs and I placed them in the front pocket of my backpack. We walked to a subway station and caught the N Train, for no reason except that it was the first one arriving. The train wasn't crowded so we sat for an hour, holding hands and relaxing. A thin Hispanic boy with long, black hair sat at one end of the train car playing the flute. I recognized a few of the hymns he played. The train screeched to a halt. A hollow announcement crackled across the speakers.

"There has been a mechanical failure. Please depart the train and wait on the platform for the next train, which will arrive shortly."

Kenzie stood, motioning for me to follow. "It's a nice day out. Let's walk around. I think I can use my phone map to get us to a bus, then on to a subway heading to Coney Island."

We exited the station, walking east awhile then heading north on Saint Ann's Avenue before turning east again at 149th Street. The area was yet another side of New York City. The buildings were similar to those in Brooklyn and the noise level only slightly less intrusive than Manhattan. What lay ahead of us, though, was nothing short of how I imagined Hell to look.

Teens gathered along the sidewalks, dressed as if they had been attending an event at the school nearby. Most wore polo shirts and slacks or newer-looking jeans. I wondered what it would be like to attend public school. The school kids across the street stood in stark contrast to the rancid landscape—clean-cut and confident.

I held Kenzie's hand as we crossed the street. My guts turned flips as we walked. I couldn't put to words my sense of foreboding, but the area gave me the sense that death lurked around every corner. Kenzie looked right at home. That wasn't to say she appeared relaxed or happy—in fact, her expression grew taut—but, she didn't seem unused to the environment. I noticed that her eyes shifted every which way as we walked straight ahead.

Beyond a chain-link fence, a slope led to an abandoned railroad bed. The summer sun reflected off of something shiny and orange. As I glanced toward the patches of weeds and dirt, I spotted several piles of discarded syringes. Needles scattered across the ground like random sticks, clumped under trees like piles of raked leaves, floating in the pools of standing water below. The area smelled worse than a Port-O-Potty. We trudged onward past the fence.

A disheveled lady with mottled brown skin and a matted, dirty afro sat in front of a crude shelter made of tarps and old sheets. The shelter overlooked the railroad bed and was surrounded by more used needles and other detritus. I watched her take out an item that Kenzie said was for cooking drugs. The lady mixed something together.

Kenzie noticed my wide-eyed stare. "She's on the jazz. If you see people like that, just stay clear.
They're unpredictable and might kill you."

The lady wore several layers of sweatshirts, blue jeans, and unlaced construction boots despite the blazing summer heat. She pulled up her sleeves, revealing arms covered in puncture marks and crimson scars. She looked straight ahead, her face blank, as she stuck the syringe into her left arm and pressed the plunger.

Panic gripped me as I noticed other people scattered around. Some tried to hide, and others lay there, motionless. In juxtaposition to the groups of teens, the people beyond the fence looked older. Much older. Most were minorities, but so were the teens. I wasn't sure if it led to my fear. My home church had been exclusively white, and I'd had almost no contact with anyone outside of the church.

"This is what I grew up around." Kenzie spoke in hushed tones. "Mom wasn't on the spike, and I don't think anyone she brought home was. It was all around us, though. When we had to clear out so mommy dearest could be alone with her latest guy, this is what we saw happening." Tears formed in her eyes, and she wiped them with her sleeve.

I hugged her from the side, and we picked up the pace toward the bus stop. Ahead of us, a disheveled African-American man emerged from a makeshift lean-to.
He had unkempt gray and black dreadlocks over skin that was lighter in spots and darker in others. The man squinted in the morning light and stomped off.

"I can't believe people are using drugs outside of a school." I blanched.

"Believe it. Welcome to the real New York. Hell, this happens everywhere."

"Can we get out of here?" I looked ahead through the streaming sunlight at a group of men sitting against a wall, nodding back and forth in a daze. "I think I'm gonna vomit."

"It's just ahead." Kenzie hustled me along. "If you gotta puke, aim toward the grass. Welcome to my life. If you hadn't come around, this is where I was heading. This could have been me, real easy."

I thought about what Kenzie had told me. While we walked to the bus stop, and during the entire ride to the subway, I prayed. I thanked The Creator for sparing my friend.

After the bus ride—which was so crowded we had to stand—

Kenzie and I boarded a train to Coney Island. During the train ride, my body relaxed. The tension melted, but it left a residual headache the size of Texas.

We arrived at Stillwell Avenue, and I gaped at the crowds and the rides. Kenzie took a bottle of Advil from her pack and gave me two. We wandered around, holding hands. I kept checking that she was still beside me.

The amusement park atmosphere drew me in, chasing away the earlier images of those lost addicts. The sounds were such a cacophony that my whole body vibrated. No state fair I had attended could compare with Coney Island. The people were such a mix that describing them all would take years. I spotted a large, black-and-green checkered blanket, folded and left to one side. I didn't see anyone near it.

"Hey, Kenzie? Think we can grab that blanket?" My eyes darted left and right.

"I can. The beach is to the left. Start walking casually." Kenzie reached over, grabbed the blanket, and followed me.

We located a spot under the boardwalk where other couples were escaping the evening heat. I laid out our blanket, and we put our backpacks where we could grab them if necessary. I was exhausted from all of the activity. Kenzie yawned. We laid on our backs, holding hands, until we fell asleep. Two hours later, we woke up snuggling. It was dusk.

"Do we get another room tonight?" I stood, dusting off some sand.

"I don't think we'd better. Let's catch the F Train back to Union Square Station and find a place to ask for spare change." Kenzie helped me fold the blanket, and we shoved it into her backpack on top of her clothes.

"Let's go." I gave her a tender kiss and we walked back to Stillwell Ave. We purchased our cards and bottles of soda.

The train was crowded with commuters. I held Kenzie in my lap. She fit comfortably, and I stroked her belly and chest as she purred. The train rocked and shimmied until we arrived at our stop.

As we walked toward the staircase, I spotted a boy of about seventeen. He had a shaved head and several earrings in his left ear. Tattoos covered his arms. He wore army pants with the letter "A" in a circle drawn on either leg with a marker. The pants were held up with black suspenders over a dirty, ribbed tank top. A large knife hung from his belt alongside a pair of brass knuckles.

Next to the boy was a girl, the crown and back of her head shaved to about an eighth of an inch. In the front she wore thick black bangs, swept to the side with thick curlicues hanging over her temples. It was the most bizarre looking hairdo I'd ever seen, to this day. She had a nose ring between her nostrils, like a bull, and several piercings decorated her lips and ears. Her thin white blouse revealed a black bra, and a sheathed knife was strapped to her calf-high lace-ups. She glared at Kenzie and me.

Behind the boy and girl were several others with shaved heads, boasting an assortment of ripped clothes and piercings. They all carried knives or chains. Some had both.

"I bet no old men act disgusting with them. We need a group like that to protect us. Those boys look strong." I looked back, but we kept moving.

"If we see them again, we'll introduce ourselves," Kenzie said with sarcasm. "I agree we should make friends with other kids. It can't hurt to have a bigger army when things happen. Those dudes scare me, though. You have no idea. If you see kids dressed that way, be somewhere else."

We boarded an N Train and, before we could sit, Kenzie pushed me toward the exit. We walked up a staircase and the whole atmosphere turned dazzling and dizzying. As we eased through Times Square holding hands, costumed characters and cosplayers approached beneath the pulsing lights of towering digital billboards. We worked our way along the sidewalks until Kenzie made an abrupt stop.

"Hey, start singing. Anything, but make it snappy. You ever see the movie Annie? You know the song 'Tomorrow?'" Kenzie asked with a serious expression.

I gave her a weird look and shrugged, beginning the iconic verse in my best church-choir voice.

Kenzie giggled and hugged me. "Someone did that to me a few days ago. Now if anyone asks, you can say that you sang Annie on Broadway."

I swatted at her playfully. "You goof." We paused to gaze at the billboards. "We should go see some of these plays."

"They're musicals mostly, not plays and we can't. Tickets cost a fortune. One day, when I have a job and a home, I can see all of these." Kenzie's voice had a wistful quality. "Up there, a block away by that shuttered store. Let's go sit there."

We walked to the spot Kenzie had indicated, took out our blanket and unfolded it. She removed a coffee can, a folded piece of cardboard, and pulled a marker from her backpack. She wrote in thick letters:

Please help us out. We got kicked out of our apartment and haven't eaten in two days. We have no money and our puppy ran away. Any spare change will help.

I read the sign. "Nice touch about the puppy. So I guess we just sit here and look cute?"

Kenzie winked, her eyes crinkling. "Not too cute. We have to look needy. But we are needy, so that's not too hard."

"What do you want to be when you grow up? You were talking about having a job. In my family, women don't get jobs outside of the house. I mean, you can get paid to talk at a conference or something, but only if your husband gives permission." I thanked a lady who dropped a five-dollar bill in our can. She wore heels and a velvety black-and-green evening gown.

"I always wanted to be a lawyer. Like that guy McCoy on Law & Order." Kenzie frowned, adding, "You can be anything you want. You don't even have to get married, if you don't want. If you could pick a job without getting in trouble, what job would you choose?"

"A singer. I know how to play guitar, too. But I've only played in the church. I saw these people on TV once in

Walmart. They were playing in a band and people were dancing. It looked like fun." I shrugged. "What's Law & Order?"

"It's a show I like. OK, then. I'll be a lawyer and make big money. You can sing and play music on the streets for throw money. Or, get something in the chorus of some musical. That'd be better. And we can live together and take in kids who were kicked out. We can get an apartment near Central Park." Kenzie turned to smile at a guy who was reading our sign.

The man dropped several bills into our can. "That should be enough to get you both a bus ticket home. You girls need to go back to wherever it is you come from before you get hurt out here alone."

Kenzie raised a middle finger at the man's back as he walked away, then counted the money. The man had dropped a hundred in twenty-dollar bills. With other donations, we had $137.63. She put all except five dollars and the change inside her backpack in a zipped pocket.

"Great night, so far. The crowds love you, Destiny."

"I'm glad someone does."

"Hey, stand up and sing something for me. You're the singer here."

I stood with her and began singing "Just a Closer Walk With Thee." My spirit lifted with the words. After two verses, a small crowd had gathered. I sang my best church solos, and people applauded and threw money in the coffee can.

Kenzie thanked everyone, and I curtsied. "We'll be here all night and tomorrow night. You've been a lovely audience. My sister needs to rest her voice now, so thank you." Kenzie blew kisses to the crowd. I started blowing them, as well.

We counted the money. It came to $217.82. It had been two hours. I sat against the wall and watched our gear as Kenzie ran into a deli. She was gone for more than ten minutes, and my heart began racing. I began to cry until she returned with two bottles of Sprite.

"You OK? You're crying."

"I'm fine. Just started worrying. You were gone a while."

She nodded. "They have a bathroom, if you need it." Kenzie sat down. I left and returned a few minutes later.

"What you were saying earlier. We should walk around the park tomorrow and practice. If I can make that much money from singing in two hours now, imagine if I had someone to really teach me how to sing." I leaned my head on Kenzie, and she stroked my arm.

"I'm sorry you got scared before."

"I'm fine. I didn't know where you were."

"I left my stuff with you and our money. I figured you'd be OK for fifteen minutes."

"I'm OK now. Sorry I panicked."

We sat quietly, watching the passing theater crowds. I'd never considered the possibility of singing as a career. Suddenly, I realized that the option existed. The exhilaration I experienced when people applauded me was intense. It wasn't like the feeling of being near Kenzie, or looking at pictures online, or of smoking pot. My stomach fluttered, and my heart swelled with pride. I had never known such excitement, not even when I received accolades in church for my musical solos.

I couldn't put my finger on the difference, but nothing felt as wonderful as the applause I received while busking. Nothing.

Chapter 6

Kenzie and I sat in the theater district until one in the morning. I sang two more sets, and we collected $329.36. My throat was raw, my voice hoarse. A warm glow surrounded me as the excitement of the long day wore off. Exhaustion and exhilaration competed for dominance in my brain. I desired a hotel room, but Kenzie talked me out of it.

"I still got $167 from before I met you." She counted on her fingers. "Now we have $496. If we get a room, that'll take a big hunk. Not everywhere is as cheap as that motel last night. We can't go back there for a while because they'll remember us. If we snuggle together on the subway or somewhere, we can eat and save more money. I'm hungry." We split the money between us, adding the stacks to our backpacks.

I held Kenzie's hand as we walked. "I'm always hungry. What's open at this hour?"

"It's the city. Everywhere's open. Well, mostly." We strolled along looking at storefronts. "What do you feel like having?"

"Pancakes and bacon. And a chocolate milkshake." I smiled at her.

We turned on a street and headed up an avenue. Across the avenue was an all-night restaurant that advertised breakfast at any hour. The lights were dim and the smell of grease permeated the air. The dining area included a long counter with tall seats. Some kind of soft, foreign music played through speakers. The cozy ambiance fit the late hour.

I ordered chocolate chip pancakes, a double side of bacon, and a chocolate milkshake. Kenzie ordered a patty melt with fries and a chocolate shake. We ate in silence, and my eyes grew heavy. Kenzie yawned, which set me off. I could have folded my arms on the counter, rested my head and slept.

After paying for the meal, we walked to the subway and boarded the A Train toward Queens. I propped my feet on the seats, my knees bent, and my back to a wall; I was too far gone to even feel scared. Kenzie leaned against my knees. We fell asleep that way, waking two hours later in Far Rockaway. We remained on the train and rode back to Harlem.

The early morning commuters began boarding. I sat up and held Kenzie on my lap as we rode to the stop where we had boarded earlier. The sun was rising. I yawned and stretched. My face flushed, my lower abdomen cramped, my eyes burned and itched.

"I need a bathroom. And a drug store. I need supplies." I groaned.

Kenzie looked at me a moment and nodded. "Me too."

We entered the corner store and Kenzie bought razors, a can of deodorant, aspirin, chocolate, and pads. I bought a package of baby wipes and a bar of Irish Spring soap. We walked to a corner café and ordered coffees. The place was down at heel, the vinyl upholstery cracking, but there was a single-person bathroom in the back. Kenzie and I entered together.

After stripping to our panties we soaped up and washed. We shaved our legs and pits before spraying each other with deodorant. After taking care of our needs, we dressed in cleaner clothes and returned to our table.

We drank the robust coffee and got refills. My eyes refused to stay shut. My nerves were in a state of hyper-alertness. After finishing our coffee, Kenzie and I walked to the park and wandered along the paths.

Up ahead, a group of boys and girls grabbed something from an old man on a bench. He was hurt. The boys were all well-muscled but they weren't dressed uniformly, except that they appeared uniformly dirty. The girls also looked disheveled but ferocious. Kenzie and I started walking away, unsure what to do about the situation. The kids spotted us, running our way, and stepping in to block our escape. I started backing away, but Kenzie stood her ground.

"The hell you want? Move." She glared with a curt command.

"This is our park. You pay a tax or join our family." The biggest of the teen males towered over her, more than six feet tall with the gorilla-like build of a weightlifter.

I inched up. "You're related, sir?"

"Our street family, dumb ass. I'm Valiant. I could watch out for you and make sure you get a lot of love." The boy reached out to grope me, but I backed away. I glanced at Kenzie.

"Get lost! We're not joining you, don't need your protection, and we're not giving you money. The city owns the park...dumb ass." Kenzie stepped back, feet set in a t-stance and hands raised like a praying mantis.

The boy laughed. "You join or we tax you. We'll take your backpacks."

Kenzie shook her head and backed off until she stood even with me, both of us beside a large boulder. "Third option." Kenzie gave the boy a stone-cold look. "Your best three bitches step up. We win, you leave us be. We lose, you get three hundred dollars."

I started to object, but she looked at me with murder in her eyes. Valiant laughed again. "Weed, Otter, Pixie—kick their asses!"

The three girls stepped up. Two were my size, five foot six, and just over a hundred pounds. One was taller, heavier and muscled. The biggest girl charged forward as the other two moved to our sides.

Kenzie met the charging girl with a front kick. The girl stopped when Kenzie's foot landed between her legs. It was like a football player trying for a field goal from the fifty yard line. Kenzie's right shin attempted to cleave the girl in two. The girl shrieked and dropped to her knees. Kenzie's foot connected with the girl's face before turning and side-kicking the girl to our right. The kick connected with a knee.

As that girl fell, I grabbed the third by her long black hair, tripped her, and smashed her face into the boulder. She bounced off, face bloody from a broken nose. Kenzie punched her in the stomach with a hard right and followed up with jabs to the breasts.

We collected our backpacks, and several boys stepped forward. An intense rage filled me. My stomach tightened and my mind fogged over, numbing me to any fear. I reached out and grabbed one of the boys by his crotch. He screamed as I gripped his testicles. Kenzie kicked the tall teen three times in the left knee. The boy crumpled, and she stomped his groin with her heel. I released the boy I had grabbed; he collapsed and hugged himself. Kenzie reached into the tall boy's pocket and extracted a fat roll of bills.

"We'll tax you for wasting our time! You don't own this park, bitch!" Kenzie snarled.

Cops came running from all directions as we tried to leave. I dropped to the ground and sat back on my heels with my hands up. Kenzie knelt with her hands behind her head. I yelped in pain as a female cop handcuffed me. Kenzie remained stoic as she was cuffed. Other cops handcuffed the teens. An ambulance pulled up, and the old man was loaded inside. Paramedics began treating our attackers.

I was put in a car with Kenzie. A female cop sat between us and read our rights. Silent tears poured down my face. Kenzie stared straight ahead saying nothing. The car pulled away, and we were driven to a station house and led to separate rooms.

I sat there, handcuffs removed, and thought about giving up. Was this my punishment from The Lord? Had my church been right about me? I'd been gone five days and was arrested, heading to prison. Tears fell harder as my chest heaved.

A female officer named Lenin and a male officer named Pitts entered the room. Lenin shoved a box of Kleenex at me across the table. I blew my nose and composed myself. The look they gave me wasn't stern, but it also wasn't kind.

"What's your name?" Pitts held a notepad, poised to collect information. "That girl with you won't talk. We need her name, too. And the names of all your buddies we picked up."

"Destiny Marie Wilbury. The other girl is my sister, Mackenzie Elizabeth. Those weren't our friends. They attacked us."

Lenin tried for a conversational tone. "We'll get to that. You have any identification? How old are you? Where are you from?"

I took a breath. "No, ma'am. Why would we? We're girls. Pastor Ruby says there's no need for an ID since we won't be working outside of the home."

Lenin gave me a harsh look. "It would make everything easier, for one. What's this Pastor's full name? We'll need to make contact with him to vouch for you. So, you're how old?"

"I'm eighteen. Mackenzie is sixteen. He won't vouch for us. He's why we came here from Florida." I was shocked at how easy the lie came.

Pitts looked up from his writing. "How's that? What brings you to the city? Where are you staying?"

"We left home because things weren't good. We're only in New York because that's where the person who plucked us up was heading. We stay in hotels when we can."

Pitts wrote with a strained facial expression. Another officer entered, handed Pitts some paper, and left. Pitts read it and took a surly tone. "You two did a number on those punks you were with. Almost killed that man you robbed. Lucky he can still see. He'll identify you both. Where'd a couple of church girls learn to fight that way?"

My mind reeled as I processed the accusations. "We weren't with those kids. They attacked us."

Lenin shook her head. "Four of those skells told us that you and your sister attacked the others because you wanted the money. They said that attacking that man was your idea. I guess you needed money for a nicer hotel, huh?"

Rage bubbled up at these lies, and I thumped the table with my fist. "No, ma'am! Honest, they attacked us. And we don't know a thing about that old man. We were walking in the park after a long night of singing on the sidewalks for throw money. We saw those other kids grabbing something from that old man. We were looking for a way to call the cops when we got attacked."

Lenin moved toward me. "Calm yourself, or I'll have you restrained."

I sat stock still and said nothing.

Pitts was writing. Lenin sat down again, leaning back. "Assuming we take your story as true, and it would explain the extra cash in your backpacks, what caused the fight?"

"That tall boy, Valiant, said we had to pay him money for walking through their park. Or, we could join them. He said that if we joined he was going to have sex with us whether we wanted it or not." I looked at both officers. "My sister said no. She told him they don't own the park. So he told three girls to attack us. My sister fought back and I helped. Then that tall boy, and another boy attacked us. I grabbed the shorter boy by his manhood, and my sister made it clear that we wanted to be left alone."

Lenin gave a curt nod. "Where'd you learn to fight that way? One of the girls might need surgery."

"Like I said, ma'am, we had our reasons to leave home." I avoided their gaze, staring at my shoes.

"I see. Well, until we sort this out you're going to a holding cell. If you want to make a phone call, now is the time."

I thought about calling Rory, Sheila, and Jeanie but I barely knew them. "I don't have anyone I can call."

"Then put your hands behind you."

I was cuffed again and taken to a bare concrete room with a concrete bench affixed to a wall. There was a metal toilet with a sink attached to the top. The cuffs were removed, the door bolted shut, and I sat on the bench with my knees to my chest. I began sobbing and praying. My parents were right, Pastor Ruby was right. I was vile, and this was my punishment.

I cried for a half hour until I had to dash to the toilet and vomit. I was throwing up, dry heaving, and in tears when a young, female officer unlocked the door. I tried turning around, but couldn't.

"Miss Wilbury? Do you need a doctor?"

"No, ma'am. I just want to go home. I'm sorry. I'm evil." I stood up, feeling dizzy, then stared at my feet.

The officer had some papers. She set them on the bench and radioed someone. Officer Pitts entered a few minutes later with a bottle of water. I sipped as I sat on the bench.

"It looks like you're telling the truth. The victim said that neither of you were even there. We showed him pictures from a cell phone. All of those humps have rap sheets. We're willing to assume that you don't have records in Florida. There's nothing under your names in the city records or the state. We need something, though," Pitts said with a stern expression.

"Yes, sir? What do you need?"

"Your sister won't say a word. She's three cells down. We need you to tell her that it's OK to talk. From what you've described, you're older so she might listen to you."

We walked down a hall into another concrete room with a bench and two officers. I looked at Kenzie and did my best impression of my mother. "Mackenzie Elizabeth Wilbury, you best answer when an adult asks you questions. You know what the Bible says about respecting elders. I told them that those kids started everything, but they need to hear it from you. They know what happened, and we aren't in trouble with them. We'll discuss your behavior later, in private, young lady." I locked eyes with her, silently pleading, and hoped she understood my unspoken message.

I was led out of the room and allowed to use the public restroom to wash up. Afterward I was told to sit to one side of the hall and wait. Kenzie came out a half hour later. We were informed that we could leave. We took our backpacks and checked them to make sure nothing was missing. Kenzie had told a cop about the stack of bills she had stolen from Valiant.

As we left, I turned to officer Pitts. "Can you do me a favor, sir?"

Pitts paused for a moment. "What is it?"

"When you give the money back to that old man, tell him that his attackers got their butts stomped by a couple of girls."

Pitts roared with laughter. "I sure will. Behave yourselves. And stay clear of that area for a while. You should consider going home. It can't be that bad."

Kenzie and I exited the station. We spotted a subway station and caught a train back to Central Park West. The pressure inside of me gave way, and I began sobbing again. Kenzie held me in her arms and stroked my face.

"I'm going home, Kenzie. My father was right about me. I haven't been gone a week and I got arrested. I guess I need more help to stop being a pervert before worse things happen. Five days away from home, and I'm fighting and almost going to jail." I sobbed. Other passengers looked at us without looking.

"Bullshit! I'm not religious like you, but I know that whatever being created this world is just and loving. I know that he doesn't make mistakes in his creations. Today sucked ass! But, damnit Destiny, getting into that fight and getting arrested happened because crap happens. It isn't punishment for being bi!" Kenzie scowled.

A squat, African-American lady with a plump face, a broad posterior, generous bosom, and a graying afro, handed me a tissue. She gave us both a sympathetic look. "Pardon my eavesdropping, honey child, but I don't believe Jesus punishes children. He loved them more than most anything! You're just a young thing! You can't be in his bad graces yet. And surely not because of who you love."

I nodded at her. "Yes, ma'am." I turned toward Kenzie, calming down. "I just, I'm all confused. I'm scared."

"Let's go to the beach. Things'll get better. We need to figure out a plan. And you seriously need to learn how to fight. I might not know about religion, but I know about fighting. I'm an expert on survival. You've got the instincts, chick. What you need to learn are the moves," Kenzie declared, giving me a firm kiss.

I leaned on Kenzie's shoulder. "I've studied biology. I saw

that in a movie once where a guy in a fight grabbed another guy down there. I'm not going home because I can't. My family doesn't want me back."

"You really laid it on me back there. One of the cops said she'd get on you about threatening me. I had to tell her you were just pissed off." Kenzie kissed me again, and we held each other.

My heart started racing, and a sudden wave of fury overtook me. "I can't believe they blamed us. I wish I'd killed those jerks!"

Kenzie gave me a steady look. "Slow your roll, chick. I know you're hurting, and I get why. But, don't kill anyone unless you've got no other choice. Fighting back, yes. But don't get carried away."

"Sorry. They totally lied about us. I want to scream or hit something."

"You weren't allowed to feel anything before. Or, at least, you couldn't express it. Don't worry, girl, I'll teach you how to kick some serious ass."

Chapter 7

The closer I grew to Kenzie, certain facts became evident. She had grown up on the streets, never knowing stability or any real sense of affection. My life had been fraught with difficulty and demoralization, but at least I'd had a bed, clothes, and food. Although I lost my mother's affections and attention when my baby brother came along, at least I'd received both for a year and a half.

Kids like Kenzie didn't survive for long on the street; at least, not in any discernibly human way. The distortion of personality and erosion of the character were swift, massive, and often irreversible. I cared about her—loved her, even—but there were walls and barriers she refused to let anyone breech.

By turns, Kenzie was cynical and callous, winsome, and desperate. For moments, she even became vulnerable. With her it was about vibes, perceptions, and boundaries. She expected the people she allowed around her to offer what she needed as she needed it. I wasn't sure she entirely trusted that I wouldn't one day abandon her. I could state unequivocally that I feared waking up to find her gone.

Despite our fears of abandonment, by mid-summer Kenzie and I were in a steady relationship. We were desperate for something beyond the streets and as far from our upbringings as possible, no matter how impossible that seemed. I was falling in love with a girl, and my parents and their cult-like church couldn't stop me. My love for Kenzie seemed more normal as time went on; but, I still had moments of self-doubt. Not every day was easy. I continued attending church in Brooklyn, and Kenzie joined me. We found the nerve, in July, to speak to Pastor Affenhoden.

We walked into his office and sat in front of his mahogany desk. "I need to confess something, sir. I'm scared, but it's only fair to your church that we tell you the truth." I studied my boots as my stomach flipped. Kenzie squeezed my arm gently.

The pastor leaned back with his hands behind his head, fingers intertwined. "It is Christ's church, not mine. But, do go on, sister Loretta."

"She and I aren't sisters. We're a couple. My parents kicked me out because I have feelings for other girls. Sexual feelings." I couldn't meet his eyes.

Pastor Affenhoden didn't sound upset. "Sister Crystal? Do you reciprocate those feelings?" My eyes lifted a bit. His demeanor remained pleasant.

Kenzie appeared startled by the question. "Do I what? I don't know that word."

"Do you love her in return? The way she loves you?" His face was relaxed, and his voice held no hint of irritation.

"If you mean do I have sexual feelings for her, hell yeah. She has my back, and I have hers."

"So you love her? And you love Crystal, Loretta?"

Kenzie looked away, adding, "I guess. I don't want to lose her, anyway. Yeah, I'm in love with her. I ran away from home because of problems. Big problems. Mom doesn't want me back. She doesn't even love me. But Destiny sure as hell does."

I looked over, squeezing her hand. "I love you, too."

The pastor thumbed his chin. "Ladies, some less enlightened people have issues with this subject. They cherry-pick a few passages of scripture and use it to make others feel less than. These same people often degrade women, minorities, and people with disabilities. It is wrong. It is horribly out of sync with the teachings of the word. So, unless you personally see a need to change how you feel, I recommend enjoying the fact that you are in love. I would caution safety in regard to sex, but I caution all teens in that. I'd prefer that unmarried people not have sex at all, but frankly my preferences don't matter." Pastor Affenhoden leaned forward. "We have group counseling sessions for teens and young adults who were abused or traumatized. It meets Tuesday evening after a dinner provided by the hospitality committee. Perhaps you could join us? We also have resources for group homes."

I looked up as tears dribbled down my face. "The counseling sounds good. We'll be there. The group homes, no thank you. I've seen what those are like. In my parents' church. We aren't doing that, sir."

"I understand, sister. If you run into trouble and change your mind..."

"We won't. There's one more thing." Kenzie smiled at me.

"Yes?" Pastor Affenhoden asked.

I blushed. "My name's Destiny Wilbury, and she's Mackenzie Guevara. We weren't sure about trusting people, but it sounds like you're on our side."

"I'll notate the records. And thank you for your trust." The pastor shook our hands. "I would like to pray for you both."

We nodded, and he prayed. It was not the type of prayers my parents offered in church. Pastor Affenhoden exuded love instead of anger.

The next day was July Fourth and we caught the F Train to Coney Island. The crowd was intense, and the heat was worse. After watching a famous hot dog eating contest, we took the subway to Manhattan and found an air-conditioned restaurant. We sat sipping Cokes, eating fries, and holding hands across the table all afternoon.

That night, we watched the fireworks. Afterward, we rode the A Train through its entire four-hour circuit—from 207th Street in Harlem, to Far Rockaway in Queens, and back. We slept sitting up, leaning on each other. The train was crowded. By July, the crowds no longer scared me; but, I remained alert to danger.

We arrived back near the Museum of Natural History at four-thirty in the morning, walked to an all-night café, and had coffee and bagels. That nightly ride became part of our routine, along with sitting by a shuttered storefront on Broadway in the heart of the theater district. I sang church songs, and Kenzie collected money.

After a couple of weeks, we bought an acoustic guitar at a pawn shop. I played while I sang. It was one more piece of baggage to tote, but it allowed me to play on the subway. We were making a few hundred dollars a day, double that on the weekends. I'd start performing on Broadway at seven each evening and finished at midnight or one.

Once the sun was up, we headed to the beach and caught up on sleep. After we woke, Kenzie taught me some martial arts. She made me execute one hundred front kicks, right-side kicks, back kicks, and left-side kicks. After that, I had to snap-punch fifty times with each fist. The sweat poured off of me, but Kenzie wouldn't let me rinse off in the ocean until I finished my work out. If I didn't execute the moves with power, she yelled at me to do them again.

When my eyes burned with sweat, I ran into the ocean and dove into the waves fully clothed. Kenzie watched my boots and socks. The water, salty though it was, cooled me down. An hour in the burning sun dried my clothes thoroughly.

Kenzie also worked on my timidity. In short order, I learned to throw attitude as well as fists. Had my parents heard my language, I'd have soap bubbles coming out of my ears. But, there was an intimidation factor in throwing out a well-timed swear word. Men, especially, caught my wrath. I would notice some boy eying me and, in return, I'd shut him down with an immolating glare and a flare of my nostrils.

Despite her physical prowess, in late July Kenzie began having nightmares. She couldn't, or wouldn't, tell me what was causing them. She'd wake up in a sweat, crying and shaking. I'd hold her, kissing her until she calmed down.

I spoke up after a few days of this. "Maybe Pastor knows someone who can help. You really need to talk to someone."

Kenzie glared at me. "I'm fine. It's nothing. I'm just having bad dreams, I'm not cray-cray, OK?"

I worried about her, but there was nothing I could do. I

held her close to my breasts and tried to use a soothing voice when her dreams turned bad.

After a few weeks of attendance, Kenzie began opening up a bit during the church group on Tuesdays. Her life had been harsh. Her mother, far from the timid flower of virtue that was my mother, was a woman of many words—most of them four-lettered. Kenzie was not a stranger to being slapped or punched. There was clearly more to tell but, as I've noted, Kenzie would open up so far and no farther. There was an emotional wall, and she allowed no one past it.

In the midst of this drama we called our life, we wandered through museums and spent hours in the parks. The art museums made my heart soar. I had never seen most of the works, but the colors and textures as well as the subjects touched something deep in my soul. The history museum exhibits left me perplexed. The information provided was often in direct conflict with my former homeschooling.

The parks, likewise, set off my emotions. The flowers with their scents and vivid color patterns made me feel closer to The Creator. So did the trees. We were in the middle of a concrete maelstrom, and yet these pockets of natural beauty allowed a momentary escape.

The other emotions I experienced were hostility and rage. We'd sit on a bench, holding hands or making out, and children would show up to play on the climbing equipment. Some might find such innocent playing to be adorable, but not me. I watched with a mixture of envy and hatred. It made no sense to me at the time. Kenzie expressed similar pain.

"Hey, those brats keep screaming for someone to push them. Maybe I should. I could shove them off the swings, and then they'd shut the hell up!" Kenzie giggled.

"We could use those toy trucks and have a demolition derby in the sand box." I scowled. "They might quit arguing about whose sand castle is bigger."

"Mama! Mama! Just be glad I'm not your mama, you whiney bitch!" Kenzie mocked as I held my belly, laughing until tears rolled down my face.

We never acted on the words, but we spoke them.

On rainy days, we napped in the libraries or watched movies. Every weekend, we would give some drunk a few bucks in exchange for renting us a cheap hotel room. During our walks in the parks, we discussed the future; in the hotel rooms, we grew closer as a couple.

Despite having been together for a few months, Kenzie and I had only kissed and snuggled when sleeping. We took showers or baths together when we had the chance, which was both cleansing and exhilarating, but we had never actually had sex.

One evening, I lay on a queen bed watching a movie with Kenzie in my arms. A lesbian couple was in the throes of passion. I turned my head. "Have you ever, um, done that stuff?"

"Yeah. A few times. At a party once with a girl I met last year. Her dad got reassigned to somewhere called Lejeune, and she moved."

"I had to sneak on the computer in my father's office to look at that. I always wanted to, but I never..."

Kenzie rolled over and kissed me on the mouth. Our tongues danced. We stood, and she unbuttoned my shorts then unzipped them.

"I don't sleep around, you know. Like I said, last time I went with a girl she left me. I want this, but I don't want to mess things up with us." Kenzie held me gently.

I pulled off my t-shirt, undid my bra, and moaned as she traced a finger over my breasts. Kenzie removed her shirt, and I kissed her chest. "I love you, Kenzie. I'm not going anywhere. I promise."

We lay down and began necking. The tension of the moment overcame us once more, and we both scrambled out of our remaining clothes. Kenzie shuddered as I kissed down her body, from her neck to her belly button. I imitated some of the action I had observed on the Internet. Her vocal responses indicated pleasure.

Kenzie rolled me over and reciprocated my affections. It

was everything I had fantasized about, as my body exploded in passion. My hips convulsed, and my spine turned to jelly as my shrieks pierced the dusty air in the room. Kenzie and I lay there after—limp, sweaty, and exhausted. A half hour later, we managed to stand and head into the bathroom. My legs were rubber bands, stretched out of shape. I filled the tub with warm water.

Kenzie sat between my legs with her head resting back on me. "Oh, baby, baby. I've never felt nothing like that. You're better than TaWanda was—a lot better. She's the girl I told you about."

I kissed her neck and rubbed her belly. "That was better than any revival I ever attended. Better than any movement of the spirit. Thank you."

After our bath we fell asleep together naked. The next day, we used our monthly passes to a fitness center. We had asked a lady at the church to co-sign for us because she used the same place. The membership cost two hundred dollars for the both of us, but it was worth the price. We weren't looking to lose weight or build muscle, mind you. If anything, Kenzie was too thin. I was losing weight, as well, from walking a lot and not eating enough. What we sought from a fitness club was the relaxation of a steam sauna and access to shower facilities.

The showers were quite nice, as a matter of fact. We received a locker key for each of us every time we used the fitness center. We'd enter a small room and lock the door. Our clothes remained on a bench, and a single shower stall was located beyond a curtain. After a quick rinse, we wrapped in large, fluffy towels and transferred our clothing and gear to the lockers. We sat on wooden benches in the steam room and relaxed. Rarely did we even speak in those confines. Kenzie would close her eyes and breathe. I took the time to offer up silent supplications to The Supreme Being. After sweating out the toxins, we fetched our clothes, had a longer shower, and left until the next day.

That morning I sat in the steam and, without warning, my mind started reeling. It wasn't the heat, but anxiety over what

Kenzie and I had done. Kissing was one thing, even sleeping in the same bed, but now I was committed to sexual sin. There was no turning back, and—if my parents were right—I was going to Hell.

I understood that Pastor Affenhoden said our relationship was acceptable, even if he didn't tacitly approve of premarital sex. I accepted that I was bi, but rational thinking didn't change my anxiety. I prayed, deciding that Kenzie and I had to break up. I didn't know how to tell her.

Chapter 8

That evening in late August, we walked in the park after spending the afternoon at the movies. We visited certain theaters when the weather became unbearable. Some theaters ran as many as twenty movies in their auditoriums. For the price of one ticket, we could watch movies all day. Between movies, we freshened up in the restroom and then sneaked into a different movie. Outside, the sun was ripping the hides off of pedestrians while we snuggled in an air-conditioned theater sharing popcorn and Dr. Pepper.

After the movies, we went out for Chinese food. Other than the occasional delivery service, I had little experience with Chinese food. I had never been inside an authentic Chinese restaurant. We caught a subway to Chinatown and headed to a place that Kenzie liked. The restaurant was a lacquered chamber, redolent with garlic, fryer grease, and licorice. We were attended to by dour old men dressed in Qing Guanmao caps, red jackets, and black slacks. Silkscreens of dragons adorned the walls. A huge statue of Hotai sat beside the cashier's station, collecting dust and stray coins.

Kenzie and I sat in the rear, nibbling on fried noodles and duck sauce while holding hands across the table. We took turns feeding each other noodles.

She chewed contemplatively. "We make a good team. Thing is that we keep talking about our future careers, our big dreams, adopting kids, all that shit. But, it's all pipe dreams. We always end up in a rundown hotel room, or sleeping on the subway, or in a squat under the Coney Island boardwalk. We aren't in school. We don't have any protection. I mean, against the old drunks and the kids who think we're prey. I can fight them off, and you're learning fast. We need a street mom, but I don't want the other crap street families are into."

I sucked on a noodle for a moment. "Yeah, I guess. I need to talk to you about that, but I don't know how to say it."

"Just say it. You've been moody today, something wrong?"

"Yes. We're wrong. Our relationship is wrong. I'm scared."

"Woah! Hold up. What are you saying? You're leaving me?" Kenzie's lip quivered as if she might cry.

"I just...I love you. I mean I really love you. But..."

"But what? Didn't you feel good last night? I wasn't kidding that you rocked my world."

"That's the problem. I wanted that so much, for so long, but..."

"Dammit bitch, but what?" Kenzie's eyes flashed with rage.

"I don't want to end up in Hell forever. What if my parents are right?"

"You know they aren't. You know that."

"My brain does. Then I get these thoughts about things. It's like I hear their voices screaming at me."

Kenzie started to stand. She stopped and took a breath. "Can we still be friends? Still stay together as friends? I need you, and you need me."

"Yes, we can stick together. I'm sorry. I don't really want to break up, I'm just scared."

"I know you are. I just don't know how to help. I want to, but I don't know how. Maybe Pastor can."

"I'm sorry, I'm being stupid. I'm happy being with you, and that's what matters. Sure beats how my life used to be."

Kenzie's eyes grew misty. "I still think we need a family around us or at least someone we can go to if things get bad. Like a street-mom, but without the drugs, sex, and crime. I don't want some thug, I want someone special. Maybe she can help you, too."

I held her hands. "Where do we look? Other than people at church the only person I know in New York is you."

Kenzie rubbed her chin. "There're some kids I met my first

week away from home, but I don't know. They're into hard drugs and shit."

I sipped tea and tried to pray. I thought about Jeanie, Rory, and Sheila. "Hey, is there any charge on your phone? I should buy one for myself." I looked up as our food was served.

She poured us ceramic cups of oolong. "Later, let's eat. I'm starved."

I helped myself from the serving dishes and took a bite of the Szechuan beef. The sensation was overwhelming, incinerating my taste buds. I gulped tea to douse the flames, cauterizing my uvula.

Kenzie's eyes crinkled at the edges, and the sides of her mouth turned up. "Careful, it's hot."

I refrained from flicking a spoonful of rice at her. "No kidding!"

We ate in silence, devouring the food. I found a rhythm for eating and drinking that kept the spicy flames in my mouth to a dull ember. The ginger milk curd for dessert helped soothe my belly.

After we paid and exited, I took the flip-phone Kenzie handed to me. "I told you about those college kids I met. Maybe we can hook up with them. It might mean moving to New Jersey, but they'd be great as street dad and moms. Rory isn't like most men. He's actually kind of sweet."

Kenzie nodded, and we found a bench. "I don't want to go back to Jersey, but sure, call them."

I dialed. After seven rings the phone was answered. "Hello?"

"Is this Jeanie? This is Destiny. You gave me a ride a couple of months ago." My stomach was churning the food I'd eaten, and I breathed deep to steady myself.

"Holy crap! We wondered how you were!" She put me on speaker phone. "Hey guys, it's that girl we picked up in Florida."

"Hey, honey. It's Sheila. I gave birth three weeks early. Our son, John Rainbow, is fine, just sort of small."

"Rainbow?" I giggled in spite of my nerves.

"Yes, we named him Rainbow. I hoped you'd call some time. I'm changing him while we talk." Sheila sounded happy.

Rory cut in. "We're doing great in school. We have a week off, second week of September. We're heading to the beach in Delaware. What are you up to, kid?"

The cheerful voices calmed my nerves. "I'm in New York still. I met this girl. Um, it's weird asking, but we need someone to talk to about things. I thought about you guys."

Jeanie took me off the speaker. "Do you and your girlfriend have any money? You should come see us. Join us at the beach, if you want. My aunt has a rooming house. Don't worry. Her partner passed on last winter, but they were out of the closet before it was considered acceptable. She'll totally understand you."

"That's one thing I need to talk about."

"So come see us."

"We'll come see you in September."

"Sounds good." We hung up.

I held Kenzie's hand. "They invited us to spend a week at the beach in Delaware. They're so sweet, and so smart. We should go. I think they can even help me figure out why I'm being so stupid about you and me."

Kenzie's eyes narrowed and her brow wrinkled. "You sure about that? You met them for like two days. I mean if you want to go see them, then let's go. But I don't want to get stranded on a beach because you're afraid. I don't want anything bad to happen to us, either. You sure they're safe?"

Despite my earlier feelings, I pulled Kenzie toward me and held her. "Rory saved me after I got kicked out. They gave me a ride, food, and let me stay at their apartment. Jeanie and Sheila are really smart. I think it's OK."

Kenzie cuddled back and sighed. "Maybe we could go to see them tomorrow. If it helps you, then let's do it. But I'm holding the money in case you don't plan on coming back."

"I'm sorry. I told you that."

"I know." She gave me a look, then hugged me tight.

We rode the J Train to Brooklyn, and Kenzie led me down

Myrtle Avenue to a large apartment complex. We climbed the fire escape to the roof of a six-story building. Kenzie waved to a boy sitting on a milk crate, reading a comic book and drinking a bottle of malt liquor. The bottle was wrapped in a brown paper sack. As the boy swigged his drink, he laughed at his comic book.

The boy looked up and smiled. "Hey, long time no see. You looking for Scully? He went to get some pies. We didn't know whatever happened to you."

The boy had a strong New York accent, an assortment of tattoos, and crooked teeth. He handed Kenzie the bottle. She had a swig and offered it to me. I shook my head so she handed it back to the boy.

Kenzie shrugged. "I'm around. This is Destiny. We've been hanging at CI a lot. Where's everyone else?"

"Ah, shit!" The boy looked up. "There was a raid other night. Big mess. Cops nicked Chrissy, Vickie, and Lucas for possession. Nothing huge, a little H and some Oxys. Me 'n Scully were getting back with food and cut out before we got fingered. No one's been coming around since then." The boy had a long pull and belched.

I looked around and saw an outlet against a wall. "That plug work?" The boy nodded.

After plugging in the phone to recharge, I sat with Kenzie and tuned the guitar. I was in the middle of "Lord I Lift Thy Name on High" when a boy appeared with five large pizza boxes. He had long, greasy blond hair and a face pocked with divots from a severe case of acne.

"Didn't know we had company. I'd have lifted some more food." The boy laughed.

My stomach tightened. "Lifted?"

The boxes were opened to reveal two pizzas with everything, one with pepperoni and two boxes of breadsticks. "Yeah. Lifted from the back of a truck. Guy didn't object after I showed him my friend." The boy raised his shirt to reveal a pistol tucked in the waistband of his jeans. "Even if most of the family scattered, I still have some kids to feed."

I looked at Kenzie, who motioned me to stay put. She cleared her throat. "If there's gonna be trouble, we'll split."

Scully sat and pulled a slice of pizza loose. He took a bite and smiled. "I'd like to think I'm better than that. The po-po didn't see a thing, and I scrambled my path some."

A whistle split the air. Scully whistled in return. The first boy's eyes were half shut as he opened up another bottle of malt liquor. The whistle came again, and three girls climbed onto the roof. Behind them were two boys with backpacks. They sat near us, and the boys took three bottles of Old Crow from one pack. From the other, they removed bags of chips, bread, peanut butter and jelly, and several packages of Hershey miniatures.

One of the girls was either twelve or just small. She had pink hair in a pixie cut, freckles, and wore overalls and boots. "Who's the new kids? I got what I could from my kitchen. Mom's passed out again."

Scully leaned over and grabbed a bottle of whiskey. He had a long pull. "This is my friend Mackenzie. I didn't catch her girlfriend's name."

I was still watching him and wanting to leave. The gun frightened me. "I'm Destiny."

Scully nodded. "Gotcha. So, over there drunk on Colt, is Mario. These girls are their street mom Dion, Rachel, and Luz. The dudes are Sal and Casey. I'm the street dad. We live up here. Except for Rachel, who lives downstairs with her drunk mama."

I inched closer to Kenzie. "Nice to meet you."

Kenzie gave me a gentle smile and everyone dug into the food. After a few sips of Old Crow, my nerves settled down. Three hours later, a few of the kids had taken out a glass tube and began smoking something. Kenzie motioned me to go, so we took our phone and left. We approached the subway stairs.

"So much for that. By the way, that was meth they were smoking. That shit isn't happening around me." She sighed, shaking her head. "Nuh-uh. Not a chance in Hell. Some pot, yeah that's good, but meth, no way."

I side hugged her. "Guns scare me. My father had one for hunting and protection, but I don't like them."

We sat on the J Train and fell asleep holding each other. A few hours later, Kenzie and I rode to the fitness club. After a quick breakfast, we caught the ferry to Weehawken then took the bus from there. An hour later, we were at the station waiting for Jeanie. As we sat eating a bag of Fritos and drinking bottles of Dr. Pepper, I kept an eye out for the van.

"That's them. Their van anyway." I bounced up and down, giggling like a kid at Christmas.

The van parked, and Jeanie clambered out the side door. She got her footing and ran over to me. "Hey, boo! Long time no see!" She hugged me tight and gave me a kiss on the cheek. I kissed her back. Her hair was a darker shade of blue.

Kenzie's eyebrows furrowed, and her mouth turned downward. "Ummm...hello?"

I put an arm around Kenzie's shoulder. "Guys? This is Kenzie."

Kenzie bared her teeth in a forced grin. She wrapped her arms around me possessively.

Jeanie grinned. "Hi. We met this sweetie in Florida. She was all kinds of messed up."

"Yeah, she is. I take care of her, though." Kenzie gave her a petulant look, like a little girl who didn't want to share her favorite dolly. I was tempted to spank her and put her in time-out.

Sheila and Rory stood side by side, looking me over head to toe. Sheila was slimmer but tired, her face drawn. She reached out, hugging me and Kenzie at the same time. Kenzie let go of me and stood looking at everyone, sizing them up. Rory hugged me. He tried to hug Kenzie but she pulled back, her eyes like a deer caught in the headlights. She grabbed me in another tight hug. He backed up without a word.

"You look stronger, Destiny. Healthier, in a way. But something's different. You sure everything's OK?" Rory's voice softened from its usual boisterous basso profundo.

"Um, yeah. I guess. I mean, it isn't easy, but we survive. I've been working out. Kenzie's teaching me stuff." I shrugged. "You alright, Sheila? You look like you need sleep."

Sheila winked at me "Joys of motherhood, imp. If I didn't have my minx and Rory to help out, I'd look worse."

We all piled into the van, and Rory drove us back to their apartment. Sheila paid their next door neighbor ten bucks for watching baby Rainbow. Rory entered the kitchen and started making food. Kenzie and I sat on the couch. Sheila sat in a recliner, feeding her son formula. Jeanie sat on a love seat with her feet tucked under her butt. Rory came out with a dish of cashews and five bottles of Heineken.

He looked at me with his eyebrows arched. "We were worried when you never made contact. The city can be a dangerous place. We hoped you hadn't been hurt or worse."

"I met Kenzie my first day. Things just got hectic. We only have her phone." I apologized. "There's stuff, though. Not trouble, not really, but...we need advice."

"Shoot." Rory took a long pull of beer.

I swallowed some cashews. "You guys still study psychology?"

Sheila burped her son. "It's my major. Rory's, too. We'll be seniors next spring."

Kenzie leaned against me and sighed. "Sorry for being a jealous bitch. Destiny's all the family I have anymore."

"That's my question," I said, poking her. "We've had trouble with some street families. Even got arrested a couple months ago. But we also have trouble with old, drunk guys. We can't get hotel rooms on our own, so we ask some person or another to pay for the room in exchange for a little cash. Most of the old creeps want in our pants, too." Jeanie nodded, and Rory scowled. "We need protection, but so far the groups we encounter are involved with drugs and stealing, or the boys want sex with us. Or both."

"Mostly both." Kenzie was on her second beer. I was a quarter of the way finished with my first.

"I wouldn't mind having sex with some of the boys. They're built. But, dammit, it has to be my choice. My choice!" I stopped myself, looking away to calm down.

Sheila looked at me with wide eyes and a big smile. "I'll be damned. Where's that girl we picked up in that parking lot? I will be damned." Rory laughed and gave me a thumbs up. Jeanie nodded with approval.

Kenzie rubbed my shoulder. "We're working on it. She's a lot tougher now. The other day, this old guy tried feeling her up on the subway. Girl damn near scratched his eyes out." She took a sip of beer. "Thing is, it'd be easier with a street family. Sometimes, though...there's got to be more than living on the streets."

Jeanie nodded. "A lot more. Things don't sound too good. You can't keep living that way."

"We got no choice. I mean, we can't move in here with you. Destiny wants to, but we can't." Kenzie sighed.

"No, that wouldn't be a good idea right now." Rory shook his head. "We're up at all hours with Rainbow, and we keep different schedules because of school."

"Yeah, and I'm not even sure if we're sticking together anyway," I added reluctantly.

Jeanie's eyes widened. "What? Why not? You're a cute couple."

"It's my fault. I'm having problems, and I can't explain it. I don't even really understand what's going on."

"Well, can you tell me what kind of problems?" Jeanie and Sheila faced me and Kenzie as Rory put Rainbow in a bassinet.

"I'm in love with Kenzie. We, ummm, well, we sleep together and everything."

Sheila grinned, "That's great. Dare I ask the problem?"

"I know in my head that there's nothing wrong with us loving each other. My heart says it's right. But, there are these thoughts...I mean..."

Sheila sighed, and Jeanie shook her head. "Yeah, I had a feeling you were going there."

"If you went back to Florida tomorrow, could you stop thinking about Kenzie?" Jeanie asked.

"No. I'd always think about her."

"Can you imagine a life where you'd be happy without her?"

"No."

"Then you'd better decide what you want. Do you want to be happy, or do you want to buy into dogmatic bullshit?"

Tears dribbled down my face, and Kenzie pulled me close. "I know what I want, but…"

Sheila interrupted, "But wanting it isn't enough. You spent years being brainwashed. Like all kids, you were fed a continual narrative. In your case, the narrative was full of misinformation, ignorance, and outright hatred. Breaking that narrative can take years. I'm still working on it."

"It hurts. I don't want to lose her. But, I don't want to burn in Hell either." I stammered through a gush of tears and snot.

"Honey," Sheila passed me Kleenex, "you're burning in Hell right now. You're torturing yourself because a bunch of puritanical dip-wads indoctrinated you."

"Then what the hell do I do?" I screamed. Rainbow began crying, and I blushed. "Sorry, ma'am, I didn't mean to yell." I stared a hole into the floor as Kenzie held me close.

"It's fine, kid." Rory waved a dismissive hand. He had just returned from the bedroom and went to comfort his son.

"We'll help you. We'll do all we can." Jeanie brought me a second bottle of beer. Kenzie was on her third.

The beer calmed me. I took a few deep breaths. "I know deep down that this is who I am. But, I've heard pastors say that humans are born struggling with temptation. Even Pastor Affenhoden says it. We're meant to struggle in order to grow closer to the Lord."

"That's accurate, as far as it goes," Sheila ate some cashews and swallowed, "but in this situation it doesn't work. Struggling against natural instinct to steal from others to get what we want—or, struggling against killing those who hurt us—is one thing. Struggling against our inherent and innate desires for love is a whole other thing. There's historical evidence, as well as scholarly interpretation, that being LGBTQ isn't sinful."

"Really? Awesome." Kenzie finished her drink. "I'm sick of Destiny beating herself up, but I can't get through to her."

I hugged Kenzie tight. "I'm sorry I'm so stupid."

"OK, first things first. Do not call yourself stupid. You aren't. Don't say it anymore." Jeanie's eyes blazed.

"Sorry, ma'am."

"Dammit, Destiny, my name's Jeanie. Hers is Sheila. Our lover boy over there is Rory. We won't hurt you." Jeanie chuckled.

Rory popped a bottle of beer and sat between Sheila and Jeanie. "We barely know you, kid, but we've talked about you off and on since we met you. Good things. We were worried about you."

Sheila draped an arm around Rory's shoulder. "Getting back to your question, first of all, the term homosexual wasn't even a concept for the earliest Christians. There were terms that denoted same-sex intercourse, but there was no word to identify someone by their sexual orientation. That's actually a very modern concept and construct. The word homosexual didn't even enter the English language until the late eighteen hundreds."

I thought about that. "Then what did the church think about people like us?"

"That depends, because unlike a lot of ultra-fundamentalist believers, historians realize that the term Christian was rather generic when Paul coined it. A lot of groups started calling themselves Christian. Some of the earliest had a wide range of views on sexuality, from openly permissive to celibate."

We moved to the dining room table and Rory served us lasagna and salad with a bottle of wine. Sheila continued between bites of food. "For the most part, there's no actual evidence for or against what the church believed. The church wasn't a uniform structure, except for belief in Christ. Matters of human sexuality have been interpreted by various academics and skewed by their own desire to accept or reject. A great deal of the trouble with this in America began during Puritan times."

I had some wine. It was strong, but went well with the food. "I never knew that. So then, The Lord doesn't hate us?"

Rory laughed. "Jesus once cursed some figs, but he never

said a word about...”

Jeanie glared, “Don’t say it. I hate that word!”

Rory looked contrite. “Pardon me, I apologize. I got carried away.”

I looked at them, shocked. “Did you just snap at the man of the house? In my family, my mom wouldn’t have dared.”

“Your family was full of shit,” Kenzie snarled.

“Yeah, but it’s even in the Bible. The man is in charge. I mean, look at them. Rory is in charge around here.”

Rory almost spit out some lasagna laughing. Sheila and Jeanie laughed, too. “Who says I’m in charge?”

“You’re the man of the house.”

Jeanie wiped her mouth and smiled at me. “He is a man, yes. And, in the kitchen, he’s in charge. Sheila doesn’t like to cook, and I can burn water trying to boil it. When it comes to paying the bills and keeping the receipts in order, I’m in charge. Sheila handles our schedules and helps Rory take notes in their classes. She also fixes the computers.”

“Huh?”

Rory nodded. “That’s right. I need help with my notes because I have dyslexia. I’ve found ways to cope, but having some help makes it easier. We all have our strengths and our issues.”

Kenzie started yawning. She’d had three beers and three glasses of wine. I was still on my first glass.

Sheila finished her food and leaned back. “Do you know what a helpmeet is?”

“Like Eve?”

“You definitely aren’t stupid. Yes, like Eve. She wasn’t Adam’s slave or submissive, she was his helpmeet. When Adam was created, he had flaws. All men have flaws. Eve was created with flaws because all women have flaws. They had different flaws and complimented each other. That’s how relationships work.”

“That’s awesome.” Kenzie giggled, a bit inebriated.

Jeanie laughed. “Do you two know what the most important part of a relationship is?”

"Great sex." Kenzie grinned, and I blushed.

"No. Great sex is fun, it's wonderful, but it isn't the most important thing. The most important stuff is 'What do you want for dinner?', 'How was your day?', 'What movie should we watch?'—stuff like that."

I stood up to help clear dishes. "That makes sense. Is that what you guys do?"

"Absolutely." Rory began loading a dishwasher as I returned to the couch.

Kenzie lay down with her head on my lap. "Are you guys sure we can't stay here? I'm liking it. I like you."

"We don't have the space or the resources, dear." Jeanie put a blanket over Kenzie.

I yawned. "We still have problems on the streets, though. Like we told you. We need a dad around to protect us."

Kenzie looked at the girls, adding, "Or a street mom."

"Yeah, or maybe both. But I'm not getting involved with the stupid stuff they do. I don't want to get arrested again."

Kenzie purred as I stroked her hair. "Thing is, we need school, too. I want to be a lawyer one day. Destiny's a great singer, and she wants to study music. How does that even happen when we're living on subway trains and eating in all-night restaurants?"

Rory brought out pieces of chocolate cake, and cups of coffee. "Well, for one thing, you don't get there by getting involved with street families. If you met a guy or a girl who wanted the same things you want, it might work. But, these street families are the exact opposite of what you want."

"I did a paper on the street family phenomenon for my sophomore psych class," Jeanie said as Rory sat beside her. "From what I've studied, the majority of these so-called street families are kids who come from decent, middle-class homes. They left that life behind to create gangs fueled by drugs, crime, and prostitution."

"Why would anyone trade a good home for a life like that? Jesus! If my mom even gave half a shit about me, I'd never have left." Kenzie's eyes took on the sad look I'd seen before during the past weeks.

"Why? Boredom, I suspect, or they're spoiled brats. It might be rebellion or a need for freedom. No one really has a handle on the why of it." Sheila stood to check on Rainbow.

"For whatever the reason, these kids turn feral. They form these so-called families. The phenomenon started on the west coast in the early nineties and moved east. The kids you see are runaways, but for every fifty of them, maybe two are running away from abuse or have been abandoned by their parents—like you both."

Kenzie's mouth opened and snapped shut as her eyes widened. "How'd you know I was abused?" She glared up at me.

Jeanie's eyes softened and her lips pursed. "Honey, it's written on your face and in your eyes. It's different than the look Destiny gives off. You can't hide what you've seen."

Kenzie sat up and snuggled into me. She wept softly.

Jeanie continued. "Most of the kids in these families run away because mommy and daddy have expectations. The brats are expected to do chores, perform well in school, and obey curfew, among other things. When they fail to meet these lofty and exalted expectations," Jeanie rolled her eyes, "the parents respond by depriving the children of cell phones and video games or, horror of horrors, grounding them."

Sheila returned and nodded at Jeanie. "Living on the streets might not be manageable if the cities weren't filled with bleeding hearts who set up shelters for the children. The shelters provide warm beds in semi-private rooms, plenty of junk food, video games and other amenities. They also provide nourishing meals. In short, the kids receive every creature comfort of home without any responsibility or rules. What you want exists, just not necessarily the way you want it."

"Sure sounds nice to me." I shrugged. "Where can we find one of those places?"

Jeanie shook her head. "The problem is that a lot of older teens have found an easy market to whom they can sell drugs. They've also found another market because the big city is full of perverts who have sick urges that involve young bodies. You said you've encountered such people. And once the young bodies are hooked on drugs, pimping them out becomes a matter of fact."

Jeanie sat beside us, holding Kenzie as she cried harder. Her voice was soft and comforting. "It's OK. No one here will let anything happen to you." I held Kenzie from the other side. Sheila and Rory moved to sit on the floor in front of us.

Kenzie tried to stop her tears. She couldn't. "I'm sorry. I just...I've had experience with that happening. I was like five the first time one of her boyfriends put a finger in me."

"Is that what those nightmares are about?" I pulled her toward my chest, where she nestled in and sighed.

Kenzie held me, shivering and crying. "Yeah. It's crazy. That stuff isn't happening anymore. But, I still see the guys when I sleep. It hasn't happened for like four years now. Not since I learned to fight back."

Rory spoke up. "I'd seriously suggest talking to a doctor. Sounds like you have PTSD. It isn't just military that gets it, you know. Sheila has it. She's getting treated for it."

Sheila helped Kenzie into her lap and stroked her face. "I grew up in Kentucky. It wasn't terrible but it wasn't always easy. My mom's folks were Jesus Freaks. They moved to Kentucky after their commune shut down. My pop was just a hard-working man. They had me and my sister and our four brothers. Pop worked sixteen-hour days to keep us going. Education and family were the lynchpin of our small town. If you didn't do your chores and homework before playing, then you did the switch dance in the front yard in front of Christ and all creation.

"There were plenty of barns, and a lot of boys took me there to play doctor. As I got older they wanted more, and I wasn't strong enough to fight them off. When I told my pop and mom, they blamed me. They said it was the way I dressed, or that I flirted too much. Mom took a belt to me once. She told me to quit acting like a tease.

"As soon as I was out of high school, at sixteen, I left home. I met Rory in freshman orientation. I was scared, at first, but he was gentle with me. I also found out that I was attracted to girls. We met my little minx, Jeanie, during our second quarter of sophomore year. One thing that helps is a class I take, Krav Maga. I think they should start teaching that in elementary schools."

Kenzie relaxed. She climbed back up onto the couch and curled up with her head on my lap. "My mom had men in and out since I can remember. Some of them used to walk in while I was in the tub—or, my sisters were. They'd say that they had to be sure we were washing all over. Sometimes at night, they'd tuck us in and kiss us. It never felt good. One of the men she brought home fingered me every night. I finally told a friend. Her father teaches people how to fight who are training to be cops. I think it's that Krav thing you just said. He taught me some moves. The next time the guy tried to touch me, he got an uppercut to the balls."

"We've all seen hard times." Jeanie stood up and stretched. "But now the three of us are healing. If you two want a family, you have one. We're family. If you want a street-mom or dad, however, I'd suggest being careful. If you find one, bring him by here. We can check him out. What you really need is to go back to school. Destiny, you need to find out how much you do or don't know from homeschooling. Get the education. That's the basis to the rest of your dreams. Kenzie, you not only need to finish high school, but you need a good university after. NYU is excellent, or maybe Princeton. You'll do better with law schools if you show that you can succeed in a competitive school."

Everyone was yawning, and it was past midnight. Jeanie brought out blankets and pillows while Sheila and Rory retired to the room where Rainbow slept. Jeanie returned to her room, and Kenzie and I fell asleep on the floor. She pressed against me as we cuddled like a pair of spoons. There were no signs of nightmares, and my dreams were pleasant.

The next morning, we all sat drinking coffee and eating

breakfast. Kenzie was rocking baby Rainbow. She was a natural, and Rainbow cooed. Everyone was discussing the upcoming beach trip.

"So, what do we have to do for your aunt? And when do we leave? Only beaches I've ever seen are in the city," Kenzie said.

"We're going the second week in September. Aunt Vi is all aces. We do like I always used to do when I'd go there for the summer as a kid. She owns a bed and breakfast. We help her change the beds. We put clean soap and towels in the rooms. We do some light cleaning and dusting, put out the cold food, and make coffee in the mornings. Rory and I can man the desk for a few hours. It's all really light stuff and gives us plenty of time to hit the beach and the boardwalk." Jeanie sipped fresh squeezed orange juice.

Rainbow dozed off on Kenzie's lap. "Sounds like a blast. We'll come the day before. Is this handsome little boy coming?"

"No. Rainbow is staying with a sitter. I need a break for a few days." Sheila yawned. "Babies are lovely, but parents have got to have a break."

After breakfast, Rory taught me the chords to some rock-and-roll songs. With his help, I found the G-7. "I know most of this is really old-school, but it still sells. Singing gospel is good for a few bucks, and if you play some of the stuff on the radio, you'll attract a younger crowd. Most kids out there busking will be playing current hits. You need some kind of an edge. Trust me, fifties rock and roll never went out of style. Plus, it has the benefit of allowing the audience to be part of the show by clapping and singing the do-wops."

While I learned, Jeanie shaved the sides of Kenzie's head to a half inch, trimmed her bangs, and evened out the back. That afternoon, Kenzie and I caught the bus back to Weehawken and took the ferry across. We stopped at a deli before heading to our fitness club.

Later that night, we played music and sang. I tried to figure out the chords on some of the new songs Rory had taught me.

I got the hang of G-7 and played "Runaround Sue" and "Johnny B. Goode." Kenzie started harmonizing on "Runaround Sue" and soon we had a crowd joining in. Rory was right, the throw money increased as did the size of the crowds. As an encore—one which gave me a delicious thrill knowing my parents and their church would not have approved—I managed to improvise an upbeat and swinging version of "Jesus Loves Me." The applause was orgasmic.

We had a string of good nights, making hundreds of dollars from the crowds. Despite her occasional nightmares, and my occasional moral qualms, life with Kenzie was an enjoyable adventure. We never slowed down, and that kept us sane.

Chapter 9

A couple of weeks later, we returned to Edison. We'd spent the previous two weeks in the libraries researching how to obtain equivalency diplomas. Kenzie was fourteen. The only way for her to receive a GED was with permission of her mother or another legal guardian. Both scenarios were impossible given our circumstances. She would have to wait for two or three years. I would also have to wait at least a year. Plus, we would have to prove residency in New York. The only way to accomplish things earlier was by obtaining fake identification.

There was nothing to stop us from taking classes online in preparation for the exams, but the tests seemed to require showing up in person. There were places that advertised a GED in exchange for money, but we had no way of knowing if these sites were legitimate.

Kenzie nibbled at a raspberry Italian ice one afternoon, her lips turning blue with dye. "This is New York. Not a thing on earth can't be bought if you have the juice."

I licked my lemon ice. "So you know someone who can for sure get us fake ID that says we're both eighteen?"

Kenzie shrugged. "No. But maybe Rory or Sheila or Jeanie know someone. I don't trust those online ads for a GED, but I bet we could pay someone to take the tests for us."

"And then what? We get into college knowing nothing except what we know now?" I sighed with exasperation.

"Well, waiting three years for something better than a damned subway train to call home doesn't really excite me."

"We can ask around, OK?" I stood up and threw away my paper cup.

When we weren't at the fitness club, the libraries, or Museums, we were in the parks or on Broadway playing music. I practiced some of the songs Rory had taught me. I even learned some show tunes from a book in the library.

One evening, I sang as a crowd gathered. "We both love farce..."

Kenzie crossed her arms. "Announce it to the world, why don't 'cha."

The crowd tittered and chuckled. "I said farce...farce!"

In between busking sessions, I kept my eyes open for anyone who looked like a good prospect as a street-mom or a bodyguard. The more money we made, the more we were harassed by street families or approached by drunken perverts. Kenzie and I protected each other, but we needed something more.

Two major changes that occurred as the money increased were in our wardrobe and hygiene. We started visiting thrift shops. Every couple of weeks, we replaced all of our dirty clothes with cleaner items and purchased new packages of panties and socks at a department store every Saturday. Don't ask me why we weren't using the laundromats instead of replacing our filthy clothes. At the time, the idea never occurred to us. We agreed that being homeless was no reason to look or smell disgusting. In fact, the panhandlers who looked as if they never bathed also made far less money.

The second week in September, we rode to Edison and arrived in the evening. After a late dinner of cold cuts and salad with Stella Artois, Kenzie and I crashed on the floor again. I awoke refreshed. Much of my anxiety about life and schooling had dissipated. Sometimes a good night's sleep fixed everything.

After coffee and showers, we all loaded into the van. Baby Rainbow was spending the week with the neighbors. We stopped at a diner for breakfast.

While eating, Kenzie and I elbowed each other and bounced around like kids at a fair. Neil Diamond crooned over a speaker system. Kenzie was eating her toast when something struck her as hilarious; she started laughing so hard she began coughing. She drank coffee to clear her throat. "That guy's family must have been dirt poor."

Rory looked up from his biscuits and gravy. "Huh? What makes you say that? I believe he was from a middle-class family."

Kenzie took another sip of coffee. "He said he recalls rubbers drying in the doorway. Who would wash and reuse those unless they were really poor?" She laughed, and we all joined in.

I shook my head. "He means boots. Like rain boots."

"They made rain boots out of Trojans?" She laughed harder.

After breakfast, we piled back into the van. I took my guitar from the case and tuned it. I was coming along with the new numbers I had been practicing, and everyone joined in with back-up vocals. Two hours later, Rory parked the van at a garage and we transferred to a shuttle. It had started to rain.

We rode the shuttle for a half hour and walked six blocks to an old diner. The exterior of the place was seedy, with cracked bricks, overgrown landscaping, and windows in need of washing. The inside wasn't as bad. There was air conditioning blowing hard enough to draw shivers, vinyl booths, and clean wooden tables. The menu was what one would expect from a diner near the shore.

As we perused the menu, Jeanie planned her strategy for the week. "Hey, since I'm the only person here that doesn't have a dance partner, where you thinking the best place for action is?"

"You mean girls?" Sheila inquired.

"What else?" Jeanie's eyes lit up with excitement.

"Yeah. Well, probably the beach," Sheila said, shrugging.

"It's raining." Jeanie pointed at the window.

"I can see that, minx. I guess you have to wait on the sun." Sheila shrugged again.

"How long for that?" Jeanie was getting antsy.

"What does she look like, a weatherman? How the hell should she know how long?" Rory got in on the conversation.

"Yeah, I know, give me a break. I'm trying to work myself up for this, you know? I mean, I can't go into this cold. Got to have some good lines in hand. You have Sheila and our baby sisters have each other. Where's that leave me?" The food came and we started eating.

Sheila gave Jeanie a peck on the lips and ruffled her hair. "You really need to relax. OK? Just take a chill. When the spirit moves you, the words'll come."

Kenzie looked at me and giggled. I put my head on her shoulder. We were watching love in motion. This was a lesson in true family relations.

Jeanie took a bite of cheeseburger. "Think we should split up?"

"Huh?" Rory looked confused.

"I said do you think we should split up," Jeanie repeated.

"What the hell for?" Sheila was also confused.

Jeanie shrugged "To play the percentages. What's my chances of finding a girl if we're all together?"

Rory shook his head. "In the rain?"

"No, meathead. On the beach, later, when the sun comes out." Jeanie laughed again.

"The chances are the same as finding one while you're with us," he said, sighing.

"Right. The word is relax." Jeanie swallowed some Coke.

Sheila nodded. "Yeah. You got it. When it happens, it'll happen. And you'll be right on it, not missing a trick. Get it?"

Jeanie ate a French fry. "Got it."

"Good." Rory finalized.

A waitress came over to make sure we had everything we needed. She was a well-constructed, college-aged beauty with a good tan and dark auburn hair. Jeanie shifted in her seat, and Rory shook his head. We ordered pie for dessert.

After lunch, we headed east about a mile. By the time we got to Aunt Vi's rooming house the rain had stopped, the sky had cleared, and the sun was pouring down. Jeanie's aunt was waiting in the kitchen. She gave us kisses and hugs and poured us each a glass of Heineken.

There were five floors in the place with four rooms on each floor. If we got an early start, we could knock off each day and hit the beach by noon. The first day was a breeze. A little light dusting and some sweeping. We ran a load of dishes through the dishwasher, and that was it. We were sprung to hit the beach.

Aunt Vi gave us rooms on the top floor. Kenzie and I headed upstairs, changed, and left, decked out in pink t-shirts and red shorts we had bought on sale at a store near Times Square. We both had on black shades and went barefoot, carrying our towels around our necks. The others were in t-shirts and swimsuits. They were barefoot, as well.

The pavement burned our feet and, when we reached the beach, the sand was even hotter. We had to stop every few feet and stand on our towels. After locating a free spot, we parked our stuff in the middle of a crowd. We were surrounded by blankets, umbrellas, kids, buckets, sand castles, and girls. Sweet Lord! So many beautiful girls!

"You guys believe this? Which one do you like for me? I'll take that redhead. No, hold up! I need to bust a move on that little honey in the striped bathing suit." Jeanie was going a bit crazy, but clearly couldn't help herself.

In the midst of all of this, Kenzie stood cool as the iceman. She stared out at the ocean like she was stranded alone on the beach. She was waiting for her ship to come in and in no particular hurry about it.

"You OK there, kid?" Rory looked over at Kenzie. She didn't move or respond.

"She's fine. She's just, you know, relaxing." I giggled.

"Yo. Destiny..." Kenzie murmured.

"Yeah, I know, relax. You're so relaxed you're gonna fall asleep standing up. If you want the truth, you look like a statue standing there. The seagulls are gonna to come sit on your head or something." I giggled more.

Kenzie gave me a look and chased me toward the water. I

dove into the waves. We wrestled and splashed around in mock combat. Our clothes got soaked. The others joined in and we had a great time, even though Jeanie didn't meet any new girls. After swimming, we spent the rest of the day lying around on our towels and sunning ourselves. Jeanie yelled to a couple of girls who were sunbathing nearby, but they ignored her. Kenzie and I fell asleep holding hands.

That night, Rory and Sheila covered the front desk from seven to eleven. Kenzie and I sat on the porch with Jeanie. There wasn't much to do except read comics and magazines. We said hello and goodbye to passing guests, but no one checked in or out. After the night auditor relieved them, Rory and Sheila joined us outside on the porch. We each had a bottle of Coke and watched people heading home from a night on the boardwalk, carrying stuffed animals, gee-gaws, cotton candy, and their sleepy little kids.

A middle-aged lady walked by with her young son and a daughter about Jeanie's age. The girl was five-foot-six and had freckles, black hair that hung past her shoulders, tanned skin, nice cleavage, and a round, firm butt. She wore boots, Levi's, a red gingham blouse, and a rainbow headband. Jeanie shot to her feet and jumped up onto the railing. She caught the girl's eye and waved shyly, speechless for a moment. The girl giggled and waved back before disappearing into the next house over.

"Damn, guys. She's the one. I know it. I felt something!"

Sheila chuckled. "She looks cute. Nice body. She's nothing like the girls you usually go for when we need a fourth, though. She looks almost pure."

"Yeah." Jeanie looked dazed. "Beautiful. Pure. I need to do something. I need to talk to her. I need to..."

"Relax." Kenzie and I interrupted her.

Jeanie threw back her shoulders and came to her senses. "Yeah, right. You got it, ladies. The word is relax." She strolled back to a chair and plopped down, forcing her eyes away from the house the girl had entered.

The next morning, Rory and Sheila had to run some

errands in town, which left me and Kenzie to make the rounds ourselves while Jeanie manned the desk. At eleven in the morning, we finished and stepped out onto the porch. There sat Jeanie with the girl from next door. The girl was a bit redder from the sun than had been noticeable the night before, but still gorgeous.

"Name's Jeanie. I saw you last night."

"Hi." The girl giggled. "I'm Skylar. Yep, I saw you too."

They were looking at each other—not speaking, but smitten. We watched them for a few minutes as they got acquainted. Skylar was from the Midwest and was visiting the area with her brother and her mother.

"I hope we're not interrupting." We smiled at them.

"Oh, uh, Skylar, meet Destiny and Kenzie. And vice versa."

"Hi. Jeanie and I were just getting to know each other."

"Hey, don't mind us."

Rory approached with Sheila. They were introduced, and the four of us walked inside carrying a few bags of groceries. Jeanie and Skylar remained on the porch. About twenty minutes later, Aunt Vi came out with us.

"Skylar? You want to join me and the gang tonight for some music and food? There's an old fifties-style retro place that has great burgers." I winked at Jeanie.

"Sure. Let me run next door and ask my mom."

"Invite your folks over. I'm just making lunch." Aunt Vi shouted as Skylar dashed down the steps.

Skylar returned ten minutes later with her mother and brother in tow. Her mother's name was Rena and her brother was Luke. Aunt Vi charmed the pants off of them. After lunch, everything was set for the night.

Skylar showed up in a red, ruffled dress and open-toed shoes looking more like she was going to the prom. Kenzie and I sported black t-shirts, jeans, and sneakers. Jeanie was in a skirt, t-shirt and sneakers. Rory and Sheila wore black jeans and blue t-shirts with boots. Aunt Vi was all spiffed up, and she looked dapper with Rory and Sheila on her arms.

The Shack was a loud, flashy place. There were old vinyl

records hanging on the walls and decorating the ceiling. A jukebox sat in one corner and, as we entered, "Rockin' Robin" by Bobby Darin was playing.

There were so many girls in the place that they were dancing with each other. This older lady with fluffy pink hair ran over in a sweater, poodle skirt, and baby-blue sneakers. She gave Aunt Vi a hug and kiss. The lady was the proprietor and an old friend of Aunt Vi. She called her a childhood sweetheart.

"Hey there, guys and gals. Name's Connie Lingus." She gave us a warm smile, showed us to a booth, and told a server to bring us Cokes on the house.

"What's that?" Kenzie asked while distracted by the décor.

"I'll show you later," I muttered.

Jeanie elbowed me and winked.

As we were getting situated, Aunt Vi said that she and Connie were going next door for a drink and would be back later. We nodded and they split.

Jeanie looked at Skylar. "You feel like dancing, babe?"

Instead of answering, Skylar stood and took Jeanie's hands as another song came on the juke. Sheila and Rory soon followed, and I led Kenzie onto the floor behind them. We started dancing, and it was like a movie.

I was stiff. I had never danced like this before. It was forbidden when I was growing up. Kenzie showed me the moves as I loosened up. Dancing with a girl was a great way to get to know her better.

After the song was over, the six of us walked to the jukebox and played nearly everything on it. We picked some slow numbers and a bunch of fast numbers. Much of it was new to me. I made a mental note to learn some of the tunes for busking.

We hit the dance floor as "Hound Dog" came on. I had a hard time of it, at first, but picked up on the back beat and start rolling. We shimmied, short stepped, flipped, changed partners once and back again. We brought everybody in The Shack to their feet. The dance floor was crowded. Skirts were swaying, bodies were rocking, the floor was shaking, and nothing could stop it.

Connie and Vi came in doing the jitterbug and everyone circled around them clapping. Rory cut in on Connie, taking over the floor with Jeanie's aunt. It was amazing. He held her by the waist and swung her from side to side around his body. Sheila took Connie by the hand and coaxed her back into the circle. Jeanie, Skylar, Kenzie, and I started a line dance going up and down the sides of the dance floor. Rory and Aunt Vi and Sheila and Connie Lingus were in the middle. We couldn't sit down.

We must have danced through every number on the jukebox twice that night before we stopped.

After Connie said she needed to close up, we headed back to the house. Jeanie and Skylar walked, hand-in-hand and smiling at each other. I walked with Kenzie, my arm around her shoulders. She looked up at me with her beautiful eyes, and it was clear that she had enjoyed herself.

The next day, after we had finished working, we hit the beach. Rory and Sheila lay together getting suntans, Jeanie and Skylar went for a walk, and I sat near the surf with Kenzie.

"It's nice out here. I could see us living on this beach. It's peaceful," she said, leaning against me.

I looked off at the horizon. "I imagine it has good seasons. I'm sure it isn't this nice all the time. We'll come back, though."

Kenzie started digging a hole with her hands and building a sand castle in the middle. "When we get back to the city, we need to crack down. I mean on school. Like Rory said the other day: we can do it, but we have to want it."

"Yeah." I agreed.

"Could we get into a regular school? We keep talking about the GED, but could we go to high school? It would keep us focused more and get us off the streets for a while every day."

My stomach started cramping and a wave of panic swept through me. "I don't know. I'm not sure I want that. I like being with you, and they'd keep us apart. They wouldn't let us be in all the same classes, you know. I'm not even sure if I would fit in. I've only ever been homeschooled and a lot of that was from The Bible instead of schoolbooks. What if people didn't understand us? I've had enough problems with that crap. I don't want to go to school and get pushed around for loving you."

Kenzie decorated her castle with seashells. "I guess so. The GED is the way to go. We have to get focused on it, though. We have to stop spending all day under the boardwalk or in the movies. The museums are good, but we have to learn the stuff inside. We can't just wander around."

"The Lord will make a way for us. I have no choice but to believe that." I closed my eyes and offered a silent prayer.

Kenzie and I spent every afternoon that week swimming, sunning, and discussing education. The whole group strolled the boardwalk at night and played games. I won Kenzie a small pink teddy bear. One morning we went to "Master Bait and Tackle" and rented fishing equipment. While Sheila, Jeanie, Skylar, Kenzie, and I relaxed on the deck of a boat with bottles of Coke, Rory caught sea bass.

That evening, Rory cleaned the fish and Aunt Vi cooked them up in garlic butter. Skylar's mother and brother joined us for dinner. The food was exquisite, but it made me tired. Kenzie looked subdued during most of the meal. We turned in early, and I slept deeply.

As the week wore on, Jeanie fell into a deep depression. Skylar was returning home on Thursday, and Jeanie began having doubts about their relationship. Kenzie and I sat with her, Rory, and Sheila on the porch the evening before Skylar had to leave town. Jeanie looked off into the distance.

"She's out of my league. I mean way out of my territory. It was nice for a few days, but this fling is flung. Besides, she's going back to Wichita tomorrow." Jeanie sighed.

Sheila looked at her sideways. "That doesn't sound like my little minx."

"Hey, she's a really nice girl. What's she want with the likes of me, anyway? I got nothing to offer her." Jeanie shook her head. "You and Rory, I take care of. But, Skylar is different. I just hoped I could find someone so I wasn't always the third wheel."

"Jeanie," Rory batted her gently on the back of the head, "you're a nice girl. And we've never considered you a third wheel. You get yourself all depressed looking for something that you already have. I've never understood it."

"Before I met you guys, I was always the one in high school without a date. I was there in the crowd, but not really there. I just never fit in. I was awkward and shy. You two brought me out of my shell. I'm still the third, though. You and Sheila will get married one day, and then where am I?"

"You're with us. If the government would allow polyandry and would recognize the rights of people to marry and love how they want, I'd marry you both. I'd love to have two spouses. A matched set." Sheila kissed Jeanie on the mouth, and they embraced.

Rory rolled his eyes. "A matched set? What are we, Tupperware?"

The next day, Jeanie walked next door and said her goodbyes. She returned with Skylar's number but indicated that she had no real hopes for a long-distance relationship. She figured it was over for them. I tried to find words of consolation, but none came.

We spent the rest of the week working and lying around on the beach. Jeanie slept a lot and developed a sunburn all over her body. Aunt Vi sensed that everyone wanted to get back home, so we finished out the week and boarded the shuttle loaded down with fudge, taffy, and great memories.

Chapter 10

After returning to Edison, we spent the night with Rory and the ladies. Rainbow seemed happy to see his parents, but he seemed as content trying to shove his head into my shirt. Kenzie and I made plans to come by once a month to check in.

"Hey, I had an idea." Rory smiled across the table at breakfast. "Can you come up with fifty bucks a month between you? I can get you both on our family cell phone plan for that. I can buy you each a phone, too, if you'd pay it back over time."

"That'd be awesome. No more flip phone and buying cards to fill it." Kenzie smiled at him and turned to me. "Destiny could use her own phone instead of swiping mine all the time."

Rory collected the dishes, and Jeanie washed them. "You'd have the Internet, too, and other tools for studying. I want you both to crack the books. I mean it."

"Yes, sir. We will."

An hour later, we were at a store buying Droid Razr smartphones. Rory said that they were top of the line. We set up the phones as part of the family plan and handed Rory one hundred and fifty dollars as a starter payment. That left us with fifty dollars, but I planned to play guitar and sing that night.

Kenzie and I caught the ferry back to the city. We made thirty dollars on the trip after I played some basic church tunes. Without warning, my head was full of wet straw. I began to sweat, disoriented as the world spun. I chalked it up to seasickness or something I ate but, after we walked off the ferry, I had an urgent need to sit on a bench. I was having trouble staying upright.

"Are you alright? You look flushed, and your face is burning up." Kenzie squatted in front of me. "I know we need the money, but you can't sing or play like this. I'm not sure where to go, but you need a doctor."

Talking made me nauseous. "I'm OK. Just achy and tired. That time of month was two weeks ago, so it isn't that. Maybe it's food poisoning or seasickness." I closed my eyes, praying my headache passed.

It didn't. I got worse. My sinuses throbbed, and my throat hurt. As we walked toward the subway, I started coughing up phlegm and choking up bile. My face was hot enough to fry bacon. Kenzie's "mommy reflex" kicked in, a pure instinct because she'd never had a "mommy." She checked her phone and found a free clinic.

"I have an idea, but you need to focus. Our parents are Rory and Sheila. We're visiting the city, and you got sick all of a sudden. If they insist, we give them Rory's cell number. We don't have insurance or money if they ask, so they have to send a bill to Rory." Kenzie flagged a cab, and our extra thirty dollars was history.

We sat in the waiting room for three hours. I spent most of that time asleep on a couch with my head on Kenzie's lap, listening to piped-in music and the sounds of people hacking and wheezing. Somewhere behind me children squirmed and a mother told them to sit still.

A tall black man with a trimmed afro rushed through the door. His fingers were covered with rings, he had several necklace chains, and his teeth were capped in gold. He held a limp boy of no more than four, undersized and bony, in his arms.

"Someone help me! My boy won't wake up!" he cried out in distress.

Several nurses rushed by Kenzie and me to offer assistance and collect details. Thirty minutes later, a swarm of police officers entered the waiting room, surrounding then interrogating the man.

A Hispanic lady with severely bruised arms, dressed in ripped sweat pants and a stained halter top, stumbled in and almost made it to the sign-in desk before vomiting and passing out. Medical personnel rushed over and put her on a gurney while others cleaned the floor.

"Junkie coming down. Or something like that." Kenzie murmured, stroking my face.

A tall, pneumatic blonde approached and led us through a hallway. We entered a chilly, sterile room with yellow-green walls. Kenzie sat in a chair. I climbed on the examining table, then curled into a ball. Five minutes later a short, swarthy woman with black hair and a tender smile entered.

"Hello. My name is Doctor Malak. You must be Destiny. And you're her sister, Mackenzie?" The voice was sweet but officious.

"Right," Kenzie replied.

"OK. If you can sit up, I need to get your pulse and pressure. This may feel odd for a moment, but I need your temperature." Dr. Malak put a cuff on my arm, inflated it, and put a thermometer in my ear. I heard a click.

"Are you pregnant?" Dr. Malak wrote something on a chart.

"Not possible, we're virgins. Plus, she had her cycle two weeks ago." Kenzie patted my hand.

Dr. Malak lifted my shirt and listened to my chest. Next came a look into my nose, ears, and throat. "Your temperature is elevated, and your sinuses are congested. I'm going to give you a script for ten days' worth of C-Chlor. My advice is to find somewhere indoors to sleep for at least a week. You can't get better if you sit outside all day, and your system is weak enough that long-term exposure to people on the subways might make you worse. Eat dry bread and drink water, juice, and herbal tea. Avoid caffeine."

Forty minutes later, we left with my antibiotics and appointments for us both to have full physicals the following month. Dr. Malak made a referral to her colleague, Dr. Coito. He worked on a sliding scale and would charge us little or nothing.

Kenzie and I walked to a corner restaurant and ordered orange juice and dry toast for me, a pastrami sandwich and coffee for her. I swallowed a pill.

She shook her head in disbelief. "That lady was reading us, I swear it. She knows we're homeless and doesn't care, except that we stay healthy. Every time I think I have people pegged, they surprise me."

I yawned. "We have to get a room. The only way I know is the church. I know I always take the lead there, but you have to do it tonight. I'm not sure I can even stay awake."

That night we attended our church group with hopes of talking someone into helping us with cash for a hotel room. Something better came up. We sat in the back near the door. I nibbled at the biscuits from the dinner provided by the hospitality committee and sipped lemonade. As we were sitting there, Veronica "Ronnie" Englekut approached us. She was seventeen years old, five foot eight, with rail-thin legs, and long red hair setting off her pale, freckled face beautifully.

"You look like warmed over death." she sat beside me. "If

you guys need a place to stay for a few days, my mom and step-dad are gone until Sunday."

"You mean it?" Kenzie almost shrieked before controlling herself. "You're a life saver!"

"Life saver? What flavor?" Ronnie giggled.

Kenzie laughed and I coughed. We sat in the group, Kenzie with her coffee and me sipping chamomile tea with four honey packets in it.

The group leader started out by asking if anyone wanted to share. Ronnie raised her hand, her face a mask of stone. "My mom and step-dad are gone for a few days. I just wanted to offer praise and say how much better I feel with them gone. Now I don't have to protect my kid sister from my step-dad every night."

The other group members all said Amen.

Kenzie raised her hand. "I'd like to ask you to pray for Destiny. She has a sinus infection." Then, she leaned over to Ronnie, adding, "Also, I thought a few weeks ago you said that you were an only child. I didn't know you had a kid sister."

Ronnie looked straight ahead. "I am an only child. Lucky for my kid sister, huh?"

Others shared and the group laid hands on my head and prayed for my health. After the meeting, Ronnie called for a car to come get us. It was a town car and the driver seemed to know her. We were driven to an upscale neighborhood full of brownstones. We entered one, and Ronnie showed us to an enormous living room. There was an oversized recliner that was big enough to seat me and Kenzie at the same time. I claimed it, leaning back. Kenzie gave me another antibiotic pill, and Ronnie covered me with a thick blanket.

"There's lots of food. I can make something hot, if you want. We can watch movies or whatever. I have school tomorrow, but you guys can hang out here all day."

Ronnie and Kenzie walked to the kitchen. Thirty minutes later, they brought me soft-boiled eggs, toast, and a mug of tea. Kenzie had a heavy glass filled with an amber liquid and a sandwich. Ronnie had a glass of Coke and a sandwich.

I took a sip from the mug and gasped. The liquid burned going down. "What the hell is that?"

"Peppermint tea with lemon, honey, and three shots of gin." Kenzie replied. "I'm having scotch, and Ronnie's having bourbon and Coke."

"The guest bathroom is down the hall to the right. There's plenty of soap, bubble bath, and bath salts. If you need to clean up, help yourself." Ronnie sat with us, turning on the TV.

I ate and finished my tea. I fell asleep without coughing much. I woke up at two in the morning, and Kenzie laid beside the chair. Ronnie was in her bedroom. I used the hall bathroom and ran a hot bath. Kenzie came in and sat beside the tub, washing me with a cloth.

"They have a washer and dryer, so I washed all our clothes. There's lots of food and a full liquor cabinet." Kenzie whispered, stroking my face. "This is better than a dream. You can rest all week. We'll leave Saturday."

I nodded. After my bath, I got dressed and Kenzie made me another tea. Ronnie stumbled out to check on us and returned to bed. I fell asleep on the floor, cuddled with Kenzie. At six thirty, Ronnie came out of her bedroom. She wore a long plaid skirt and a white blouse with a skinny black tie.

Ronnie packed her backpack with books. "If anyone calls, let the machine get it. I have your cell numbers so it won't be me. No one's coming home so you can stay here, as long as you don't leave the house. Help yourself to whatever food you find."

Kenzie looked up from where we lay. "Do you have a copy of your reading list for English class?"

"Sure. I'll get it out for you," Ronnie said, gazing at us with curiosity. She reached into her backpack and pulled out three sheets of paper.

Kenzie looked over the sheets. "Thank you. We're thinking about trying for the GED and reading some of these books might help. It can't hurt, anyway."

Ronnie left. Kenzie and I fell back asleep. At eleven we woke up, cleaned, and I had another tea. Kenzie poured a rum and Coke. We turned on the TV, and I fell asleep again.

I woke up at three thirty and had some water. Kenzie was sitting at a table in the dining room with Ronnie. I noticed that Kenzie's eyes looked glazed. She had a heavy glass in front of her with scotch in it. Ronnie was drinking milk. I took a seat.

"She lives!" Ronnie smiled. "Sleep well, Destiny?"

"Yeah. I'm still tired, though." My sinuses were clogged up and my temples throbbed. "Are there any more of those eggs?"

"I'll make you some." Ronnie walked to the kitchen.

Kenzie smiled at me and giggled. "I'll make you more tea after you eat. It'll help you sleep."

"How much have you had to drink? You sound like you're slurring. You should slow down."

"I'm not slurring. It's probably just your hearing because of the cold. I've only had like three glasses. It's nothing. We have this awesome place to stay for a few days so why not relax?" Kenzie kissed me. I smelled the alcohol on her breath.

Ronnie came back a few minutes later with toast and apricot jam, soft-boiled eggs, and ham. "Kenzie asked me for some book suggestions. I'm going to make a list. Right now I'm reading If Beale Street Could Talk by James Baldwin. I finished Maya Angelou's I Know Why The Caged Bird Sings last night. You should read those. They're really good. Baldwin wrote about Harlem. I don't go up there because my step-dad would beat my ass. I'm going to soon, though." Ronnie drank her milk, adding, "Anything by Dickens or Shakespeare is a must read. And Hawthorne's The Scarlet Letter. You'd both love that one."

Kenzie walked to the kitchen and brought me back another spiked tea. She had a glass of Coke. "I want to read those. We need a math tutor, too. And we have to study science and social studies. But, I doubt we can afford a tutor for any of that."

Ronnie cleared the dishes away. "I'll tutor you both. I won't even charge you. Hell, if it gets me out of here for a few more hours a day, I'm glad to do that."

I returned to the oversized recliner and fell asleep. I woke up with my nose running like a faucet. My chest hurt, and my stomach was sore. I cleaned up and ate some wild rice and chicken with mushrooms that Ronnie had cooked.

The next few days passed with sleep, hot showers, and eating. When I was awake, I noticed that Kenzie was drinking more. She was never quite drunk, but she was on the border. I was concerned but decided not to say anything. After the third day, I asked her to quit spiking my tea.

Saturday morning, my health had improved. I still had to take antibiotics, but my coughing was minimal. Ronnie helped us pack our backpacks and left with us.

We walked to the subway after stopping at a drugstore to buy several packets of tissues and a bottle of multivitamins. The weather was crisp and sunny as we walked to the Museum of Natural History. The sunshine refreshed my body.

"I love this place," Ronnie said. "You both should come here every few days and take the tours. Be sure to ask the curators questions. It's like an entire course in science was built around this one museum. Mr. Glupan, my earth sciences teacher, doesn't teach anything that I can't learn right here. Sometimes I think school's a waste of time. In fact, as your tutor, I'm directing you to come here at least three times a week and dedicate four hours to an exhibit. Plus, you are to attend the planetarium twice a week. It might seem repetitive, but repetition is the key to learning things."

Ronnie walked with us through the entrance and paid fifteen dollars for the three of us to get inside.

Kenzie kept an arm draped around me. "I love the dinosaurs and the earth history. Who would have thought that the whole world is four and a half billion years old?"

"My homeschooling texts say that the world is six thousand years old. That Adam and Eve lived with the dinosaurs." I gestured toward the exhibits. "I guess someone got it wrong."

Kenzie's eyes narrowed and her mouth turned down at the edges. "Your homeschooling texts probably say that being gay is a sin, too. One guess who has the wrong end of that stick."

Ronnie turned toward us. "I have to say that I don't really get it with you two. I like the boys in my classes. I mean, there's even this one I'd like to go to the prom with. But, I've never understood homosexuals. Like, which one of you is the guy?" The sincerity in the question touched me.

Kenzie's head tilted up and her eyes registered annoyance before softening. "It isn't like that, chick. We're both girls. We happen to love each other. We get turned on by boys sometimes, but we feel more comfortable with each other. I believe if a person isn't into dating girls, they should date boys. Or, whatever."

Ronnie smiled and shrugged. "No offense. I just don't get it."

Kenzie smiled back and gave me a passionate kiss. "None taken. You don't have to get it. You just have to accept it. Even if it isn't your personal brand of vodka."

We walked exhibit to exhibit. I made mental notes about topics that interested me. We stopped in the cafeteria, and I had a glass of apple juice. Kenzie and Ronnie had coffee.

"Maybe I won't go home. I could stay with you both. We can really be sisters. I mean, not just at church. I don't like being at home," Ronnie said wistfully.

Kenzie puffed air from her lips. "If you want to be sisters, I'd like that. But, living on the streets isn't sane when you have a nice place to live. I'd kill for a house like that."

Ronnie pouted. "OK. I've survived this long, I can make it another year. But we're sisters now, right?"

"Forever." I raised my juice in a salute. "Maybe in a few weeks we can introduce you to our brother and sisters from New Jersey."

We walked through some more exhibits before attending the show at the planetarium. It was incredible. I had missed out on a lot of information growing up. The planetarium made me feel indescribably small. There was no doubt in my mind that a divine being had created the universe, but that was the extent to which my homeschooling made any sense. I could have sat through the program every day without getting bored.

After we left the museum, we walked to a deli for turkey sandwiches. Ronnie paid for our meals. We made plans to meet her the following day at church to set up a tutoring schedule. She left after dinner and returned home. Kenzie and I took the subway to our usual spot and sat by the storefront. I didn't feel like singing much, as my throat was still raw, but I played guitar. Kenzie sang a few songs. Her voice had a soulful, earthy quality when she belted out "Puff The Magic Dragon." We made two hundred dollars before quitting and heading to an all-night restaurant for chicken soup and coffee.

"You're still sick, chick." Kenzie broke saltines into her soup. "I know it's not going to get us ahead, but for a few more days we have to find a hotel. If we keep it around one hundred a night then we might be able to save fifty from our collections."

The suggestion irritated me. "I'm better. We can ride the subways like always."

Kenzie glared. "No, you aren't. You need rest and somewhere warm. I can't let you sleep outside or even on the trains." I glared right back.

We rode to Brooklyn and talked a lady into getting us a room for the night at a hotel. We came in the side entrance, took the elevator to the fifth floor, and fell asleep after locking our door.

The next day, we woke up at seven and cleaned up. Kenzie washed every nook and crevice of my body. I returned the favor. Afterward we cuddled for a while before dressing. At nine, we headed to church. On the way, we bought a small notebook and a pen to make out a schedule.

From the chaos that had been Kenzie's life, and the misogynistic domination that had been mine, a phoenix was forming. Out of the ashes of two worlds scarred by abuse, a majestic and noble creature would one day soar.

Chapter 11

That first Monday morning, we sat in the library reading room. We made a decision to each read two or three books a week. Instead of napping, I started reading Go Tell It On The Mountain, by James Baldwin. Kenzie sat reading Maya Angelou's I Know Why The Caged Bird Sings. Baldwin's tale stirred emotions in me that were hard to express. From the look on Kenzie's face, and the occasional trickle of tears, I figured that she was going through the same process.

At four, Ronnie walked into the room. She nodded her approval at our selections and checked them out for us. We left the library and walked to a quiet coffee shop nearby. Ronnie took out her math books and started explaining her algebra homework to us. I understood it, but Kenzie was clearly out of her league. We decided to ask Pastor Affenhoden if he knew anyone who could help Kenzie catch up on the math she had never studied.

The social studies Ronnie started us on was easier for us both. We could learn that material by checking out certain books in the library. We agreed to do that the following day.

Kenzie and I fell into a steady schedule. On Monday, Wednesday, and Friday, we arrived at the library when it opened at nine. We read novels until noon, then went out for coffee; from one until four, we studied social studies. Ronnie joined us after her school let out, tutoring us from four until six.

On Tuesdays and Thursdays, we spent the entire day at the American Museum of Natural History. I took notes about the exhibits, at first; then, Kenzie learned how to take effective notes.

Saturday was our day at the art museums. We would

wander from exhibit to exhibit and admire the classic works. I found a great interest in the Rubens. The paintings set off something inside of me that I couldn't express—at least, not without blushing. Kenzie found more enjoyment in the paintings of Modigliani and Van Gogh.

Every night except Tuesday, I played music from eight until one in the morning in the theater district. Tuesday, after the church group, I played guitar on the subway. My repertoire grew. As it did, so did our earnings.

One Saturday afternoon, we invited Ronnie to join us for a matinee performance. Rory, Sheila, and Jeanie were in town with baby Rainbow. They were attending a lecture at Columbia and planned to come see Kenzie and me on Sunday.

That morning Kenzie and I sat in the library reading King's sermon titled Some Things We Must Do. It was inspiring and about personal accountability. I was impressed when he mentioned not being able to afford fancy perfume but still being able to afford a bar of soap. That was us. Using the showers and steam room in the fitness club, the bathroom sinks in restaurants, cleaning up when we had hotel rooms, and buying packs of clean underpants and socks was all we needed.

We discussed the sermon with Ronnie as we walked to our spot in the theater district. She pointed out that while certain statistics in the speech had changed over time, the general tenor of the speech remained accurate. She mentioned that many people enjoyed playing the victim role, but that the changes King suggested were the best answer to current racism. The playing field would be leveled with a few basic changes on either side of the ideological fence.

After church one brisk November day, Ronnie, Kenzie, and I caught a subway to Harlem. We walked to Morningside Park near Columbia University and saw our new family standing outside. Jeanie rushed over and grabbed Kenzie in a tight embrace. She gave her a gentle kiss.

"Hey there, sweetie. How's tricks?" Jeanie looked beautiful. Her hair had grown to her shoulders, but she kept her short bangs. It was still blue.

"I'm doing alright. Studying hard." Kenzie grinned.

Jeanie turned and hugged me until my ribs started to give. "And you? Things going well?"

"I'm studying hard, too. Otherwise, yeah I'm fine. There's a lot to think about, but, I'm good." I put my hands in the pockets of my winter coat.

Sheila and Rory hugged us both tight and let us hold Rainbow. Rory was dressed in a black overcoat and black dress shoes. It was the first time I had seen him in slacks and a tie. Sheila was dressed up, too. So was Jeanie.

"Guys, this is our new sister, Ronnie. She attends our church. She let us stay at her place when I was sick. Ronnie, this is Rory, Sheila, Jeanie and Rainbow."

"I've heard so much about you. Nice to finally meet you." Ronnie hugged each of them. She reached over toward me to hug Rainbow, and he gave her a big smile. Ronnie took him, and he tried burying his face in her leather jacket.

"If everyone is good with Italian food, I'm buying." Rory led the way.

As we walked, I noticed a guy sitting on a bench reading Welcome To The Monkey House by Vonnegut. From the square face and chin to the close-cropped sandy hair, he appeared to be my age. He was medium height with a deeply tanned, muscular build. His clothes gave him an older appearance, however—loafers, tight black jeans, a black dress shirt open at the collar, a stylish leather jacket and a fedora. He also wore mirrored sunglasses. I admit that he stirred a response in me that few males caused.

Our family walked to a subway station and rode to midtown. The place Rory had chosen was upscale and pricey. There were autographed pictures on the wall of various famous diners including Frank Sinatra, Tony Bennett, a radio talk show host, and several opera singers. Kenzie, Ronnie, and I were under-dressed for the establishment, but with the others taking point—we sort of blended in. Rory asked for a private room, and one was provided. He slipped the maitre'd a fifty-dollar bill.

After Rainbow was situated in a folding bassinet, the waiter appeared with a tray of negronis. The drinks were placed beside Rory. He asked the waiter to bring antipasto, calamari insalata, and stuffed artichokes. The waiter left and Rory passed around the aperitifs. The drink had a strange, but delicious taste. Kenzie's eyes lit up and her smile widened when she took her drink. As we began to settle in, Sheila looked at me.

"You said you had things on your mind lately? Care to share, honey?" She reached over and patted my free hand.

"Nothing major. I was sick for a week. After that, we decided to get serious about our studying. Ronnie's tutoring us, and our pastor has a special math tutor for Kenzie. But, well, some things I'm learning don't jibe with what I was taught growing up. Like the age of the earth and when people actually came around. Also a lot of astronomy is inconsistent with The Bible. I'm confused."

"You also question whether you're sinning sexually, being who you are?" Rory got to the point.

"Sometimes. Not as often now."

Sheila rubbed my hand. "It takes time. About the science, I can't explain that. It's true, the Bible doesn't match established facts. The best I can do is that The Maker's timetable isn't ours. They don't line up perfectly."

I shook my head and nibbled some artichoke followed by some soppressato. "So, once again, everything they taught me is crap."

"You have a serious problem with your broad thinking." Ronnie sighed, eating some calamari. "I'm sure that at some point you heard about love, about honesty and loyalty, and things of that nature. Those concepts aren't wrong. I'll admit that it sounds like your parents and their church screwed up Christ's teachings."

Kenzie's shrugged. "I don't understand hardly anything in the Bible. Some of us are retards."

Ronnie glowered. "First, don't ever let me hear you use that word again, baby sister. The correct term is mentally challenged. Second, you aren't. If you don't understand something, ask." Kenzie sulked and chugged the rest of her drink.

I shook my head. "It's still confusing."

Rory smiled and ate some roasted pepper. "Kid, if you try watering down The Bible to the point where the common clay understands it, you end up with a great deal of misinterpretation and a whole mess of hatred and bigotry."

Kenzie stopped pouting and gave me a side hug. "They forced you to think the way you do. If you didn't puke back the correct responses you were beaten, or worse. It isn't easy to change after years of that. I'll work on not seeing myself as stupid."

The waiter returned and brought escarole monacino, broccoli rabe with garlic and olive oil, pork rollatine, and linguine puttanesca. We all dug in. Rory ordered three bottles of wine, and—while Ronnie and I had a few glasses—Kenzie kept refilling her glass. The others seemed stable, but Kenzie's eyes and head drooped.

While eating, we discussed literature and the history of the Harlem Renaissance as well as Ellis Island, and the role immigrants played in shaping the city. Rory, Sheila, and Jeanie were well informed. I even learned about connections between Italian families in Florida and New York City. I made some notes about books to read and movies to view. One name, Joe Pistone, came up a lot in our conversation.

After a three hour dinner, and a dessert of panna cotta and cassata with espressos, we walked through the city. Ronnie caught a cab home. Rory pushed a stroller with Rainbow inside, and Sheila walked beside him. Jeanie walked between me and Kenzie. Kenzie was tipsy and mellow. I was full and sleepy, as well.

"This is when I start to really love this city." Rory looked around at the neon lights, the passing people, and the shops. "Dusk is the time to be here. And it improves as the hour grows later."

I held Jeanie a little closer. "I like this cooler weather. But sometimes at night it feels sort of, I don't know, scary out here."

Rory stretched his arms out as if to embrace Manhattan, "I wouldn't necessarily choose the word scary, but I know what you mean. McKay, Thurman, Hughes, and Hurston wrote about a Harlem—a city, in general, that no longer exists. But the more this city changes, the more it remains unscathed. There's a charming insalubrity to this place that will never dissipate. It will beautifully fester just below the surface and forever draw me back to these environs."

"That's poetic, man." Kenzie giggled, loose and silly.

"That's my deep love for this city, baby sister." Rory spun around looking at the sky.

We walked forty blocks before Rory took us into the foyer of a much nicer hotel than Kenzie or I ever frequented. The lobby was covered with beautiful artwork and had several statues that were either Greek or Roman in design. There were chintz armchairs and sofas, and dedicated employees manned the glass elevators. Rory informed us that our stay was paid for as part of the conference he was attending. The room which we entered was a one-bedroom suite. The king-sized bed was covered with little tasseled pillows at one end, and a fluffy purple and gold comforter. There was a separate dressing area with an upholstered bench and a three-way mirror. The tub in the bathroom had gold faucets and a matching toilet.

The main room held a full length couch, a large-screen television, and a queen-sized bed. A small refrigerator held a full assortment of snacks, soda, juice, and miniature bottles of alcohol.

"Is this stuff in the fridge for everyone to share?" Kenzie eyed the little liquor bottles with interest, but she didn't need any more to drink.

Rory snapped, "Absolutely not. The hotel charges a fortune if you touch those items so please don't."

He and Sheila changed Rainbow and got him into his crib while Kenzie and I had a bath. We soaked for a while in the deep tub, getting out once we started to yawn. The white towels were the biggest I had ever seen and the fluffiest I had ever felt. After drying off and changing into clean panties and t-shirts, Kenzie and I crawled under the blankets on the queen-sized bed. Jeanie joined us a half hour later, as there wasn't another bed, and we slept curled up together.

The next morning, I woke up feeling refreshed. Kenzie and I shared a mischievous glance over Jeanie's sleeping body before we attacked, kissing and tickling her until she squirmed awake. In turn, she grabbed each of us and playfully smacked our butts. We giggled and curled up close to her.

"How's things been going with you?" Kenzie asked, kissing Jeanie's cheek. "When we were at the beach a couple months ago, you seemed sort of sad."

"Things are better, sis." Jeanie said. "I've been seeing someone professionally. There isn't anything specifically wrong, either. I just have issues with my self-image. I never used to fit in. I know I seem older, but I only just turned eighteen. It wasn't so long ago that I was your age."

I sighed, cuddling closer. "Well, we aren't really that young either. It's weird. The world sees us as fourteen and fifteen-year-old kids. I stopped being a child about four years ago. My church and my family expected me to be a small adult, unless it served their purposes to claim that I wasn't. And, from what Kenzie tells me, she grew up at ten years old. That was when she finally put an end to that creep molesting her."

Jeanie smiled and kissed my cheek. "You have a real understanding of this for someone who hasn't had much formal education. You're pretty smart, sis."

Kenzie held Rainbow as Rory and Sheila packed. "Thanks for letting us stay here. I've never been in a place this fancy. I could get used to living like this real easy, though."

"That'd be possible if you keep studying. We certainly can't afford to stay here, or anything like it, unless we attend a conference that's footing the bill." Sheila snapped her suitcase shut. "If you get a law degree, I imagine you'd be able to attend plenty of conferences every year."

After breakfasting on bagels and lox with cups of rich, creamy coffee in the hotel restaurant, Rory, Sheila, and Jeanie drove home with Rainbow.

Kenzie's eyes sparkled. "This was cool. This place is my dream. This hotel right here."

Chapter 12

It was a mild afternoon for autumn, so Kenzie and I walked to the park and practiced some martial arts. As we worked out, her attacking and me defending, I noticed the guy from the night before. He was reading a copy of The New York Post. I tried not to stare, but something about him intrigued me. His eyes were both sad and fierce. He wore Nikes, stone-washed jeans, a navy blue sweater with a charcoal-gray blazer, and the same fedora adorning his head. His sunglasses were folded in the breast pocket of his sweater. On his wrist was a gold watch with diamond chips on it. Everything about him spelled quality and success.

The guy raised his eyes from his paper about forty-five minutes into our workout. He was looking right at us. After another fifteen minutes, Kenzie and I started walking away. "You got the rhythms down, chicks, but you zig when you oughta zag."

"Excuse me. Say what?" I asked, confused.

"You're hooking your feet at the end of the kicking sequences. You'd do better to snap the kicks."

Kenzie's nostrils flared as her eyes narrowed. "Yeah? Can you do any better?"

"Straight from the fridge, gate. But really, I should tend to my own." The guy returned to his newspaper.

Kenzie shrugged as we headed to the subway. "Yeah, right."

For the next two weeks, we began adding a martial arts workout to our learning schedule. One day, I was the aggressor; the next, I was on defense. I began to develop some instinct for defending myself in a variety of ways. Kenzie began teaching me to recognize certain cues and attack instead of merely reacting.

Each day as we worked out, we saw the guy in the park sitting on the same bench. He was always well-dressed and had the same intensity in his eyes. I began to notice certain other things about him. He always carried a large backpack, filled to capacity, and a leather courier sack that could be slung over his shoulder. Every day, he read a different book or a newspaper. A large cup of coffee or a twenty-ounce bottle of Pepsi was always within his reach.

Whenever we spoke, which was not a daily occurrence, he was friendly but formal. His manner of speech was like nothing I had ever heard with expressions like "What's the action?" and "Drop that into low gear and run it around the block once more." I couldn't identify my feelings for him, but they went well beyond prurience. Other than Rory and a few church members, I found that trusting men came hard for me. This man, however, had an air about him that made trusting him seem natural.

During this time, I also began utilizing my training. As Kenzie and I continued looking for a street family that wasn't predatory or a danger to us, we met several people our own age. Most of them were involved in the drug trade or the sex trade. Even so, some were friendly, and even affable.

Anna, a pretty and petite blonde, was a twelve-year-old runaway from Maine. Mikey was fourteen, thin but muscular, from southern Texas. They had problems at home. Anna's parents were divorcing, and Mikey's father was in and out of prison. Anna and Mikey hung out in the park together, and that's where we came to know them. Mikey was making a few hundred dollars a day by performing in online videos. His arms indicated where most of the money went. Anna stuffed bags of drugs inside her bra and transported them for one of the street families.

Mikey approached one afternoon with his aww-shucks smile. "You gals got anyone for protection?"

I looked him over. The chiseled butt, the rippling abdominals, and the self-flexing pecs made him appear older.

The bruises on his arms made him look desperate. "We watch out for each other. We don't need protection. Thanks, anyway."

Mikey flexed. "Well, my boss knows people. And if I recruit a few teens to shoot videos, my salary doubles. If you work for him, he protects you."

Kenzie shook her head. "She said, no thank you."

Mikey winked. "You sure? You have the kind of looks our customers want."

I stood and squared my shoulders. "We said no. That's not our thing. We see you around with your girlfriend, and you both seem nice. Take no for an answer, OK?"

Mikey sauntered away, thumbs in his belt. I never heard from him again. I hope he made it, but I have my doubts. His offer was one major reason that Kenzie and I needed a street family.

We were sitting on a bench a week later, making out, when four cops arrested Anna. They frisked her, then pulled her shirt up. Although they found the drugs she was carrying, I was shocked at their lack of concern for her right to privacy. As they put her in the rear of a wagon, I started to protest. Kenzie clamped a hand over my mouth.

We scrambled away. "Shit, Destiny, you better watch yourself. Yeah, that was some bullshit flashing her like that, but you don't get involved. I thought I was teaching you better." Kenzie glared.

I snarled. "She's always been nice to us. Screw the cops! Men like that think they're so tough. Bastards."

Kenzie held me while I raged. The incidents and others made it apparent to us that we needed someone to look out for us. Someone not dealing drugs or making pornographic films. We weren't interested in robbing old people or anyone else. We wanted safety while we studied and pursued our dreams. Someone like a parent, but better.

A few days after Anna was arrested, we met Candace outside of a deli. She was sitting against the wall, crying, looking forlorn. Her stringy black hair contrasted with the milky white skin. The eyes, crater-like and desperate, were hollow with hunger.

Kenzie stared. "You alright? Need help?"

The girl nodded but said nothing. She glanced at us, then dropped her eyes. I figured that she was mentally challenged. "What do you need? Should we call someone?" I emphasized my words.

The girl shook her head. Her voice was so soft that I had to strain to hear her. "Got a smoke? A drink? Some cash?"

Kenzie and I looked at each other. I knelt down. "We can buy you a sandwich and a Coke."

"I gotta get out of here. If Kermit and his family see me, they'll kick my ass. They told me I'm eighty-sixed from this block. I need money for the subway."

Kenzie scowled. "Who's Kermit?"

"He owns this block. I was part of the family, but they kicked me out because I didn't want to be with him. All the girls are his."

I stood up. "Is he around? I'd like to meet this guy. We need to clear some things up. What's your name?"

"Candace." She stood, as well. I noticed the fear in her eyes. "I'd better split. They're coming." She started walking in haste, but Kenzie stopped her. She shoved Candace behind us.

From the east came a group of teens being led by a boy who stood six feet tall. He wore a dirty Kermit The Frog t-shirt. Behind him were twelve others, mostly female. The boy in the lead walked toward us with his shoulders hunched and fire in his eyes. Behind him was a pudgy, dough-faced female. She was an inch taller than Kenzie, with a mop of blonde hair in need of a wash.

I sneered. "You Kermit?"

He stopped. "What's it to you? You don't want to be around this little bitch. You'll get hurt. Trust me."

Kenzie laughed. "If he's Kermit, I guess that skank behind him must be Piggy."

The girl stepped forward. "What the hell did you just call me?"

Kenzie reached into her side pocket and clicked open a switchblade. At the same moment, I lowered my center of gravity and punched Kermit in the manhood. Everyone backed up as Kermit fell to his knees. I kicked him in the face.

Kenzie looked at the crowd. "I called you Miss Piggy. You could be the town slut for all I give a shit. Miss Candace here told us all about you. You kicked her out. We're claiming her. We're her street moms now. Come near her again, and Kermit gets castrated."

I stepped forward and shoved the girl backwards. "Let's dance, bitch! I haven't killed anyone in a few days."

The teens turned and ran, leaving Kermit and Piggy to deal with us. I assured Candace, "This idiot doesn't own the street. The city owns it. And you don't have to have sex with anyone unless you want to." I turned to Kermit. "Get to stepping."

Kermit hunched over then staggered away, leaning on his girlfriend. I turned with Kenzie to face Candace. "You're free now. If you have somewhere to go, get lost."

"Thank you. I thought those guys cared about me." She began crying.

Kenzie handed her some Kleenex, and we walked with her to a church. An older lady at the front desk appeared to recognize Candace and came around to hug her. We left and caught the subway to Times Square. As I set up to busk, we chatted.

I tuned my guitar, preparing to play. "What do you think about that guy we keep seeing in the park?"

Kenzie unfolded our blanket. "He's cute. He acts tough, and I don't think it's entirely an act. Why? You like him?"

"I was thinking about asking him for protection. We need someone. Eventually, we're going to get arrested again—or, worse."

Kenzie pondered that thought. "I'm cool with that."

We sang until one in the morning. The money was nothing great, but not every night was. We made enough for sandwiches and coffee with a bit extra to save.

The next day, we introduced ourselves to the

guy. Thanksgiving was approaching, and Kenzie and I were going through a dry spell. The previous night we'd cleared eighty dollars, which was far less than our average.

The weather was colder and people weren't responding to my mixture of church music, rock music, and country ballads. Ronnie was out of commission with bronchitis which left Kenzie and me to study alone during the days. I was desperate for a night off the streets and the subways. Kenzie agreed. It was ten o'clock at night, and we were down to our last two hundred dollars.

I whined at Kenzie. "I've got to get a warm room tonight. I can't take another night of this bone-aching cold! We haven't been able to get a room for ten days!"

Kenzie gave me a kiss and we cuddled closer on a park bench under our blanket. "I know. But if we spend everything we have and run into trouble, we're screwed."

I shrugged "That guy is sitting over there. We both agree we like his looks. I'd do him, or let him do me, anyway. I've never offered that, and if you say no then I won't. Maybe even just offering would be enough. He looks like he has money." A palpable fear tightened my chest, but my mental need for a warm hotel room insisted on overriding the sensible part of my brain.

Kenzie's eyes widened, then she giggled. "Some church girl you are."

"Alright then, I'll go to hell."

"You're too sweet to be Huck." Her voice softened, but her eyes registered fear. "On a serious tip, if you want to ask him, I'll try to play along. You talk first, and I'll follow your lead."

We folded our blanket and put it in Kenzie's pack. I approached the boy. He wore a navy porkpie hat instead of his fedora, a black bomber jacket over an electric-blue shirt, gray chinos, and well-polished loafers. He was on a bench under a floodlight reading Slave Girl by Sarah Forsyth.

As I sat on one side of him and Kenzie sat on the other, a group of girls passed by dressed in red and pink. They looked passion-driven but fierce, with full-blown lips, mascara, and long eyelashes. I tried not to show irritation at the intrusion. Kenzie and I knew the Alley Cats by reputation. They were the female members of the Blade-Runner family. We stayed clear of the girls because, despite our ability to fight if necessary, we rather enjoyed eating solid food. Hard ass barely scratched the surface when it came to those chicks.

I was about to introduce myself to the guy when from another direction came a group dressed in motorcycle boots, tight jeans, and black vests over tight black shirts. The patches on the back of their vests read "Mighty Musclers." They all sported sunglasses, despite the late hour. They were joking and laughing with each other.

Kenzie eyed them hard, and they returned the glare. We had dealt with them before, and they had agreed to leave us alone after one of their members ended up on crutches for two weeks.

The Musclers and The Blade-Runners were not friends, but they had a truce going. In the thick of battle, they supported the same umbrella organization. The Runners were far tougher, but The Musclers were more apt to fight dirty. I checked the surroundings to assure myself that we weren't about to be caught in a turf war.

After a few minutes, I cleared my throat. The guy marked his place in the book and turned to give me a look. "Hi. We've been seeing you around. My name's Destiny Wilbury. This is my girlfriend, Mackenzie Guevara."

I tried to act cool, despite my nerves. Kenzie stared straight ahead, her face a stone mask.

"What's shaking, and what can I do you for?" The voice was a velvet-smooth, baritone. "Vinnie Il-Cazzo is the tag my folks hung on me." He turned to Kenzie. "Any relation to Ernesto?"

Kenzie spoke to no one in particular. "I don't know any of my mom's family."

Vinnie chortled, shaking his head. "Forget it. I doubt you and Che ever met."

I took a breath. "You have any spare change? Anything?"

I pleaded. "We're hungry, and we can make it worth your while. We need to get a room for the night, too. I'd do anything."

Kenzie re-animated and turned, batting her eyes. "Just enough money for coffee would be great. We're just so cold, Vinnie." My eyes widened at how flirty Kenzie was acting. I noticed her hand reaching for his back pocket, stopping short as she registered that no wallet was there.

He looked stern, his eyes narrowing. "I'm certainly not about to lay any bread on either of you until I tune in your frequency." He scowled at Kenzie. "Nice try, doll, but only a total Clyde keeps his wallet in the rear." He looked us both over, before turning back to me. "If you're hungry, I would dig buying you both some eats. And if I dig the flip and the riff of what you just offered, I'll just say nowhere later on the solicitation. Not that you aren't both hotties, because you are."

"Sorry, sir. It's just that I got kicked out of my house almost six months ago. Kenzie, too. We've been doing OK, but we ran out of funds." I took a breath. "We need help. Please."

Vinnie stood up and grabbed his sack. "Copacetic. Allow me to escort you to a greasy spoon and purchase comestibles. I can even secure a crash pad for the night. You can boil up, and catch some shuteye. Say another word about hitting the sheets in exchange for that, though, and I'm going to have to get strident." Vinnie glared at us. "If you're warm to my form and want to spend time together, that's another matter."

He returned his book to the side pocket of his courier bag before adjusting his backpack. We started walking with one of us on each of his arms.

Kenzie looked up at Vinnie. "I'm sorry for my part, too. You're a nice guy, Vinnie. Thanks for helping us out."

He shrugged. "Don't count on me being nice, but don't sweat it either. I help where I can."

Vinnie pointed out an all-night restaurant, and we crossed the avenue. "That joint has decent grub for a choke and puke. The prices are next to nothing, and you get your money's worth. I dig the ambiance, however."

It took me a moment to adjust to the lighting. The bulbs were a fluorescent yellow. A soft recording of a jazz quintet played in the background. The tables were plastic, made to imitate wood, as were the booths. The smell of hot oil filled the air. I understood why Vinnie enjoyed the ambiance. The place was both cheap and soothing.

Our server's name was Lucretia. She was a solid, older lady with glistening ebony skin and a knotted bandana over her hair. Her face was round with cherubic cheeks, and she had a bright smile. Kenzie and I ordered cheeseburgers with fries, coffee, and apple pie. Vinnie ordered a piece of pumpkin pie and coffee.

"If we perambulate toward uptown, I can likely land us a room. Nothing swank, but it won't be roach bait. I have to beat tracks in the early bright, but I can shell out for two nights. That way you can pull a Van Winkle before cutting out. I'll lay my cell digits on you in case you want to hook up after my meeting."

"You're unbelievable," I said. "I'm sorry I offered you sex like that. We've never done that before, it's just that we're desperate right now. For shelter, not for sex."

"We'll converse on that subject later, chick. And if this job interview works out, maybe I can help you chicks out steady." Vinnie finished his pie and ordered another piece. "You dolls have moxie, I'll give you that. And moxie is a righteous turn on."

Mackenzie looked across the table. "You sound like a street dad. You got a family?"

"I have sisters, but they don't live around here. And I don't know where my parents are. I'm not a papa yet. At least, I better not be. There's been no word indicating such."

I smiled and explained, "She doesn't mean family like that. Some kids we've met are part of street families. They have an older teen who acts as the street dad. Like those guys in the park earlier. Usually an older girl acts as mom. The family protects each other and lives together as a group. The dad's in charge."

He took a forkful of pie, chewing then swallowing. "I dig the flip. Solid. No, I'm not part of that scene. If you want me to watch over you and take care of you, I mean sure. Why not?" Vinnie shrugged, appearing unsure of what to make of our offer. "One thing, though. I'm not too hot on that dad term, dig? I like you both, but not with a dad sort of vibe. That'd be straight creepy."

"I really am sorry about what I asked." I blushed. "We haven't been doing so well with busking lately. Must be the cold weather. Last month, I was wowing the crowds with old-school rock and gospel."

Kenzie yawned with a small coo. "It's all good about the dad thing. We'll just say you're in charge."

Vinnie motioned the waitress to order another piece of pie. "Solid, I dig that. Why label everything? And Destiny, you have to change up the riff to fit the seasons. I'm sure that music you were swinging in the summer and even into the fall was solid jive. The cats and kitties always dig that riff. But, shortcakes, it's the holiday season now. Tomorrow you should try swinging some traditional carols on that ax of yours. Your main squeeze here should join in on the backup vocals and get the crowds singing with you. You'll rake in next to a heap of bread."

We finished eating, and he paid the bill. He slipped the server a twenty-dollar bill as a tip. Vinnie hailed a cab and we rode fifteen blocks to a moderate hotel. It was one in the morning when we secured a room. The desk manager was happy to take cash and Vinnie's word that he was nineteen. The room had a king-sized bed with a dark blue, quilted bedspread, and a desk with a chair. There was a television and a landline. The bathroom had a deep, clawfoot tub. As we settled, Vinnie looked over at us.

"OK, dolls, get stripped and into a hot shower. You need it, trust me. Then we're going to have a chat and get you to bed." He yawned and started taking off his jacket and shirt. He was removing his loafers when I noticed Kenzie, backed against the wall and frozen. The corner of her mouth twitched, and her eyes glazed over.

Vinnie looked up at Kenzie, turned his head, and looked at me. "She alright?" He sounded concerned. "Seizure? Should I call someone?"

"She'll be fine in a minute. It isn't your fault—how could you know? But, the comment about getting undressed and into the shower triggered her." I embraced her, squeezing her arms—firm, but without aggression. "Shh. It's OK, baby. You're fine. No one will hurt you. Destiny is here."

Vinnie shook his head. "Please accept my deepest apologies. I wasn't clued in. I can clear out. I'll catch forty on a bench or the trains. Or, if you'd rather, I can just crash in the chair until the early bright."

Kenzie relaxed in my arms, shocked by his offer. She smiled at Vinnie. "No, you paid for the room. I'm sorry I freaked out."

"It's cool. I dig the riff. Some cat caused you distress and now your gauge gets blown when certain notes go discordant with your mental circuitry." Vinnie looked less tough. Almost pained.

"Huh?"

"Someone hurt you, and it sets off an alert in your brain when circumstances remind you of the incidents surrounding the hurt. I've seen it before."

"Oh. Umm, yeah. Before I took off from home, my mom had men around. A few wanted to watch me and my sisters have a bath and stuff." Kenzie relaxed a little.

"I dig. Well, if you'd rather, you and Destiny just change in the bathroom and boil up. I'll wait out here."

"It's OK. I trust you. You don't seem dangerous. Would you really have slept somewhere else?" Kenzie began untying her shoes.

"I still will if you want. Don't want to blow my girls' radiators. What kind of a caregiver would I be if I ignored your distress?"

I pointed at him. "That right there is why we trust you. No one we've come across gives a damn about that. They just want sex."

Vinnie took out a cell phone and began texting some people. While he did, Kenzie and I stepped onto the bathroom and undressed. A half hour later, we were pink and glowing with vitality. Kenzie and I smelled far better and looked much cleaner. Vinnie sat in the chair in a pair of black silk pajama pants and a t-shirt. He gave us stern look as we stood there naked and shivering in our towels.

"If memory serves, and it does, you both tried to prostitute yourselves. That never happens again."

"It won't. I promise, sir." I stared at my feet, afraid of what I knew was coming.

"I assure you that it better not. That kind of jazz is a one-way ticket to doomsville. You said you want me in charge. Well, now you have it. You ever go that route again, and I'll roast your butts!" Vinnie's eyes flashed with gentle fury. "Get your pajamas on, vixens."

Kenzie's eyes glistened with tears, and she nodded. I grabbed a clean pair of panties from my backpack. Kenzie did likewise. "It won't happen again, I swear. We don't have pajamas. We usually sleep in our clothes or panties and t-shirts."

Vinnie handed us each one of his shirts, which fit us like dresses. We changed in the bathroom, and he tucked us into bed and kissed our foreheads. After he settled in the middle, we curled up beside him and were sound asleep in minutes. Three hours later, he climbed out of bed. After dressing, he took a small bottle of something from his backpack. He unscrewed it and took a sizable drink. Next, he took a photograph from his backpack, kissed it, then returned it. Prior to leaving, he wrote a note and left it on the desk. When we woke up at ten, we read the note.

Here's fifty dollars for each of you plus my cell number. Get dressed and take your backpacks to the following address. Get change on the way by ordering breakfast. Do your laundry and put on clean clothes. Wash what you put on this morning and rewash anything that's extra dirty. Have a nice lunch and meet me at the dinosaur exhibit in Natural History at four. Be good, V.

Vinnie was something incredible and rare. At that moment, we had no clue how special he truly was or how much he would change our lives.

Chapter 13

Kenzie and I showered and dressed. We put all the toilet paper rolls and the extra miniature soaps in my backpack before leaving.

"I can't believe Vinnie. Guys like that usually terrify me, but there's something about him. It's like he really cares. I hope he wasn't serious about spanking us, though." Kenzie snuggled next to me.

"I think he was serious as a heart attack. We deserved it, too. I know what you mean, though. He's like a teddy bear. He roars like a grizzly but comforts like Paddington." I gave her a soft kiss.

"Who's Paddington?"

I stood up and adjusted my pack. "A British bear. You should read the books. I had a stuffed Paddington, but I had to leave him behind."

"Your parents kept your teddy bear? What assholes!"

We left the hotel and walked to a corner café for breakfast. Afterward, we caught the subway toward second street on the upper east side. The train was half full so we each had a seat, comfortable and holding hands.

I held my guitar case in my lap as we rode. "I like Vinnie. Man, he's built. If I'd known a guy like that back then, I'd have made my parents happy."

Kenzie laughed. "If he ever met your dad, I bet he'd kick the man's ass. Those douchebag church elders, too."

I smiled for a few moments, picturing that. "I'd like to watch that. I get this weird feeling that he has a lot of secrets."

Kenzie leaned over and snuggled against me. "So do we, chick. I was scared at first, but it's like he went out of his way to make us feel safe. He didn't even demand anything from us. You're right about his looks, too. If I was looking for a man, he'd be the one I'd want."

I giggled and squirmed. "I'd sleep with him. Well, sleep isn't the right word."

Kenzie laughed and gave me a light push on the arm. "I'm shocked. You sound like you know something about boys. I'm also jealous."

"There's a lot that my church got wrong, but they taught kids about the birds and the bees." I kissed her cheek. "No need to be jealous. You're the only girl for me. Actually, I was thinking about Ronnie and Vinnie."

Kenzie pointed at me. "Now that's not a bad idea there."

We got change at the laundromat and bought little boxes of detergent. While our clothes washed, I sat outside and played my guitar. I started with "Jingle Bells" and "Frosty The Snowman." By the time I started playing "I Heard The Bells" and "Good King Wenceslas," a crowd had formed. Vinnie was right about the seasonal music. The crowd threw money into my case and sang along. Kenzie put the first load into the dryers while I was led the crowd in "Twelve Days of Christmas." I was a smash.

After the first load of clothes dried, we changed in a restroom. We threw our dirty clothes into a washing machine with our sweaters and jackets. I performed my second set outside, feeling the chill as my winter coat washed. We cleared over one hundred and fifty dollars in the two hours we did our laundry. After everything was dry, I bought us sausages and sauerkraut at a German restaurant. After, we walked to a candy store to buy chocolates.

When we arrived at four, Vinnie was standing by the triceratops in The Museum of Natural History. He looked suave in his designer clothes. Kenzie and I were raggedy in comparison; but, for once, everything we had on was clean.

"Hey." Mackenzie side hugged him. "We did our laundry like you told us. I hope you don't mind, but we took all the toilet paper and an extra bar of soap from the room."

He chuckled "As long as you don't take towels or bed linen. The hostelries don't dig that action. Kiting the toiletries isn't a big thing."

"Thank you for everything, sir. I didn't know if you'd be here." I stood on my tiptoes to kiss him on the cheek. "We bought you a present."

Vinnie opened the box of opera fudge that we'd bought for him and ate one. He kissed us both on the foreheads, "If you're still hip to my lick, I think we should down some comestibles and confabulate. Last night, time wasn't on our side. I also need to secure us another night at a different snooze and split. I'm not sure we should use that same place again."

He stood and took one of us on each arm. We walked a few blocks and caught a subway to the Upper East Side. Vinnie led us into a Turkish restaurant and got us a table. I looked around the place and perused the menu. My eyes moved up to meet Vinnie's. The prices were steep.

He winked at me. "Line your flue, and fuel the furnace. If there're leftovers, we can pack it for later snacking."

We ordered hummus, spinach tarator, borek, hunker begindi, and manti. We washed the food down with mineral water. I had never tried any of the dishes, and they took getting used to. Turkish food, I learned, was not bland by any means. I noticed Kenzie's mouth screwing itself into odd positions, at first, as she tasted everything.

Vinnie took a sip of water and crossed his arms over his chest, giving us a look of authority. "Let's get down to polyvinyl chloride tacks, chicks. From whence do you hail and why are you on the lam? Straight from the fridge, why did you put the bullseye on me for your bodyguard? From what my pallie Ralph tells me, countless other options abound. Why not them? How much do I risk by dealing myself a hand?"

Kenzie looked sideways across the table. "Do you speak English?"

Vinnie chuckled. "You want a smack on the keister? It ain't Turkish, gate. I asked where you're from and why me. Don't get to thinking you're Mendy Weiss."

"Who?"

"Just answer my questions. I need the scoop."

I fixed my eyes on the table, afraid to say something wrong. "I'm from Florida, sir. My parents kicked me out."

"Why?"

"They don't understand that I'm bisexual, sir. Father told me I wasn't allowed to come back unless I submitted to the church beliefs. I came to the city and met Kenzie."

Kenzie looked at Vinnie with sad eyes. "I wasn't getting smart with you. I've never heard the expressions you use. I used to live in Jersey City. It was bad. I got hurt a lot until I got tired of being pushed around and yelled at. I got tired of the sicko creeps my mom dated trying to touch me. So, I packed a bag and left. My mom said that she's fine with that."

Vinnie thanked the waiter when he brought the appetizers. We ate in silence for a few minutes.

"Why me? Why not the other cats who group together?" He sighed. "I'm a loner, dolls. I like to read, work out, and exist in my own stratosphere. Plus, I've got some heavy chips down on side bets. I'll help you, but why me? Hep me to that knowledge."

I took a bite of the spinach dish. "We've looked at other street families, sir, but it isn't so good. Most of them are criminals. I'm talking about purse snatching, beating up old people, using drugs, that sort of thing. We even got offers to make dirty movies. We don't want to get arrested because someone stole an old man's wallet. And we don't like that most street-dads think of their daughters as sex partners. That's creepy, like you said. Except for my offer last night, we aren't whores, sir."

Kenzie blushed and ate a bite of humus on a pita. "I saw you in the park and told Destiny that you looked like you had money. The way you dress says a lot. After seeing you every day, we thought we should chance it. It worked out good, too, except for you threatening to spank us. We earned that, though, and probably worse."

Vinnie stared, unblinking. "Savvy. Well, you dealt the cards, so let's play the hand. I'm glad to find us places to lay our heads and just as happy to help you stay safe. I'm not much older than you both. I'm sixteen, despite what my ID reads. I've been blowing it solo eight to the bar for too damned long." He nodded at Kenzie, "I was forced to grow up too fast and take care of myself. Life has dealt me one lousy hand after another, but I've learned how to bluff. As of this morning, I landed a gig. I'll be in action every day, except Sunday."

We listened attentively, continuing to eat our food.

"You both need to be in school. Either that, or we need to procure you each a GED. If you aren't in school it could attract attention from cops or other undesirables. That I can't allow. I already have a GED. I expect you to lay low and stay out of trouble when not in school. I won't bail you out of jail if you do anything stupid. If you get into any serious trouble that brings attention my way, you'll think what I said last night was nothing. That's not a threat. You can bank on it. For a lot of reasons, I can't stand people abusing kids, but there's a broad line between abuse and a well-skinned ass. Don't test me on that. If you agree to my terms, we can hang out tonight. Tomorrow, after work, I can take you shopping. I'll teach you everything I know about survival skills so that you can fly solo. Take it or leave it."

"We'll take it. We get that we have to obey you." Mackenzie put her hand on Vinnie's. "We're already working on our GED. We have a tutor you should meet once she recovers from bronchitis."

I felt a strange sensation in my belly. My breathing hurt a bit as my heart raced. I looked at Vinnie then back down at my plate. I couldn't collect my thoughts. Kenzie must've sensed my distress.

"You OK? You look sick." She rubbed my thigh, then told Vinnie, "She had a sinus infection a couple of months ago."

I shrugged. "I'm fine...just...never mind. I'm fine. Yes, sir we will behave and not cause any trouble."

Vinnie reached over and lifted my chin with a light finger. "You don't have to call me sir. It sounds like you came from a real strict home. The mention of homophobia...I hate that word, says it all. I read enough to know. I was laying the boundaries, but I wasn't trying to crush you. Smile for me, sweetheart."

I smiled. "You have no idea how bad home was for me. I get these moments where I feel like I'm stuck in a cage."

"Solid. I dig the flip. It might take time, but you'll get there."

Kenzie glanced between us, then held our hands. "Why don't you like the word homophobia? It's what her church was."

"No, ma'am. Negative. Phobia means fear. Clydes like that don't fear homosexuals, they hate on them. Prejudiced is the word. Intolerant assholes. Soulless bastards. There are a lot of words that apply, but homophobia isn't one of them." Vinnie took a healthy swig of water.

Our entrees arrived, and we dug in. I didn't realize how hungry I was until I started. Eating cleared the last of the residual fear from my system. Vinnie and Kenzie were clearly famished, and we continued without further conversation. As Vinnie paid in cash and left a huge tip, Kenzie let out a tremendous belch.

"That was about six point four on the Richter scale, doll." Vinnie helped us with our coats. "You dig the grub?"

"I've never had anything like it. We should come here again." I stifled a yawn. "That pastry thing we had was delicious."

"That was borek. I dig it, too. Phyllo dough dishes are difficult, but they never fail to satisfy." Vinnie held the door for us, sounding alive and spirited. "Back to where we were, we can discuss your schedules for studying and work tomorrow. For now, want to see a movie? Go skating at Rockefeller? What sounds good? I could get us a room instead and a bottle of something. Do you two smoke out?"

My eyes widened. "We both smoke pot when we can get it. I was afraid to ask if you smoked it. You've mentioned spankings a few times, and I enjoy sitting."

Vinnie chuckled and ruffled my hair. We walked to a different hotel than we had used the previous night. He paid two hundred dollars cash for a room with a king-sized bed on the fourteenth floor. The desk clerk agreed to forgo needing a credit card if Vinnie put down an extra hundred for security.

Vinnie pocketed the room key-card. "Let's hit the stores before we head upstairs. You both need some pajamas. Maybe some other things."

We left and caught a cab to Macy's. He bought me a pair of pink Hello Kitty pajama bottoms and a matching t-shirt. Mackenzie opted for a long, Winnie The Pooh nightshirt. After paying, we returned to the hotel. On the way, Vinnie gave a homeless guy thirty dollars to buy us a bottle of Jim Beam.

Kenzie sat watching TV while Vinnie texted some people. I texted Rory about our new situation. Hey, guys, Kenzie and I met this boy named Vinnie. He's not only handsome, but he's caring and seems to understand our situation. We asked him to watch out for us and he agreed. So far so good.

My phone pinged two minutes later. Rory here. Bring Vinnie by as soon as you can. We'd like to meet him. Be careful, kid. Not every well-wrapped package is a treasure. Stay safe.

After we cleaned up, Vinnie placed three ice cubes in glasses, poured some bourbon, and a splash of club soda. The bourbon left a pleasant sensation in my stomach. Kenzie relaxed with her first sip. She had three glasses for my one. Vinnie lit a pipe and we smoked a couple of bowls of pot. The window opened so we blew the hits outside.

The effects of the pot took a few minutes to kick in. One minute, I was looking out the window at the street below; the next, I was in a cinematic dream sequence. The air compressed around me and the heat of the room formed a cocoon. Kenzie put an arm around my hips and stood beside me, staring off into space. The clock read nine-thirty, but I was exhausted. Vinnie was already in bed with his eyes closed. Kenzie and I fell asleep with one of us cuddled into Vinnie from either side.

I awoke at four thirty in the morning. Vinnie slipped out of bed and tried not to wake us. I pretended to be asleep. Kenzie cooed and rolled over toward me. We cuddled together in the void Vinnie had left. In the dark of the morning, I watched him open the bottle of Jim Beam and take a healthy swig. It made me nervous, but I wasn't sure whether to say anything to him later. He took the photograph from the front pocket of his backpack and kissed it. That was twice I'd seen him do that.

Pulling on his pants and shirt, Vinnie checked his appearance in the mirror and brushed his fingers through his hair. He dabbed on some cologne and wrote us another note.

Girls, be out of the room by ten. Here's food money. I'll meet you at four outside the big library. I'm getting us reservations for Thanksgiving dinner. You might check out some stores and see if you can find any backpacks you like. If not, we can figure out a way to order some. You need new shoes, too. Don't worry about price, just find some, and I'll get them for you. If there's any change in plans, text me. Behave yourselves, V.

I closed my eyes. Kenzie woke up at eight thirty. We cuddled for a while before dressing in jeans, hoodies, jackets, and sneakers. I pocketed the note, and Kenzie pocketed the money. We exited the hotel and grabbed a cup of coffee before boarding the subway toward Times Square, rested and ready to start another day.

Chapter 14

I had watched the Macy's parade on television every year. Most people have. Seeing the parade in person was an experience that words can't do justice. Kenzie and I squeezed in between people for a spot near the front, despite our backpacks and my guitar case. The floats were exceptional, and the hot air balloons were awesome. Kenzie squealed with delight as Snoopy flew by chasing The Red Baron. I waved with excitement at Hello Kitty.

The musical acts were phenomenal! I adored Neil Diamond, and a group called Fresh Beat Band had Kenzie and I dancing. Even seeing Sesame Street made my heart swoon. Kenzie giggled, but she was into it too. As I watched the performers, I hoped that it would be me performing in the parade one day. At the end, came the spectacular denouement. The pièce de résistance, as it were. Kenzie and I bounced like five-year-olds, enamored at Santa's appearance. Some magic never wears off.

Once the parade finished, we worked our way back through the crowd. People packed together like sardines and more than one hand grabbed my butt. I clipped a teenaged boy on the chin with my elbow, but there was no real way to tell who was groping whom. Kenzie shrieked when someone tried feeling her up. In time, we escaped the dense throng of bodies and took a side street. After a short subway ride, we walked through the park and hunted for an empty bench.

We found one a block further, and I played guitar for ninety minutes before stopping. Sticking to traditional holiday classics allowed Kenzie to do much of the singing. She was in excellent voice, and the crowd responded with appreciation. As an encore, I played "I Heard The Bells on Christmas Day."

While putting my guitar away, I considered taking some professional lessons. Kenzie collected the money and shoved it in her backpack.

I put on my pack. "I wonder how much it would cost to find a guitar instructor. I really could use lessons."

Kenzie adjusted her shoulder straps, "More than we make, I'm sure. You're great, and one day you'll get lessons. You deserve it."

"I love performing." I bought us each a hot chocolate and some chestnuts from a vendor. "Nothing sounds as wonderful as applause. Nothing."

"The crowds love you, Destiny," she said, gazing at me with bright eyes. "On another subject, we should buy Vinnie something for Christmas. I was thinking about getting Ronnie something, too. But I can't decide what to get them."

"What about a romantic dinner for two and tickets to a show? Maybe we can double date."

Kenzie grabbed a New Yorker from a bench. Her eyes lit up. "I've heard of this one. Godspell. You might really like that one. It's about The Book of Matthew. The music is rocking. And there's this opera I've heard of called Porgy and Bess. One time in music class, we listened to a song called 'Summertime.'"

I smiled. "Matthew's a great book. Kind of funny that it's Christmas and, from what I've heard, that musical picks up with Christ's adult years. Still, that sounds cool."

She appeared shocked. "You know it, then?"

I shrugged. "I've heard a couple of songs from it, but I've never seen it performed."

We walked several blocks to a business that dealt in surplus tickets. I purchased four tickets in the third row, center orchestra to each of the shows. The Godspell tickets were for the Thursday before Christmas, and Porgy and Bess was a Christmas Eve matinee. Our cash holdings dropped to an all-time low of three dollars, but I knew we could recoup the money. After buying the tickets, we perused some outdoor adventure stores and found one that was several stories high.

Kenzie and I searched every aisle of the giant camping store. I was amazed at the sheer enormity of offerings. We located the aisle we needed and tested over fifty backpacks.

The need to decide left my mind cluttered. "I don't know which one we want. Nothing with a metal frame, I guess. Even with those taken out, we have more than thirty options."

A lady with long hair resembling clumped straw approached us. She wore jeans and a flannel shirt. "Can I assist you?"

Kenzie toyed with a pack that was as broad across as she was. "We're looking for backpacks and boots. We've never bought backpacks like this before. What's the best brand?"

The lady inquired in her cheerful voice, "What do you plan to use them for? Day hikes? Camping? Mountains or trails?"

"We need something that can hold two weeks' worth of clothing plus books, toiletries, and some food," I said, examining a thick, light-blue pack.

"I see. So, long trips then. I can recommend four different backpacks." She showed us the selections, each of them cost more than busking would bring in two days.

"We'll think about these and ask our dad."

After looking at the packs, we tried on over twenty pairs of boots each. We found a few styles that we loved. The lady helped us with our decisions. She assumed that we were planning a long camping trip. But, we weren't going camping. This was survival gear. Survival in the city. The packs would hold our entire lives. The boots had to last.

We left after a while and headed to the library; we sat outside while I played my guitar. I made a quick sixty dollars. After busking, we took a stroll down an avenue to meet Vinnie.

There were a number of boys about our age standing against buildings or leaning on street posts. Most of them were skinny with hungry, vacuous eyes and arms that displayed purple-black contusions. Those opaque eyes that saw both everything and nothing were frightening. These kids were not like street families, or anyone else I had encountered in the city. Kenzie informed me that they were rough trade. Male prostitutes who were so desperate for money or drugs that they didn't care who did what to them. They needed food, shelter, a shot of heroin or meth, or someone to love them enough to help. Kenzie looked inured to the scene, but I found the situation sickening. I offered up several silent prayers for these lost souls who made my life, desperate as it was, appear cozy in comparison.

That evening, we sat across from Vinnie in a restaurant with a soft lighting and subdued sounds of merriment from surrounding tables. The first course was autumn squash soup with citrus yogurt and a pear and pecorino salad.

"Last night, we told you about ourselves. But what about you? Where are you from and what's your story?" I asked, digging into the vibrant salad.

"I was birthed in a suburb two shakes and a shimmy outside the urban blight. My bodily metamorphosis took place there until I was nigh on twelve. My parents were cool. My father's sharp enough to shave with, and he's flushed out in hearts where compassion is concerned. My mother, she's always stayed back and kept it mellow. Thing of it is, they grew up watching our nation take beating after beating, both economically and socially. Their own parents were a real mixed bag, and that shaped them."

Vinnie ate before continuing. "If you dig the riff, my mother is the quiet, retiring sort. But, behind that persona is a woman who has no problem handing corporate America their collective asses. My father isn't exactly boisterous, but neither is he shy. He taught me from the age of five where the cracks in the system are—and how to dynamite those cracks — to bring down the corporate walls and destroy the rich bastards who get fat on the backs of poor ham-and-eggers."

"Huh? You learned how to use dynamite at five years old?" Kenzie said, shocked.

Vinnie's chin quivered and the sides of his mouth rose. "Not strictly correct. I was speaking metaphorically. This nation, if you haven't figured it out, is by the rich, of the rich, and for the rich. If you don't have the do-re-mi then you're S-O-L. That being so, people have developed ways and means to take back from the rich that which rightfully belongs to the poor."

"So you're Robin Hood?" I giggled.

Vinnie grew animated as he discussed this part of his life. "In a manner of speaking, doll. Lord Loxley stole from the rich and gave to the poor. Me and me and mine are also the poor. So, we robbed from the rich and gave unto ourselves and each other. There are many ways to accomplish that, and I can hip your wig to many of them."

The waiter brought us poached turkey with mushroom-leek stuffing, cranberry relish, and turkey gravy. There were traditional sides of candied yams, mashed potatoes, and a broccoli rabe risotto to go with it. I had never had such a feast, and Kenzie's face said it all for her.

She dished up her share of the food. "Where did you move when you were twelve?"

Vinnie leaned back with his hands interlaced on his belly. "The short answer is that we moved to New England. A small dot on the map. Before we moved, my parents went through a period of deep depression and anxiety. They were completely tuned out most of the time. Later on, I learned that they were also under investigation, as were a number of family friends. Shortly after, my parents started receiving disability checks. Before anyone could link them to any criminal activity, we pulled a fade."

Kenzie took a bite of stuffing. "What were they into that had the five-oh on your ass?"

Vinnie's eyes softened, revealing a deep emotional pain. "Plenty. Allow me to continue. Once we moved, I made a few friends. One, in particular, was a girl from a few doors down. She was beautiful. Her name was Stephanie Ann Baker. I was smitten like a kitten from jump street. But her father was a brutal drunk and getting close to Steph was next to impossible. Eventually, her mother needed to escape and asked my parents for help. One of my sisters was already in college, but the rest of my family helped Steph, her sister Caroline, and their mother escape.

"On the way to helping them get free, Steph and I grew closer. She was my first, in a way. It was just swapping chews, and a lot of feeling each other up, but it was phenomenal. The Baker ladies were escaping, however, and the romance was short-lived. I've never met anyone like Steph. I have one photo and my memories to hold me."

"Is that the picture you kiss every morning? Yeah, I've seen you," I said, blushing.

Vinnie ate a few bites before answering. "I assumed you both to be asleep in the early bright. Yes, that's her photograph. After we returned home, my father made a few calls. Myron Baker disappeared. It turns out that, among his other activities, old Myron was trafficking in illegal aliens. His disappearance brought police attention and, with that, my parents cut and ran. I stuck around awhile. I had found an interesting doll with whom to bide my time. Julie was no Steph, although they'd been acquainted. Steph was wholesome where Julie was feral and randy. But I grew to love Julie, in a carnal and prurient way.

"My sister, Tori, and her boyfriend left for college. I was on my own. My sister, Gina, had her boyfriend make me a fake ID. I made tracks for Florida and got my GED. My parents sold our house and furniture, arranging for my sisters and I to each receive twenty grand for college. I don't see college in my near future, however."

The waiter brought us maple-bourbon pumpkin pie and coffee. I tried to formulate a polite question. "Were your parents involved with the human trafficking you mentioned? Is that why they ran?" I looked away, hoping I hadn't crossed a line.

Vinnie sighed, his grip tightening on the coffee cup. "Not directly, no. But part of how they operated involved being closely connected to people who had their fingers in those pies. It was explained to me that the people who came to America were paying back the cost of the trip, plus housing and their document papers. I'm a quick study, though, and I know the truth.

"Once everything fell apart, I started dating several chicks. Julie Dimitrion was just one of them. When I moved to western Florida and obtained my GED, I not only made plenty of bread but I had arm candy by the dozens. After moving back to my original neighborhood near the city, I met a guy who hipped me to a gig that pays decent. I thought life was perfect, being alone and easy-breezy cool. Then, I met you both. Once more someone needed me, and again I couldn't say no."

We finished dessert and had more coffee, then I inquired, "So do you know where Steph Baker moved to?"

Vinnie paid the check, leaving a two hundred dollar tip. "I don't. That was necessary in order for them to truly escape. I only have vague knowledge that Heather Baker was from a small town in Nebraska. One day, I might beat my kicks eight to the bar and look around the area."

"That was the best meal I've had in a long time. Maybe ever." Kenzie patted Vinnie's hand. "Thank you."

"I'm glad I had you both to share a meal with. Three days ago I turned...ummm, nineteen according to my ID. I was alone and blowing the blues. Now I have you both in my life, and that's the most swinging gift ever." He yawned, gazing at us both. "Enough of my depressing story. What kind of action did you chicks get into today?"

Kenzie finished her coffee. "We watched the parade, played some music, and looked at some stores. The backpacks we like are expensive. So are the boots."

"Savvy. You can pay me back half of it when you earn the bread." Vinnie smiled. "Or perhaps I can hep you to how I operate. Then it won't cost a dime."

Kenzie's mouth dropped open. "Hold up, hold up! You saying that you can get that stuff for free? I don't want to be involved with robbing a store or anything like that."

"You won't be involved. I know some people who get stuff F-O-T. I duke them a fraction of the shelf price. In this case, I might can suggest that with the holidays coming up they could help me out on this deal." Vinnie stood, motioning for us to follow. "It's part of what I was telling you about how my parents operate."

We walked toward Fifth Avenue to look at the window displays. "What's F-O-T?" My heart beat faster.

Vinnie laughed. "It means the items fell off of a truck."

Kenzie squinted with irritation. "I'm not the smartest girl who ever lived, but if the items fell off of a truck then shouldn't the driver pick them up and put them back on the truck? Or, if the items are damaged, shouldn't he report that?"

Vinnie threw back his head and roared with laughter. "I asked that same exact question when I was five," He calmed down to a slight chuckle. "The term is an expression. For the most part, the store's upper management turns a blind eye when a truck driver pulls in and items vanish from the inventory. They collect insurance on the stolen items, plus they get a cut of the bread on resale. The drivers get an extra couple hundred clams to take a powder for a few. It's a well-run part of most retail businesses."

"So, the items are stolen. But the evidence trail leads nowhere because no one actually wants it to lead anywhere. Therefore, you're buying hot merchandise for less than market value and have probable deniability if it comes to any questions being asked. Is that the gist?" Kenzie smiled a little.

I gawked. "Look at you with the big words all of a sudden."

"I watch Law & Order. I understand these things." She shrugged, smiling.

"Give the girl a cigar." Vinnie ruffled Kenzie's hair. "Not hot merchandise, though. Lukewarm items, at best."

I hugged Vinnie from the side. "I won't tell on you."

"Copacetic. I get most of my clothes F-O-T. I have for years. There's a catalog from a place up north, too. It requires a hefty initial buy-in on merchandise, but no further cost ever to replace or trade in items. I'll show you later."

Everywhere we walked, the city was decked out in lights, tinsel trim, and decorated trees. A Santa stood on every other corner, ringing bells and seeking donations. The glittery department store windows were enchanting. Vinnie dropped a ten-dollar bill in every Santa's kettle, and he gave a few homeless people twenty-dollar bills as if it were nothing.

"These festive window displays are a tradition dating all the way back to the 1870s. Macy's was the first retailer to start the trend," Vinnie said as we stood by the first window.

We strolled from window to window, from store to store, and I grew fascinated with the animatronic storylines. Although clearly a come-on to purchase gifts at the stores, the displays touched something deep inside of me. I experienced the feelings I imagined children felt at the holidays—if their childhood hadn't been torn asunder.

After strolling by each store, we bought hot chocolates and searched for a hotel. As we walked briefly through the park, Vinnie reached into his backpack and took out a bottle of Chopin vodka. He poured two shots into each of our cups of cocoa. Kenzie's face lit up as she sipped.

"Where you score all the drinks? You always have a bottle on you, but you aren't old enough to buy it. Not even with your ID. You just ask someone in the park or what?" Kenzie asked, mellow with her spiked cocoa.

"I don't need to go that route often. I have other means by which to procure whatever libation I might require." Vinnie turned toward a moderate hotel. "I'll introduce you to some cats tomorrow night."

I hugged Vinnie and kissed him on the cheek. Kenzie smiled and followed suit. "Before we go in, I want to do something."

After undoing my guitar case and tuning up, Kenzie and I performed a soulful version of "Happy Birthday." Vinnie watched us both, then put on his mirrored sunglasses as gentle tears fell. He hugged us both when we finished.

The hotel was nothing extravagant, but neither was it a dive.

We paid for a room on the twelfth floor and took the elevator. As advertised, Vinnie's ID showed that he was nineteen. The desk agent was willing to accept cash in exchange for a room. The room had a king-sized bed with a cranberry and gold comforter, a desk and chair, a dresser with a TV, and a large bathroom with fluffy towels. I turned on the tub to get the water hot.

Kenzie and I undressed and spent forty-five minutes in the steaming water. When we emerged in our pajamas, Vinnie was reading American Roulette by Richard Marcus. He poured Jack Daniels into three glasses with a splash of Perrier. We toasted his birthday and fell asleep.

The next morning, Vinnie was gone when I woke up with Kenzie in my arms. We found his note.

Girls, I have to make the scene with a cat in Queens later. I won't be back until after midnight. Either we can hook up tomorrow or you can meet me somewhere tonight after my appointment. Text me, and let me know. Here's fifty dollars. Get cracking on the schoolwork today. Stay gold, V.

Kenzie and I showered and changed our clothes. We grabbed the extra toilet paper and toiletries before exiting. I found us a place to get hot, open-faced turkey sandwiches on white bread with gravy. Mariah Carey was singing from the speakers in the ceiling. While we were having pumpkin pie and coffee, I cleared my throat.

"If we study for a little while and get in some performing, we could ride to Rockaway and meet Vinnie tonight."

"I'll text him." Kenzie pulled her phone out, thumbs dancing across the screen. "Hey, I got a text from Jeanie. You did, too."

I checked my phone. Hey, you two. We're going to be out that way in a couple of days. We want to meet this guy you told us about.

Kenzie smiled. "Vinnie says to be at the station by one in the morning. He said we can ride the A Train tonight and wander around some in the parks."

"Jeanie and family are coming next week. If we can make

enough, I was thinking about a scarf, gloves, and hat combo for Rainbow. Maybe some perfume for the girls, and a tie for Rory." I paid the bill, smiling from the plans. The joy of the season was gripping me.

"I think Christmas is the happiest season of them all!" Kenzie looked buoyant.

I spun around in circles with my arms out. "Andy Williams would likely agree with you on that."

Chapter 15

As the weeks wore on, Kenzie and I came to love Vinnie. He was a hard guy to figure. You had to look deep, and listen carefully, to read him well; there was more than one volume to him. He wasn't comfortable letting people into his most private thoughts, or near the guarded layers of his heart. To look at him, though, one got the feeling that he was always busy inside his head. His eyes expressed unfathomable emotional pain, and the way he carried himself was a challenge to the rest of humanity. Despite his internal turmoil, it never ceased to surprise me how Vinnie offered such an air of cool to the world. His cell phone was forever chirping with people needing help, needing hope, needing him. He seemed to revel in that role. He changed Kenzie's and my life.

The day after Thanksgiving, Black Friday, Kenzie and I found the library closed. We walked to a huge bookstore and took novels from the shelves. There were oversized chairs for people to use while perusing selections. I sat in one and read Uncle Tom's Children by Richard Wright. Kenzie read Alcott's Little Women. After a few hours, we left and found a place to play music. We stopped to purchase a cheap tambourine for Kenzie to use.

With the introduction of some percussion, the money increased. The crowds gathered, shouting for more. Two girls asked if they could join us. One played violin and the other clarinet. We agreed, and the sound was magnificent. After playing for four hours, we split $600. Kenzie and I played for two more hours, adding $150 to our bankroll. I was exhausted.

We stopped at a fast-food restaurant and loaded up. The food revitalized my circuits. After a walk through the park to admire the lighted trees, we rode the A Train to Queens. I slept most of the way, and Kenzie stayed awake to guard our gear.

At midnight, we waited at the station for Vinnie when a group of teens approached. The oldest guy was dressed in jeans, combat boots, and an army jacket. He had a long greasy hair and looked vicious.

The guy stopped before us as his family clustered behind him. "You girls alone?"

Kenzie gave the guy a cold look. "No. We have the entire cast of The Lion King sitting here with us."

He gave a forced chuckle, his eyes scanning my body. "My name's Contagion. If you need protection, we can do that."

I stood up and lowered my hips a bit. I breathed in and breathed out. "Look—Contagious, is it? We have someone who looks after us. He'll be here soon, and he's the jealous type. So get lost, asshole!"

One of the girls stepped forward, and I moved a metal trashcan between us—ready to shove it into her legs. "All of you, get to stepping. I'm not in a good mood. I don't want a big cop scene, and I don't need another felony on my record!" I stepped back into a boxing stance and raised my fists.

Contagion snorted in disbelief. "Yeah, right. Felony for what?"

I grinned as Kenzie stood to move behind me. "Some jerk named Anthrax was annoying me. I accidentally threw him off of a bridge in Central Park. I was charged with felony assault and got probation because juvie was full."

Contagion's eyes widened, and he backed up a step. "Anthrax? Like The Blade Runners' war chief?"

I took a step forward to close the gap, pushing the trash can between myself and the others. "Right. Next time you see him, ask about the cane he uses."

The group filed past us and kept going. Kenzie sat beside me on the bench and laughed. "You told a fi-ib. I'm gonna tel-el."

I stuck out my tongue. "Someone taught me well. I read

about some teen getting probation for that the other day."

"Moving that trash can was a good idea. You're getting better at that."

We were locked in an embrace and necking when Vinnie showed up. He called our names more than once before we stood. He was dressed to the nines, as usual. I made a mental note to ask him how he managed to change his outfits so often, keep his clothes so pressed, while living out of a backpack.

"Evening, gates. Let's percolate. Hope you weren't waiting too long." His eyes were half closed and his shoulders drooped.

Kenzie covered a yawn and leaned on me. "Long enough. We showed up and had some trouble. There's an assclown around here calling himself Contagion. He thought we looked like easy marks, but our pit bull here told him where to shove it. One of his bitches took offense, but we made it clear that we wanted to be left alone."

Vinnie's eyes opened wider and his face registered concern. With the deftness of a magician performing a card trick, a pair of brass knuckles appeared in his right hand. Contagion and his family didn't return, and no one else showed up for the train.

The fourth car was a third full, so we dozed all the way to Harlem and back to Midtown Manhattan. Kenzie used Vinnie's lap for a pillow, and I leaned on his shoulder while we napped. As false dawn approached, he led us to an all-night corner deli for breakfast.

Vinnie chewed while lost in thought. "This arrangement we've set up is a solid gasser, chicks. I had a notion, however, that might boost us from a three-aces hand to straight flush in hearts if you dig the flip. But, I need your input.

"I'm making plenty of bread at my job. I even get bonuses, which that was part of what tonight was about. If we can find a hotel that's not a complete dive, or a pay-and-lay, I might can get us a monthly rate. That way we don't have to always be on the move. We can stash our gear, and you'd both have a permanent place to crack the books."

"That'd be awesome!" Kenzie smiled. "We can help out with the costs."

I nodded. "We made $450 last night. Most nights is less than half that, but we usually make $300 on the weekends. These two girls stopped and asked to play with us. It made a big difference. I never realized how much a violin and clarinet could improve my guitar playing."

Vinnie took off his sunglasses and folded them, signaling for more coffee. "That's far out! I'll allow that you can perform and help out. But homework and schoolwork first. Savvy? You need to tune your dials to the GED certificates."

"We can't even get those for a couple of years." Kenzie sighed. "We're too young. We don't have ID cards like yours."

Vinnie winked. "Give it time. As you grow closer to the goal, a path may appear. There's much to discourse where that's concerned."

"I'm tired." I yawned. "Can we talk about it tonight?"

"Plan on it. I'm going to make like a newborn and head out. Stay safe." Vinnie paid the pill, giving us a thumbs up while clicking his tongue.

Kenzie and I finished our coffee and walked to the library. When we arrived, there was still a two hour wait until the doors opened. We held each other and fell asleep, leaning against a wall. Once the library opened, we slept some more in the reading room. We woke up at two in the afternoon and texted Ronnie.

She replied. I'm a lot better. I still need another three days, at least. I'm looking forward to meeting this guy you keep texting me about. I want both of you to write essays about the books you just finished. Study your math, then go to the planetarium.

We texted Vinnie and made plans for dinner at a burger chain. After walking to the right area, we found a spot to sit against a wall. I played guitar, and Kenzie rattled the tambourine. By the time Vinnie arrived, we had made forty dollars. The three-block stroll to the restaurant was pleasant after sitting on the sidewalk.

We ordered triple burgers, fries, and sodas. Vinnie handed over three vouchers that he extracted from a fat envelope. No money changed hands.

Kenzie bit into her burger. "Hey, did we just get our food for free? Where'd you get those?"

"Later." Vinnie winked at us and ate. "So did anything interesting happen today?"

Kenzie swallowed then said, "Well, we were walking in the park earlier, and this dude in an overcoat stepped in front of these three old ladies and flashed them. The first one had a stroke, then the second one had a stroke. The third lady's arms were too short, so she didn't." Vinnie shook with laughter.

After dinner, we took a walk through some more industrial neighborhoods near Hell's Kitchen. As we passed several trucks unloading merchandise for department stores, Vinnie stopped to talk to a tall, muscular man with a bald, seamed head.

Vinnie took on a cordial, businesslike tone. "Excuse me, sir. I'm a friend of Vasily Mogilevich. He around?"

The man paused in mid-lift. "I don't know no one by that name, buddy, but let me radio my boss." He set the package down, pressing a button on a two-way radio. After a couple minutes, he turned toward us. "Boss says he ain't heard from him lately. Asks why you need him."

Vinnie gave the man a solid look and produced three one hundred-dollar bills. "I was eyeballing two backpacks for my chicks here. Also two pairs of hiking boots and some bomber jackets. Vasily and I used to conduct business on discounted merchandise. I thought he might have some bargains tonight. Was worth the inquiry, anyway."

Another man approached and grabbed the first man's package. The tall man took the money that Vinnie proffered, folded it, and put it in a pocket. "I don't know this guy you're looking for, but actually, I have some good deals going myself. If you don't think your friend would mind you doing business with me, that is. Wait here." The man disappeared into the back of a store.

Ten minutes later, another man approached us. He was distinguished in a black suit, an overcoat, and a black fedora. He shook Vinnie's hand. "So you are a friend of Mr. Mogilevich?" The voice was nasal and understated. He thumbed the side of his chin as he spoke.

"You could say that." Vinnie nodded. "A family friend. He's my godfather. But, I can't reach him on his phone."

The chin was thumbed some more. "Well, he left town for a while. It was an emergency. Likely he has no cell connection. But make me a list of the items you need."

The man handed Vinnie a pad of paper and a pen. Vinnie wrote a list.

"Very well, sir. I can fill this order tonight." The man gave us a broad smile as Vinnie handed over another two hundred dollars. "Until your godfather returns, you come see me. If I hear from him, I shall let him know you are looking for him."

We walked away and caught a subway to Brooklyn, checked into a nice hotel, and got settled. Once we were clean, Kenzie and I changed into our pajamas and sat with Vinnie, who wore silk boxers and a t-shirt.

"This might take a bit to explain." Vinnie poured us each three fingers of Jack Daniels mixed with the slightest dash of soda water. "My parents, as I may have mentioned, are urban pirates. My sisters and I were raised on the practice."

"Pirates?" I giggled. "As in Arrrr, yo ho and a bottle of rum!"

Vinnie chortled. "Similar. But not quite. We operate on dry land and don't wear hooks or eye patches."

Kenzie snuggled under the bedspread. "So did you ever meet Long John Silver or Jack Sparrow?"

Vinnie tucked us in then sat, facing us on the bed. "Never met Captain Silver. I have met Jack Sparrow, though. A couple of years ago at Disney World. My family took Steph Baker, her sister, and her mom there to hook up with some people who moved them elsewhere. That isn't the kind of piracy to which I refer, though. Tune your ears in, gators. Let me lay it down for you.

"Let's start with grocery stores. My father used to work as a stock supervisor at different stores. He would help himself to items every day. Because he worked in a refrigerated environment, he always wore a bulky sweatshirt. That made it easy to slide food items up the sleeves or into the waistband of his jeans. There were other scams, too. A lady my parents knew had a method for securing prepaid Visa gift cards. We'd use those to pay for groceries.

"As for my mother, I never saw her shopping without a large handbag. My sisters would each carry one, too. In those crowded aisles, especially the ones with pyramids of cans, all sorts of goodies would be transferred from shopping cart to handbag. Small bottles and jars would often have the same size cap as the larger, expensive sizes. If they had the price stamped on the cap, my mother or father switched caps, getting the larger size for the cheaper price.

"In the produce department of an organic food store near where I lived, there were brown paper sacks for the potatoes. My mother would slip a few steaks or some pork chops into the bottom of a bag and pile some potatoes on top. She would have a man weigh the bag, staple it, and mark the price. Some grocery stores even carried packages of socks, underpants, and t-shirts. My mother always stocked up."

Vinnie paused, sipping his drink. "My job was to act as look-out and shield my parents from the eyes of nosy employees and other shoppers. In extreme cases where the risk of capture was great, I would feign clumsiness and knock over a display tower of cans. Or, I might fake a temper fit in front of an approaching store manager. Sometimes, in stores where we weren't known, I acted lost to distract the manager just long enough so my mother could escape with the plundered items."

"So your family used five-finger discounts. I'm glad you didn't get arrested," Kenzie said.

"That isn't all we did. That's barely the tip of the iceberg." Vinnie chuckled. "Whether leaving quickly or making purchases, we always used the self-checkout, and we always left through the gardening section if there was one. When using self-checkout, one can never tell what was or wasn't scanned. It's easy enough to place all the items together. Then, after paying for only a portion of the swag, leaving through a rear exit often helps avoid passing through electronic sensors."

Vinnie refilled his glass and Kenzie's. I still had half of my drink left.

I yawned while asking, "So, what's with the meal vouchers?"

Vinnie's eyes lit up and his mouth curled in a huge grin. "That's another angle I often play. You know how items in the store say that you can receive a free replacement if you're not totally satisfied? Well, I'm never totally satisfied. Plus, I keep a notebook in my pack. When I'm in the store I copy down serial numbers, UPC codes, and expiration dates. That way I can get coupons or replacements without actually buying the item."

Kenzie giggled. I shook my head laughing. She said, "You're a bad ass!"

Vinnie wiggled his eyebrows. "The food vouchers is simply a matter of emailing corporate offices or calling restaurants and complaining, Tell them you asked for no onions on a burger and they put them on. Tell them service was slow. They almost always replace the meal or send gift cards and vouchers. Even high-class establishments offer gift cards if the story you tell is good. Like you got steaks to-go, and they overcooked them. If they don't offer to send you a gift card or a voucher, then you crank up the iPad or laptop and email the corporate office. That gets vouchers for sure."

Vinnie put our empty glasses on the dresser. "I have several PO boxes in the boroughs, plus friends in a few states who forward my mail. I can get stuff in various names sent out every week. I'm always updating my envelope file."

Kenzie and I fell asleep, and Vinnie positioned himself between us. The next morning, I woke up later than usual. Vinnie had left for work. My head throbbed. Kenzie groaned and pulled me close. We lay there for a while before showering, dressing, and heading to the library. Vinnie had left us fifty dollars, and we used it to buy breakfast and lunch.

We spent the morning and early afternoon reviewing math. Kenzie was coming along. Afterward, we went out for coffee and studied science. The GED was starting to look possible, but I needed a way to get us each a fake ID. I figured that Vinnie could make that happen.

Chapter 16

Three days later, Ronnie was feeling better. She texted Kenzie and me.

I hope you have your essays ready for me to review and are prepared to discuss what you've been reading the past couple of weeks. Also, I plan to quiz you on both math and the basic facts taught at the planetarium. Be at my place before lunch.

Kenzie and I spent an hour sitting in a hot bubble bath before getting ready to go. She nestled between my legs, as usual, with her head resting on my breasts. I stroked her, and we relaxed. Vinnie was at work, and we didn't have to check out of the room until eleven. It was a quarter of nine.

"Not to spoil a wonderful bath, but we have to meet Ronnie for lunch." Kenzie murmured and stood.

We dried off, dressed, adjusted our gear, and left. We looked like proper schoolgirls in our sneakers, pink tights, black and white plaid skirts, and white button-up shirts with gray hoodies. Vinnie had taken us shopping one evening. We both had a better understanding of how the F-O-T process worked. He also told us not to approach anyone dealing in such goods unless we were with him.

Ninety minutes later, we met Ronnie for a lunch of clam chowder and grilled ham and cheese sandwiches. While eating, she read our essays on Richard Wright and Huckleberry Finn.

"You're both reading up a storm! I like how you're seeing parallels between current events and the troubles that faced Wright growing up. Your choice to include other writers of color from that time helps illustrate your points." Ronnie's voice was still raw from her recent illness. "With Huckleberry Finn, I agree that part of the draw is a desire to be shed of urban life and to experience the freedom Twain describes. Furthermore, I like how you tie Jim's escape from slavery to the escape of real authors of color from the social constraints of racist society. It may be a sad fact that they relied on the kindness of whites to assist them, but it's a fact, nevertheless."

Kenzie sipped some coffee, then said, "We both read some books by this dude named 'dumb ass.' The Count of Monte Cristo and The Three Musketeers."

I giggled. "I thought Annette and Cubby were Musketeers, but they weren't."

Ronnie glowered at us. "The author's name is Doo-MAH, not dumb ass. It's French. You're both smart enough to know the difference between Musketeer and Mouseketeer, little miss wiseacre!" She shook her head. "So, did you like the books?"

"They're exciting. I imagined myself watching the action," Kenzie said.

Ronnie started clearing dishes and we helped. "That's the beauty of classic literature. It takes you on adventures and lets you escape."

After lunch, and a discussion of planetary science and basic algebra, Kenzie and I joined Ronnie on a trip to the drug store. Neither Kenzie nor I used certain items that Ronnie swore by, but we perused the shelves anyway.

I looked at the label on a bottle of feminine wash, shaking my head. "Seriously, at fourteen dollars a bottle who cares if my crotch smells like flowers?"

Kenzie giggled. "Dr. Coito might the next time we have a check-up."

After shopping, Ronnie, Kenzie, and I walked around looking at holiday display windows and watching the ice skaters in Rockefeller Center. As evening approached, we headed to a pizza parlor and introduced Ronnie to Vinnie.

There was already a pitcher of beer and two large pizzas on a table in the rear of the place. Vinnie waved to us. He wore polished loafers, black chinos, an electric blue silk shirt, and a leather jacket. He had exchanged his porkpie for a black bowler and, as usual, wore mirrored sunglasses.

I gave Vinnie a kiss and a hug as he stood. "Vinnie, this is our tutor, Ronnie."

Kenzie hugged and kissed him as well. "She says we're doing well with our studies."

"They sure are. So you're the Vinnie they speak so highly of." Ronnie sat next to him, placing her back to the wall.

Vinnie took her hand, turned it palm-down, and kissed the back. "Yes, ma'am. Vincenzo Cassiel Michelangelo Il-Cazzo, at your service."

Ronnie blushed. "So elegant you are. That's a truly lost art. Most guys don't know the proper way to greet a lady."

We all served ourselves and poured glasses of stout beer. We chatted as we ate.

"Dolls," Vinnie said, "I normally have action on Saturday, but there's some sort of executive to-do about supply and demand tomorrow. My services aren't required, and I thought we might take the opportunity to go clothes shopping and replace any threads that are down at heel. I have new backpacks waiting for you with a friend of mine. Please feel free to join us, babe." He winked at Ronnie.

Kenzie drained half her glass of beer in a gulp. "Actually, our friends Rory, Sheila, Jeanie, and Rainbow are coming to the city for a day. They invited us to join them for breakfast and a walk in Central Park. I'm sure they'd join us to shop afterward."

"Copacetic." Vinnie smiled. "Are they cubistic or would they be hep to urban piracy?"

"Piracy?" Ronnie looked at Vinnie, tilting her head. "You mean like stealing?"

Vinnie raised his glass to her. "No, ma'am. I mean piracy. Yes, I am known to help grocery stores reduce their overstock but, in this case, what I have in mind requires a bit more finesse." He draped his arm around Ronnie, and she didn't object. I winked at Kenzie.

"What's the plan?" I smiled.

Vinnie poured a third glass of beer. Kenzie was on her fourth. Ronnie and I were still sipping our first. "The plan is to trade-in older and worn-out threads for newer items. It involves a technique my father taught me." He wiped foam from his mouth. "I enter a Goodwill or a Salvation Army store. After perusing the racks and finding an outfit I like, I step into the changing room and remove all the price tags. I leave my old threads in the room and walk out wearing my new outfit. Since people donate the clothing to those places, the prices they charge are obscene. I feel no serious guilt pangs over taking for free what the stores receive for free. Plus, they receive my old clothing in exchange. Fair trade is no robbery."

Ronnie laughed. "You're a real hustler, buddy." She turned and kissed Vinnie. He returned the kiss with relish.

Vinnie paid the check. "Must you return home tonight, Ronnie, my dear? The girls and I shall be retiring to a moderately priced hotel, and I invite you to join us. Also, prudence requires me to ask if you're seeing anyone steadily."

Ronnie blushed again. "I don't have a boyfriend, no. I should go home, but I guess I could tell my mom I'm staying at a friend's place tonight." She pulled out her cell phone and dialed.

Two hours later, we were sitting together in a hotel suite. Between the four of us, we managed the price. Kenzie and I had the foldout couch in the main room. Ronnie and Vinnie shared the queen-sized bed in the bedroom.

As Kenzie and I flipped through the TV channels, Vinnie and Ronnie headed into the bedroom. The muffled sounds of grunting filled the air. Kenzie and I put on our pajamas. We settled on an old movie called Bananas. After a while, Vinnie and Ronnie joined us. He'd changed into silk lounging pants and a tank top. She wore a red thong and her t-shirt. The movie ended, and we sat on the queen bed drinking bourbon and soda.

"So, other than clothes swapping, and five-finger discounts, what other sorts of piracy do you engage in?" Ronnie asked, resting her head in Vinnie's lap.

Vinnie stroked Ronnie's cheek. "A big item I had growing up wasn't even entirely a scam. There are gin-joints all over that cater to the yuppie riff-raff trying to hustle their way up the escalator of big business. Many of these establishments have a hot buffet or several warming containers of hors d'oeuvres served free as a come-on to drink their overpriced booze. My mother and father would take me and my older sisters, Tori and Gina, to the bars on the weekends. My folks would sometimes take half-empty glasses from a table and use them as a prop to ward off the wait staff. Usually, though, my sisters and I ordered Cokes. The bars even offered free refills.

"We would walk around sampling the free food until we had eaten our fill. If the food was easy to transport, like pigs in a blanket or chicken strips, my sisters would cover me as I dumped large quantities into plastic Ziplock bags. I would stuff the bags in my sack, or inside my mother's purse. Furthermore, these bars were good places to cop things like bottles of mustard and ketchup, shakers of salt or sugar, toilet paper, silverware, and cups for home. We'd each carry a knapsack or an empty purse and load up after we'd cased the joint. I'd make sure to pack soft clothes like t-shirts and socks to buffer glass items from breaking."

Ronnie laughed. "You turn me on like no other guy I ever met."

"Destiny and I kite food like that at church every week. We bag up the cookies and fried chicken." Kenzie giggled.

I yawned and excused myself. After kissing Vinnie and Ronnie goodnight I took Kenzie by the hand and retired to the foldout couch. Kenzie and I smiled at each other as the sounds of moaning issued forth from the bedroom once more. We fell asleep cuddled together.

The next morning, Kenzie and I woke up early. Ronnie and Vinnie were still asleep. Kenzie filled the tub while we dumped our backpacks on the couch and stripped off our pajamas.

She whined, "My head's throbbing. This is seriously the worst headache ever."

I hugged her and gave her a loving pop across the butt cheeks. "Well, golly-gee, I wonder why? You finished half a pitcher of beer at dinner and had three glasses of bourbon later."

Kenzie held me close and squealed when I smacked her butt. "It's not that. I can handle my liquor. I probably just have a cold. And only Vinnie can spank me."

I glared. "Oh yeah? I'll do it some more if you keep whining, young lady. You're probably right, maybe it's just a cold. Drinking doesn't help, though. There's a reason that The Bible counsels against strong drink."

Kenzie closed her eyed, breathing in the steam as I held her. "Just drop it about the drinking. You drink, too. It relaxes us."

An hour later we dressed in frayed jeans, our most threadbare t-shirts, and hoodies that had seen better days. Vinnie dressed in faded slacks, and a button-up shirt with a small stain on it. His sports coat had a few worn spots. Ronnie had on the same clothes she'd worn the day before.

Kenzie and I sorted the contents of our backpacks and threw away socks and panties that had holes in them. We repacked, headed downstairs, and caught the subway to the Garment District. Vinnie stopped us along a street near a truck.

"You Il-Cazzo?" A short, squat man called out. He had a severe crewcut, a pinched face, and eyes that were a bit too close together. His arms and legs were massive.

Vinnie approached the man. He handed him two twenty-dollar bills. "You say it. I say it."

The man handed him a large box. Inside were two cranberry and orange backpacks. They were long and well-constructed. Kenzie and I transferred our gear into the packs and had plenty of room to spare. Inside each pack was a zippered pouch hidden in the lining. We split our cash and put it inside. We put our cell phones in their dedicated pockets and adjusted the straps.

Next, we exchanged our beat-up sneakers for top-of-the-line hiking boots. The boots were dark gray and black, cushioned, and felt wonderful on my feet. Kenzie bounced around on her toes like an elf and smiled.

The final item was two sets of dark orange rain gear. We rolled it up and put it into our new backpacks. We looked at

Vinnie in silence for a moment, then hugged him at the same time. He smiled and hugged us in return. Ronnie watched the proceedings with a huge grin on her face. She took out her cell phone and snapped our picture.

After returning the cardboard box to the man by the truck, we started walking toward the restaurant where we were meeting Rory and family. We paused by a park bench and left our old sneakers for whom ever might need them. Kenzie slipped a five-dollar bill in each shoe. Vinnie nodded his approval.

He lectured us. "You chicks catch on fast. Always spread the dineros and help cats on the skids. As bad as you may have it, someone always has it worse."

As we walked, Ronnie kept looking at us. I began to get nervous.

Kenzie adjusted a strap on her pack. "Yes, sis? Is something wrong?"

Ronnie started to speak, stopped, and started again. "No. I'm just trying to decide how to ask you both something." She sat on a bench outside the restaurant.

I sat beside her and Kenzie sat on the other side. "Just ask. We don't have any secrets."

Vinnie stepped away to text some people. Ronnie watched him go, then said, "I understand that Vinnie is looking after you. He explained it to me last night. Anyway, this morning we were talking. I know we're sisters, but would you like me to be your street mom?"

Kenzie smiled wide. "I'd love that. I mean, if you aren't too strict."

I leaned over and put my head on Ronnie's shoulder, batting my eyelashes. "Can I get a raise in my allowance, mother?"

Ronnie pushed me away with a giggle. "Not much changes between us. Except that if you don't get your schoolwork done, there will be consequences. And I expect a card and present every May for Mother's Day,"

Vinnie returned and nodded at the sight of us. "I guess we

reached an agreement, chicks. Copacetic."

"In honor of this celebration, we'd like to give you both a couple of early Christmas presents. We bought them a while back with busking money." I handed them the tickets to Godspell and Porgy and Bess.

"No way!" Vinnie looked shocked. "Far out! My father was into opera. I've heard Porgy and Bess a number of times, but I've never seen it. And I've heard recordings of Godspell, too, but I've only seen the movie version. Thank you!" He kissed us both and hugged us tight.

Ronnie hugged us both as well. "I'll take you to my salon before the shows. I don't go a lot, but this calls for getting dressed up to the nines."

"We haven't been using them lately, but we have monthly passes to a gym. We can bring a guest for free. Mostly we used the gym for showers and the steam room before we met Vinnie. If you want to join us before the salon, we can sit and steam."

Kenzie looked beyond Ronnie. "Hey, there's Jeanie."

Kenzie and I hopped up and greeted Jeanie who was walking down the block. She was dressed up, as were Rory and Sheila. Rainbow was decked out in a red and green suit with a miniature Santa hat.

"Happy Holidays, you guys." Kenzie hugged and kissed them each in turn. I hugged and kissed them, and Jeanie almost crushed my ribs with her return hug.

"This is our protector, Vinnie. You remember Ronnie? She's our street mom now," I announced.

Rory and Vinnie circled each other, sizing each other up as men are wont to do— a simple, primal ritual. Can I take this dude out if the need arises? I watched this testosterone-fueled rite with interest.

Rory extended his hand. "So, you're the one caring for my kid sisters?"

Vinnie took the offered hand and they shook solid. "I do my best by them, gator. I care for these chicks deeply, in fact."

We entered the restaurant, and Rory announced our reservations to the hostess. We were seated and served strong, rich cups of coffee. After we had ordered our food, we caught up on each other's lives.

"So, you're nineteen?" Rory asked Vinnie.

"According to my ID card I am." Vinnie smiled. "My GED records indicate as much."

Rory took a bite of lox omelet. "I get you. You sound like you know the city well. Are your folks around here?"

"My parents used to be—kind of, sort of." Vinnie shrugged. "We lived in the suburbs just outside of the boroughs. After that, we moved to New England and from there I went to Florida. My mother and father might be on a southern Pacific island right now, but I couldn't swear to that."

Sheila fed Rainbow some formula. "That sounds exciting."

Vinnie looked at his coffee. His eyes shifted and for a moment he looked sad.

"It had moments, for sure, but, in the end, it was too exciting. It was a strange time growing up. Exciting, much like watching a hostage situation on TV." Vinnie looked up and, with a slight shake of his head, broke from his reverie. I glanced at Kenzie and Ronnie, but they weren't sure what was wrong, either.

Everyone finished eating, and Rory split the bill with Vinnie. We walked along the avenues, admiring the holiday decorations, and browsing the stores for present ideas. After fifteen blocks, we decided to walk through the park.

Vinnie smiled as he walked in the middle of our group, talking about the glory days. "When I lived near the city, my family regularly ventured to this area. There were always great places to score fantastic meals and make the scene. Probably still are. Gina and Tori, my sisters, would look in the society pages to locate weddings, bar mitzvahs, social groups holding open houses, and the like. You dig? They were aces at locating family occasions where plenty of delicious comestibles would be consumed.

"Jay Quinn, from my old neighborhood, had an eighteen-

year-old son who would show up at the back of
the synagogues a few hours after an affair had begun.
Williamsburg in Brooklyn is hot for that, but that line-up plays
in Manhattan, as well. Jay's son would hit the places with a
story of how he wanted to bring some leftovers of 'authentic
Jewish food' back to his fraternity or sister sorority. It often
worked, and he'd return with enough grub to feed a small
army. My family always got an invite to dinner after these
excursions."

Kenzie and I hugged him. He ruffled our heads and
continued. "In the case of my family, we would dress to fit the
occasion. Then we would schmooze our way in long enough
to hit the buffets. I found that remarks such as, 'I'm Louie's
cousin' or 'Gee, Dorothy looks simply marvy' worked great.
Lines like 'Betty doesn't look pregnant' tend to be frowned
upon at weddings. Gina, Tori, and I could work this free-load
like nobody's business. We would chatter back and forth while
stuffing ourselves. My parents would be on the other side of
the room, holding their own."

Everyone laughed as Vinnie told his tale. I shook my head
and tried to breathe, but I was laughing too hard. "We have got
to try that!" I dried my eyes.

Rory chuckled. "Your family sounds like a bunch of first-
rate scrounges."

"We're urban pirates," Vinnie said. "Gina's almost finished
with her bachelors' degree and owes hardly anything. Tori and
her fiancé, Fisher, are in New Mexico at the university. They
live virtually for free. As for me, I'm practically minting the
cash. Well, to be honest, someone else mints it. But, I have
plenty."

As the day wore on, Rory, Sheila, and Jeanie loaded up on
presents from the stores. They left at four to return home.
Ronnie left to go home, too. She took Vinnie's cell phone
number and arranged to meet us at church the next day.
Vinnie, Kenzie, and I walked to a huge thrift store full of
clothing.

The process worked as Vinnie had stated it would. I found a

pair of Gucci jeans that didn't appear to have ever been worn, a pink blouse with the tags still on it, and a teal-blue cardigan. Kenzie picked out a pair of dark-blue corduroy overalls, a double thick purple cotton t-shirt, a light-blue chamois shirt, and a fleece-lined suede vest. We changed in the dressing room and left our old clothes on the bench.

Vinnie had traded his outfit for a pair of Ralph Lauren gray slacks, a cream-colored dress shirt, and a black Pierre Cardin sports coat. He motioned toward the door as he left the men's dressing room. We followed him outside. Nobody said a word to us, or even looked our way.

He gave us each a hug. "Girls that's as easy as piracy gets. You can change out your old clothes every few days and have an entirely new wardrobe inside of a month."

We strolled on Fifth Avenue, one of us on either side of Vinnie, before deciding to check into a room early. Vinnie stopped on the way and talked to a man sitting on a bench. He slipped the man a few bills, and the man entered a wine store. He returned with a bottle of Moscato d'Asti. Vinnie took the bottle and told the man to keep the change.

He led us toward the subway and said, "You chicks are in for a treat. This is my favorite wine."

Kenzie shrugged. "A friend of mine stole some Boone's Farm and some Wild Irish Rose once. It was OK. I prefer vodka."

"That isn't wine! That's evil torture! Moscato d'Asti is exquisite."

The F Train took us to Brooklyn, and Vinnie paid for a night at a hotel near our church. The room was adequate and had a king-sized bed with a cream-colored comforter. There were the usual furnishings, and we set our new packs on the desk. Vinnie laid down on the bed, closing his eyes with his hands folded on his chest.

I had purchased two small, lilac-scented candles earlier. I filled the tub, poured some wine in the plastic glasses the hotel placed on the dresser, lit the candles, and opened a music app on my phone. After turning out the lights, Kenzie and I sat in the tub together—relaxing, as had become our ritual.

We began to doze off. Sitting in the warm water with Kenzie resting against me—the candlelight, glasses of wine, and Bertie Higgins crooning on my cell phone—I enjoyed a moment where every aspect of my life felt connected and perfect.

After soaking until our fingers and toes wrinkled, we rinsed in the shower, and slipped into bed beside Vinnie. In the morning, he woke up before either of us. I kept my eyes half-shut and watched him remove the photo of his lost love from the front of his backpack. He kissed it and put it back. As I watched in the dark room, he took out a pint bottle of bourbon and had a swig. Vinnie undressed and walked to the bathroom. I went back to sleep.

Later that morning, we dressed in our new outfits and walked to church. Ronnie stood outside, her cheeks pink from the nippy air. She and Vinnie kissed each other and led us in, holding hands.

The sermon was on Romans 14. Pastor Affenhoden discussed a live-and-let-live philosophy within certain wide parameters. I was still shocked, after all the months, by his liberal interpretations. It was so far away from all I had known growing up.

It turned out that Vinnie hadn't attended church in quite some time. His nods and expressions led me to believe he enjoyed the sermon.

We sat eating the potluck meal afterward. "I attended church with Steph Baker and her family before all Hell started popping," Vinnie said. "The pastor at that other church had nothing on Pastor Affenhoden. Of the two, Affenhoden is superior in both interpretation and clarity."

Vinnie gave me a huge grin when I bagged up sliced ham and chicken drumsticks. After lunch, we departed into the crisp, wintery air. Two blocks along, a homeless family sat huddled under blankets. Kenzie and I opened our backpacks and handed the two little girls and the little boy each a twenty-dollar bill. Vinnie did us one better by handing the mother a hundred-dollar bill. We also handed over the bag of chicken drumsticks. There didn't appear to be a father. I was growing used to seeing this situation, and it never ceased to break my heart.

Chapter 17

After assisting the homeless family, Vinnie, Ronnie, Kenzie, and I went for a walk to look at hotels. Ronnie said that she knew a few with weekly rates that weren't likely to attract prostitutes or disreputable characters. I suggested that Kenzie and I might be disreputable, or at least poor white trash, and received a hard slap across the rear of my jeans.

Ronnie's eyes narrowed and her mouth tightened as she stood with her hands on her hips. "You're my street daughters. You are ladies. You're not trash. Are we clear on that, Destiny Marie?"

"Yes, ma'am." I rubbed my butt, lowering my eyes as tears formed. My stomach clenched and, for a moment, I couldn't breathe.

Kenzie hugged me, then Ronnie hugged us both and kissed our cheeks. "I know how both of you struggle. But, unless you stop saying the words, you simply reinforce the negative self-image. Dammit, you're both beautiful girls. Your parents are the dirtbags, not you."

A few minutes later, my stomach felt normal again. The wave of anxiety passed; I pushed it back, telling myself to toughen up. I wasn't home anymore, and it was stupid to be upset. My new family was different.

After looking at several options, we settled on a hotel that agreed to take cash every week. The cost would be twenty-seven hundred dollars a month. Kenzie and I barely made half of that every week. Vinnie made the full amount—and more—weekly. We agreed to a sixty-forty split. Kenzie and I would also buy our own breakfast and lunch every day, except for family meals.

We moved in and unpacked our gear into the big dresser. Vinnie set his books next to the TV and told us to read any of them we liked. The bulk of them were biographies and true crime. He did own some classics, however.

Kenzie ran a finger over the book spines. "You read everything, don't you?"

"Mostly. I have eclectic tastes." Vinnie set up a miniature bar next to his books.

I started sorting my clothes. "We're trying to read as much as we can. There's so much out there, though."

"Stick to the good stuff. Like with liquor, everyone is an imitator, but only the originals did it best."

Vinnie hung his clothes in the closet and claimed half the dresser. Kenzie and I put our clothes in the other half, tucking our blanket from the beach under the desk. We put away our toiletries, and Kenzie set her stuffed animals on the bed. She still had the teddy bear I had won her at the beach and a stuffed penguin from before we met.

We sat on the bed, looking around the room. There was a large picture window that faced an apartment building. A family of four sat in a kitchen, sharing a meal. In another apartment, a lady washed dishes. I closed the curtains, then turned to Vinnie.

"What do you mean by 'good stuff'?"

He poured scotch into glasses and said, "Well, every cat and chick who can tap on a keypad seems to be writing these days, and a lot of it is schlock. Like Probing Uranus for Gold by Seymour Butts. And Pledging Rituals at Vampire Sororities by Heywood Jablome. I mean, come on. Stoker did Vampires first—and best. Shelley did Frankenstein. Tolkien covered the fantasy genre. If you want wizardry, read The Once and Future King by T.H. White. The Star Wars books aren't dreadful, I suppose. But no one writing today comes close to Bradbury. That cat was an innovator."

Ronnie piped up from a large chair in the corner. "You're a literary snob? Isn't reading anything better than not reading?"

Vinnie leaned down and kissed her. "There are those who

would argue such. For me, it's the difference between steak and potatoes versus a candy bar. Both fill you up, but one is more satisfying and provides lasting sustenance."

Ronnie returned the kiss and asked, "So, what's next on the agenda?"

He tossed off his scotch, replying, "If you chicks are up for it, I'd like to hit an AA meeting and then buy some groceries. We need some nosh to go with the libations."

"You're in AA?" Ronnie laughed. "Could have fooled me. You have enough liquor here to satisfy W.C. Fields. And, we're sitting here sipping scotch. Or, am I missing something?"

"I only make my appearance at the open meetings, and those explicitly state that all are welcome to attend. Even if I have attended closed meetings, the only requirement for membership is a desire to stop drinking. There's no time limit to that desire." Vinnie winked. "To be quite honest, my reason for attending is this." He grabbed his courier's satchel, extracted a false leather bottom, and removed several thick stacks of twenty-dollar bills and a small stack of fifty-dollar bills.

Ronnie gasped. "Have mercy!"

My eyes bugged out as did Kenzie's. "How much money is that, dude?"

"It's roughly twenty-one hundred. Not one of these is real—although, no one can usually tell." Vinnie put the money back, followed by the false bottom. "At AA meetings, they pass a basket and it's the only place I know that allows one to make their own change. I drop in a twenty and remove nineteen. Sometimes I take twenty-eight dollars if a ten gets slipped into the one-dollar bills."

Ronnie looked askance. "You rip off AA meetings? That's pretty low. Don't you feel bad for the people who attend those?"

He shrugged. "I do, and I don't. If I thought I was ripping off square johns, regular guys, I wouldn't do it. Thing of it is, doll, most of the money they collect goes to a giant umbrella organization. Anyone with a brain knows that someone at the top is getting theirs from all the collections. I'm just getting mine first."

Kenzie laughed. "I was reading an article in a magazine a few weeks ago about how computer scanners are so advanced now that you can make perfect copies if you have the right paper."

Vinnie gave her stern glance. "Don't even think about it, doll. I had the same notion a couple years back. A friend of mine, his brother was doing that. But my godfather taught me better. I don't even make these bills, and they're the last ones I have. No, ladies, making bills on a scanner is the act of an imbecile. The process is far more complicated and labor intensive. It's actually an art form. To be good, really good—not just scanner or photocopier-adequate—one must make negatives. One must precisely carve masking materials and burn metal plates. The lining up of plates must be exact to the last nanometer. The mixing of the inks alone is a grueling task. I'm not that good, not by half. So please, don't try making your own prints."

We finished our drinks, and Vinnie pocketed two twenties and his envelope of coupons before we left. The crisp air felt delicious as the scotch played with my brain. We walked to a subway station and waited amongst the crowds.

"One thing, chicks." Vinnie looked serious. "In all the piracy I'm teaching you, never ever take on a square john. You know, a mom and pop business. Only take on big corporations, restaurants that mark up the price ridiculously, places like that. I admit these meetings are a gray area, but ultimately they make a heap of bread, and someone somewhere is getting a big cut. Also, always tip wait staff well. If the meal is free, then you tip at least fifty percent of what you would have paid. No reason to screw a hard-working employee. Especially since they survive on their tips."

All three of us nodded, and Vinnie led us onto the train. We rode standing due to the crowds. Vinnie motioned us to exit at a mid-town stop, and we walked five blocks to a building with a large basement conference room. There were at least seventy people in attendance. Against one wall was a table with pizza, subs, cake, cookies, and coffee. We helped ourselves to food and sat in the rear aisle.

As we were getting settled into our chairs, a lady rang a bell. The room grew quiet. There were announcements about other meetings in the area and some sort of an election for meeting support staff. After that, people recited a prayer, there were some recitations of printed text, and a speaker was introduced. Her name was Brie Stilton.

Within the first five minutes, I was transfixed...on Kenzie.

"Hello, my name is Brie and I'm an alcoholic." Brie sounded relaxed and was stunning in a pink taffeta dress with a pearl choker and blonde hair swept into an elaborate bouffant.

"Hi, Brie!" The crowd roared back.

"I started drinking when I was eleven. My home life was beyond dysfunctional, and I needed an escape. My mother often brought men home, and those men routinely messed around with me, if you catch my drift. If I drank, I didn't feel anything—and trust me, I didn't want to feel. I don't know if my drinking affected my choices in friends, but I mostly hung around with girls. One thing that was not a choice was my sexual attraction to other girls. I was told those feelings were wrong and drank more to try suppressing them. It didn't work." Brie looked around the room at the knowing nods.

As I studied Kenzie, understanding dawned in my mind. When the action of life was heavy, or we were desperate for shelter, she rarely needed a drink. However, when we had been at the beach in Delaware, or at Ronnie's house, or with Vinnie—safe and relaxed in a hotel—Kenzie drank more. It occurred to me that when we had downtime, her mind began processing and rehashing the horrors of her childhood. When we were too busy to think, she was fine.

As Brie was finishing her story, a basket full of cash came around. Vinnie dropped in a counterfeit twenty-dollar bill and took change. Another basket came from the other direction and he did it again. No one even paid attention. Ten minutes later, he headed toward the exit and we followed. Once outside, Vinnie counted out fifty-eight dollars.

"That was fun," Kenzie said, nibbling a piece of cheese pizza. "That lady had a hard life. I feel bad for her. At least I can stop drinking anytime I please. I don't even drink all the time. And I certainly never got arrested for it."

I changed the subject. "So, where to next?"

Vinnie winked at us. "The grocery store. I need to take off after we get the groceries back to our room. Got some people to see, and you chicks aren't invited. Christmas is next week."

Kenzie smiled at me. "Then we'll go out and busk. We might do some shopping, too."

Ronnie sighed. "I have to get home later. My mom and step-dad invited some friends over for dinner, and one of them has connections at Yale. Like I give a crap about going to some snobby university. Mom expects me to go to an Ivy League. I just want a small school for undergraduate study."

We walked fifteen blocks to a grocery store. Vinnie loaded up on groceries and snacks. With his coupons, we paid less than ten dollars for well over eighty dollars in merchandise. I helped him place most of it in his backpack. Kenzie and I distributed the rest into ours.

I couldn't stop giggling. "You have got to show me how to get coupons like that."

He winked. "If you have a laptop, it's a snap, gator. It's one of the easiest hustles."

Two hours later, Vinnie had left and Ronnie headed home. Kenzie and I lay on the bed, necking and touching each other. She stood and poured herself three fingers of scotch. "Want one, Destiny?"

An uncomfortable sensation disturbed the pit of my stomach. "No, thanks. I thought we were going out for the evening."

"Relax! I'm just getting loose. Why are you being so damned uptight? I'm not a drunk, OK? Those people are weak. I'm not." She finished her drink in a gulp.

We left and caught the subway to Broadway. It was easier having the guitar, one backpack, and no other gear. I started out playing the classic Christmas tunes and followed that with some rock and roll. The crowds cheered with enthusiasm. We played until ten o'clock and made over three hundred dollars. I texted Vinnie that we were planning to be back by one. He replied, Must discuss curfew.

Kenzie and I headed back and looked at the store windows while making notes. She pointed toward a mannequin in a window wearing a terrycloth robe. "That dark blue robe would be a great gift for Vinnie."

"I was thinking that, too. And some aftershave. I don't know if he smokes, other than pot, but we could get him cigars." I tried not to look too much at the one-piece red pajamas with a drop seat. I thought it would look cute on Kenzie.

Excited, she added, "I think we should get Mom some perfume and some scented bubble bath. We could also give her and Vinnie an overnight alone."

We made it back by a quarter to one. Vinnie was awake and reading. He looked at us over his book, Black Widow by Ramona McDonald, and put it on the side table. "I'm still getting the hang of this guardian gig, chicks, but I see no reason for you to be rolling in this late. Even with studying, you can still do your music and whatever and be back by ten. Unless you have a good reason to be back later, do that." Vinnie's tone was sharper than usual.

Kenzie pouted. "We're used to staying up late. We make more money after the shows let out."

"I make plenty of bread. I'm more concerned about your safety than your ability to bring in the do-re-mi. You asked me to be in charge. I agreed, so curfew is ten unless we're together or there's an emergency." Vinnie fixed us with a stern gaze.

I nodded. "Yes, sir. That's fair."

Kenzie sighed and began to sulk. "No. No, that isn't fair. We can handle any trouble. We've been handling ourselves for months, dammit!"

Vinnie shot daggers at her with his eyes. "I said ten, young lady! Do I need to bare your ass, and we can discuss this across my lap?"

Kenzie looked down and shook her head. "No. Fine. But, it isn't fair."

We took out our pajamas and changed. Vinnie closed his eyes and fell asleep. We crawled into bed on either side of him and snuggled. I was sound asleep when movement roused me. The clock read four-thirty. He kissed his photograph before opening a twenty-ounce bottle of Pepsi and drinking about a third. He filled the empty space with bourbon.

Vinnie departed, and I slipped out of bed and sat at the desk praying. Several matters vexed me, and I couldn't clear my thoughts. Vinnie never seemed drunk, but he drank all the time. Kenzie drank more frequently, as well. I didn't know what sort of job paid the kind of money Vinnie was making, but it was clear that he had connections in less-than-honest circles. And Kenzie's attitude was the straw that broke the camel's back. I sensed imminent danger but I couldn't put my finger on what was the nature of the danger. My stomach knotted, and my temples throbbed. I prayed for some sort of clarity.

Kenzie woke and stood behind me, rubbing my shoulders. I sighed, content, and finished my prayers by reading a few Psalms in the free Bible the hotel provided. She began undressing for our bath. "He's being an asshole about the curfew thing."

"No. He just cares about us. He's the man of the house...well, whatever this is. He has the right to tell us what to do. You want bullshit rules? Talk to my parents. There wouldn't have been a warning. You back talked them, you'd get slapped and then the belt."

She didn't disguise her irritation. "I didn't sign on to be bossed around, dammit. I just want protection from the gangs and the creepy old men. I want someone to buy us good food and keep us warm at night. I don't need a man in charge, no matter how you were raised. We aren't little girls, you know? And he isn't that much older than you."

"Yes, we are. In any sane situation, we are kids. I look at those brats in the park that we make fun of, and I'm jealous.

They have people around them who care. When did I ever get that? Or you? I stopped feeling cared for the day my younger brother popped his head out. Vinnie's clearly not used to making the rules, and he's winging it. But, with this curfew thing, he's right.

"Look, sweetie," I turned her around and held her shoulders. "We asked Vinnie to protect us. He's protecting us. He isn't walking away. And if being in by ten is what it takes to keep him from abandoning us, then I'm fine with that. You can't ask Vinnie and Ronnie to protect us, then not follow their rules. Ten isn't such a bad curfew, you know? Now quit your damned sulking."

Kenzie's eyes filled with tears. "Or what? You going to kick me out of the family?"

"No. Don't you even go there." I scowled, then released an exasperated sigh that blew back her hair. "I love you, and I'll never abandon you! We need structure, though, and you know it."

She snarled, turning around to walk to the bathtub. "Fine."

I'd had enough. "Mackenzie Elizabeth Guevara! You're being a bitch!"

She gasped, howling, when I spun her around and slapped her left cheek. I sat on the chair, pulling her with me. She tried to get away, but I held her and slapped her butt four more times. Her cheeks turned pink before glowing fiery red.

"I'm sorry! I don't like being told what to do!" Kenzie bawled. I sat her up, holding her while she sobbed.

After a few minutes of snuggling, she calmed down and her breathing was even. "I understand that. I really do. I don't like rules either, but I know enough to respect them. He's the man of the family."

"I'm sorry. I didn't mean to make you mad. Can we not tell mom and Vinnie about this?" Kenzie stood, and we walked to the bathtub.

I rubbed her shoulders as she leaned against me. "Of course we can. Just stop with the sulking, honey."

We sat in the hot water for a while before dressing and

heading to the library. Ronnie met us for tutoring at two, and we busked from four until nine before heading back home.

Chapter 18

The week before Christmas flew by. Every day, Kenzie and I studied math and read novels before busking in the Theater District. We also made two trips to the planetarium that week. Whenever we attended, I'd feel small; that place always made me feel insignificant. Despite any issues I had with my parent's church, and I had many, I knew a greater force had created the cosmos. That, I imagined, was the allure of the planetarium for so many—being one dot in a vast and infinite tapestry.

When we weren't preparing for the GED or busking, we were shopping. We stashed our gifts for Vinnie at Ronnie's apartment. We stashed her gifts in our hotel room. The Thursday before Christmas, we met Ronnie at the fitness center. We were attending Godspell that night.

Ronnie, Kenzie, and I undressed in the locker room and wrapped ourselves in oversized towels before entering the steam room. The hot, humid air took my breath away as we sat on the wooden benches and relaxed. I inhaled deeply through my nose and exhaled through my mouth as my body sweated out toxins. Ronnie chatted about our afternoon plans.

"I notice that neither of you wears makeup. I'm not much for it, either. But it brings up a point. Do you know if you have allergies to any of it? At the salon they'll wash and style your hair however you like, but I'd suggest not having them make up your face." Ronnie sat back, breathing in steam.

"I've never worn it." I said. "It's bad enough having short hair, as a girl—at least, where my parents are concerned. If I'd tried makeup, they'd have thought I was a whore. I would have been standing at dinner for a week."

Kenzie smiled. "I used to own some bright red lipstick. I lost it somewhere. I like nail polish, too."

"Oh, for sure we're getting manicures and pedicures. I like how you both wear your hair, although I'd suggest seeing a stylist every couple of weeks, Kenzie. You need to keep up the sides. And Destiny, I think you'd look great if they feathered your hair a bit. Like a retro eighties look," Ronnie said, laying back and closing her eyes.

Three hours later, we were sitting in revolving chairs inside a salon. Several men sashayed about in striped pants and gray vests with mauve scarves around their necks, bringing us espressos and assisting the stylists. I'd been given the most luxurious shampooing of my life. Kenzie and Ronnie looked euphoric as they lay back with facial masks. The end result was that my hair was teased and moussed, and I looked ready for a photo shoot. Kenzie looked younger, fresher, with her hair styled so that it hung across the left side and swept back. The right side was shaved to a quarter inch from the temple, around the ear to the neck. Ronnie had her hair fashioned into an elegant boho braided up-do.

We went shopping afterward, and Ronnie bought me an emerald-green velvet dress with a plunging neckline. Kenzie opted for a midnight-blue, wrap-around dress. She also bought us shoes and other accouterment. We took a town car to Ronnie's brownstone, changed clothes, and helped her choose an outfit. She decided on a black satin evening gown and sapphire earrings.

Vinnie met us at a French restaurant, dressed in black from head to toe except for a silver tie. He bowed gracefully and took Ronnie by the arm. They entered in front of us, and he slipped the maitre'd a picture of Benjamin Franklin. We were seated and waited on in short order.

I started with a tasty salad made from watermelon and feta cheese with mint. There was also a baked pear prepared with bleu cheese. Vinnie and Ronnie ordered escargots. I tried one and wasn't impressed. We ordered Cornish game hen as our entrée. The flavors were delicate, and the meal was delicious.

Ronnie and I had two glasses of red wine, which was enough, but Kenzie finished half a bottle and didn't seem drunk. Vinnie drank quite a bit, as well.

We cavorted to the theater and looked around inside. The architecture was breathtaking —a marble floor and staircase, huge murals in the corridor, and Neo-Grecian plaster moldings. Ronnie gave us a quick art lesson and explained that most Broadway theaters of any renown were once part of the vaudeville circuits.

The crowd was elegant with men dressed in everything from tuxedos to slacks and sweaters. The women were also extravagant but, to my eye, we outclassed everyone.

I turned around in slow circles. "I feel as if we just entered a fairytale, and I'm a princess."

Kenzie's eyes twinkled in amazement. "No arguments here. This is beyond anything I could have imagined." Vinnie stood by, looking suave, as Ronnie held his hand.

After a few minutes, we found our seats and the show began. I was awed from the start. The story, while familiar, was told with such nuance and imagery that it gave new meaning to the gospels. My parents would have found the performance blasphemous, but I gained new insights. Kenzie was into the music, tapping her feet and smiling. Vinnie and Ronnie held hands, also seeming to enjoy themselves.

After the show, Vinnie took us to a corner restaurant for coffee and cheesecake. He and Ronnie were wrapped in each other's arms, kissing. Vinnie broke it up, turning toward me and Kenzie. "So what'd you think, dolls?"

"That was so incredibly cool! I've never seen a show like that!" Kenzie bubbled.

I added, "I agree. It makes believing in Jesus fun and joyful. The way I was taught growing up was scary and judgmental. But this was like they were testifying to the audience about how interesting and exciting life can be as a believer."

"Yeah." Kenzie nodded. "They were telling us about not just being a church Christian, but about forming a community which carries on the teachings of Jesus. Kind of like you talk about doing, Vinnie."

Chilled and relaxed, he replied, "My methods aren't always Christ-like, but they're whatever's needed to hold the corporate marauders at bay, chicks. The end result is helping the poor and downtrodden. If that's the mission of The Lord, then so be it."

"So you girls are saying that it's the effect Christ has on others which is the story, not just the blood atonement and only saying the words of a believer. That's insightful." Ronnie gave us a big smile and nodded. "And sometimes the ends justify the means."

"Exactly." I pushed away my empty plate. "Jesus was crucified, but through the agony and pain of seeing that, we are more drawn to carry his message of community and caring instead of judging others."

Kenzie smiled at me. "Not judging ourselves." I looked away. She squeezed my shoulder gently.

Ronnie finished her coffee. "That's why I enjoy church with Pastor. He's always preaching about helping others. He's big on Matthew 25 and Romans 14. I was blessed to be born wealthy, even if my home life sucks and my birth father is doing time in a federal prison. I have to use my blessings to bless others."

Vinnie turned in surprise. "Your father's in prison? You never told me that. What was he accused of, if I might ask."

"He did something on Wall Street. I don't know all the details, but he had information he shouldn't have had."

He chuckled. "Insider trading. Not my bag—but, hey, if it made you money why not?"

Vinnie paid the bill and led us all outside to a cab. We took Ronnie home and returned to our hotel room. Kenzie and I hung our dresses up and climbed into bed in our underwear. We curled up together and fell asleep. At some point, Vinnie joined us; but, by five in the morning, he left for work. Kenzie and I slept until ten.

We repeated the process, minus the salon, a couple of days later. Porgy and Bess was incredible in different ways than

Godspell but spectacular in its own right. The story was sad, the history behind it brutal but, in the end, there remained a glimmer of hope.

It was grand getting dolled-up in fancy dresses and jewelry, having dinner at an upscale restaurant and attending a musical or an opera. Neither Kenzie nor I had ever rubbed elbows with high society, but Ronnie had often enough. She knew the etiquette and formalities. She served as our guide.

After the matinee show of Porgy and Bess, Kenzie and I left Ronnie and Vinnie to enjoy the evening. We had last-minute purchases to make and gifts to wrap. The thought of the upcoming celebrations excited me, like a small child. Ronnie wasn't difficult to shop for. Two ounces of Chanel, and a pink angora sweater dress with ice-blue, satin tights were our main gift for her. We also bought her a box of assorted chocolates.

Vinnie was trickier. He was mercurial by turns, and we weren't sure how to meet that. In the end, we went two directions at once. We bought him a bottle of Aramis cologne with its spicy, floral scent, and a bottle of Agua Lavender Puig, which was more delicate. We wrapped his new robe and a box of twenty Macanudo Inspirado Churchills.

I purchased pajamas, a manicure set, and a portable DVD player for Kenzie. I had no idea what she had chosen for me. After we finished, we headed downtown to busk and have sandwiches. Vinnie and Ronnie were meeting us at eleven for midnight services.

On the way to the subway, Kenzie and I walked through the frozen night handing out chocolate bars, fudge, and other sugar-laced snacks to the shells of humanity huddled in doorways. Wild eyes stared back from crapped-out faces, the occasional voice offering thanks. There's simply no place like Manhattan on Christmas Eve.

The candlelight service was exquisite. The choir sang carols and Pastor Affenhoden read from Luke. After the sermon, the entire congregation joined in singing "Silent Night." There was a cake and coffee gathering following that. I bagged up extra cookies to hand out on the way home.

Ronnie returned to her brownstone, while Vinnie, Kenzie, and I walked to our hotel. As we walked, I handed fistfuls of cookies to every homeless person we happened upon. At one corner sat a man dressed in a rumpled tan, shadow-striped suit. By his feet sat a Doberman. Kenzie reached down to pet the dog and the man looked up at us.

"Don't," he murmured. "Her name is Karma, and she'll bite you in the ass."

We left the rest of our cookies and backed away in haste. A half hour later, we were in our room changing into our pajamas and drinking spiked eggnog. Vinnie lit a bowl of pot, and we smoked together. The effects were quick, and I began to yawn. Kenzie and I climbed into bed. We fell asleep in each other's arms as Vinnie rustled about.

We woke up at eight in the morning to the smell of coffee. Vinnie sat in the desk chair reading A Christmas Carol by Dickens. He set it down and smiled.

"Merry Christmas, dolls! It looks like Santa came." He motioned with a thumb to a huge pile of presents.

Vinnie spoiled us that first Christmas. We each unwrapped a bottle of Acqua di Gioia. It smelled divine. Next, were giant black teddy bears which were at least three feet tall. Kenzie and I unwrapped matching leather biker jackets and black leather, calf-high, laced boots. Vinnie sat in his new robe smiling, hands behind his head, and puffed one of his cigars.

Kenzie received a copy of The Motorcycle Diaries by Ernesto Guevara. Inside Vinnie had written I doubt you're related to Che, but you should read this anyway. I received sheet music to Godspell for guitar. We opened one last present. Vinnie and Ronnie had purchased us Apple laptops. He promised to help us set them up for studying and piracy.

Kenzie opened my presents for her, and I opened hers for me. She had bought me a stiletto in a leather, belted leg sheath, a bottle of lilac bubble bath, and a gold necklace with half of a heart on it. She wore one with the other half. She'd also bought me a stuffed Paddington bear to replace the one I'd been forced to leave behind when I was kicked out of my house. I wept tears of joy and hugged Paddington for all I was worth. We kissed deeply, holding each other before drawing in Vinnie. The three of us gazed out the window, not saying a word and hugging each other. Across the way, children played with toys as their parents cooked breakfast.

We cleaned up and dressed in our new clothes. Vinnie wore tight black jeans, loafers, a blue silk shirt, and a black tie. Perched on his head was a blue homburg. He smelled of Aramis. Kenzie and I wore red, satiny tights, black leather mini-skirts we had received from Ronnie, our new boots, and our leather jackets over pink, long-sleeved t-shirts. We sported matching sunglasses and dabbed our perfume behind our ears and on our necks.

Arriving at church, we saw Ronnie waiting in her new dress and tights. She was a sight to behold with her hair done up in a chignon, her cheeks glowing from the nippy air, and a big smile for us.

"Merry Christmas, girls. Merry Christmas, Vinnie my love." She kissed us each on the cheek and led us inside.

After we were seated, Ronnie informed us that she had made reservations at an upscale restaurant. We were having Christmas dinner and taking a carriage ride through Central Park. Excitement coursed through my body, and Kenzie bounced in the pew.

The service was full of carols and discussions of renewal in the spirit. Pastor Affenhoden suggested that the congregation seek to do more for the poor and deprived. After we were dismissed, Ronnie called a cab and took us to eat. She and Vinnie sat together playing footsie as did Kenzie and I.

Christmas dinner was a feast and a half. We began with a roasted fig salad and lobster bisque. Next, was goose with asparagus and parsley potatoes. After a bread and cheese course, we had a plum pudding. We drank lime seltzer with the meal and coffee with dessert. I ate until I was stuffed. Kenzie looked as if she needed a nap.

We walked to Central Park and climbed into a classical English carriage. The coachman wore old-fashioned riding boots, knickers, and a topcoat with a top hat. We rode through the park, staring at the trees, and enjoying the brisk air on our faces. After the ride, the four of us returned to our hotel and rested while watching Christmas movies on TV. Ronnie headed home at seven, and Vinnie texted family and friends. Kenzie and I had a long, hot bubble bath with glasses of sparkling wine. Perry Como crooned from my cell phone as we soaked. We fell asleep early.

The day after Christmas was peaceful in the same way the Atlantic at sunset is peaceful. I lay in our big bed as Kenzie rested against my breasts. Vinnie had already left for his job at five that morning. The air was still and the noise outside muffled.

As we stood, we faced a family with a mother and father and two teenage boys in the apartment building next door. The building was so close that I could have opened our window and hit theirs with a rock. They were in the kitchen eating breakfast. I started laughing until tears filled my eyes as Kenzie stood on the bed, faced the window, and performed a slow, sultry strip tease. Once she was naked, she turned and wiggled her butt at everyone. The family lowered their blinds and several other families closed their curtains.

I gasped, trying to stop laughing. "Why did you do that? You goof!"

Kenzie giggled, "I've been wanting too for a while, but Vinnie's always here and I don't want to get in trouble."

I regained control. "I won't tell. Trust me, that was a riot!"

The best Christmas of my life was over, but I didn't feel sad. The love and memories would sustain me.

Chapter 19

As the months passed, and our relationships grew closer—as friends or lovers, as a family—I began to unravel the paradox that was Vinnie. He was a loner in the realest sense. He found comfort immersed in a book with no outside forces bothering him. He had little interest in sports, social media, or any of the other activities that kept our peers distracted. If he wasn't reading, he was devising new scams, or he was executing scams that already existed. He worked every day except Sunday; otherwise, he was happy to be left alone.

Yet, despite his desire for solitude, he still needed people in his orbit. Kenzie was much the same way. Both of them wanted the accoutrements of the loner, but alone they were anxious, even fearful, of solitude. Alone, they couldn't be themselves.

If Vinnie was alone, those in his orbit would be lonelier, more lost and without a beacon. He knew it, and those of us around him knew it. Vinnie was a nucleus among those he loved and cared for. He covered every ass, dried every tear, lent out the hubris, rigged the tempo, and made the rules. He made sure everyone was well fed, had enough to drink, and was cared for. With everyone satisfied, he retreated into his silent reverie and his reading.

Kenzie was similar, yet not. She needed action in a way Vinnie didn't. But the action didn't necessitate crowds surrounding her. It sustained her to always have somewhere to go and something to do, even if it was just me and her. She needed a purpose to drive her, a goal to reach. If there was even a moment's pause, she grew introspective; her introspection often necessitated a drink. Or several drinks.

Once drinking, she'd slip further into her dark thoughts.

Ronnie had her own issues. She barely discussed them and seemed to roll through life. She consumed alcohol but, unlike Vinnie, she drank in moderation—same with smoking pot. Her grades were excellent and, despite an unenviable home life, she was well-adjusted. The more she came around, the happier we all were. She let Vinnie take the lead, yet she guided the three of us when we faltered. She was the perfect, nurturing maternal force.

Then, there was me. I was changing. At times, I'd climb out of bed after Vinnie had left and before Kenzie was awake. I would read The Bible, pray, and look at myself in the mirror. It had been close to eight months since I had been kicked out, and I wasn't the same. Physically, I was stronger, and more sure of myself. Emotionally, not so much. If there was danger, or a need, I could play the tough role. I had been in several altercations and won them all. Even so, if Vinnie got terse or Ronnie's tone turned strict, I shrank inside my shell.

In church when Pastor Affenhoden turned to discussions of fire and brimstone, even briefly, I felt myself wanting to hide. I couldn't stop my fear. I forced myself to bottle the emotions and tried to focus on the events of the moment. I was in love with Kenzie, but even that scared me. Drinking and smoking pot helped blunt the emotional edges, but something inside kept me from going too far down that path.

New Year's Eve had been a gay affair. Ronnie had her brownstone to herself because her parents were gone for three days. She invited us to join her there for a celebration. We invited Rory, Sheila, and Jeanie; they accepted, agreeing that Rainbow should stay with a sitter.

The afternoon before our party, Vinnie, Kenzie, and I hit four AA meetings. He dropped twenties in three of them. The fourth meeting was in a church and had well over three hundred people in attendance. Vinnie dropped in a fifty and took a large stack of bills in exchange. I was happy enough eating the snacks and drinking coffee.

"You know," Kenzie said to Vinnie as we walked toward a

subway, "if you let us have a few of those bills we could hit more meetings at the same time."

"That tune wouldn't play the hit parade, gator. I'm actually the assistant-treasurer at a meeting as of two weeks ago. I exchange fifties there before the cash goes into an envelope for the bank. The rest of the ersatz bread will be exchanged soon. You chicks just lay low and play your cards straight. Let me deal the doubles." Vinnie ruffled Kenzie's hair until she purred.

That night we all sat around eating crudités and dip, pâté and crackers, assorted cheese with bread, and drinking flutes of Asti wine. Soft jazz played in the background as we all talked about the past year and our aspirations for the new one.

"It's hard to believe that it was eight months ago when we first met you. You were shaking, and terrified, and couldn't even meet my eyes when we talked. Look at you now, kid." Rory's eyes lit up as he sipped his wine.

A sense of bittersweet melancholy swept over me. "I'm still scared sometimes. I have a long way to go, but Kenzie's really helped me learn how to survive. And, I'd never have stuck it out if it wasn't for you three teaching me the truth about my faith. Mom, Vinnie, what can I say. You both give me the boundaries and structure I need."

"All I did was make suggestions," Ronnie chimed in. "You girls took the ball and ran with it. I'm proud of you."

Kenzie downed her glass of wine and filled it again. "I wouldn't have made it without you, Destiny. I was ready to give in and become another loser on the street when you showed up. You brought these three into my life, and introduced me to church, which brought us Mom. Vinnie, I love you. I buck and I fight, but I still love you."

Sheila cleared her throat. "I'm glad to have you all in my life. I put in an application for graduate studies in New Mexico. So did Rory. Jeanie can finish her undergraduate there. If it comes through, well, you all have an open invitation any old time."

Jeanie gazed at us. "I love each of you. You're my strength, and my hope for a better tomorrow. Seriously, I mean it."

Vinnie listened, contributing little, but soaking in what everyone else said. After we'd all shared, he lifted his glass. "Seems to me that none of us came from great shakes. We all got a first-hand dose of dysfunction early in life. Now, we have each other. We're a perfect family of imperfect souls. Street families, from what I'm finding, all have names. My suggestion is that we dub ourselves the FEBU family."

Kenzie sipped her third glass of wine. "Feh-boo? What's that mean?"

"It's an acronym for Fuck Everybody But Us! It stands for complete loyalty and unconditional love amongst our members. The rest of this world can get knotted." He raised his glass once more.

Rory also raised his glass. "That's strong. Quite powerful. I like that, indeed."

"I think I have something in my eye." Jeanie rubbed away a few tears.

Sheila raised her glass. "Happy New Year, my beautiful FEBU family."

We enjoyed the evening and the cozy atmosphere, drinking and eating together. After the wine was gone, Vinnie brought out old-fashioned glasses of Jack Daniels with a splash of soda water and a few ice cubes in them. We watched the ball drop and drank toasts to each other. Ronnie brought up Barry Manilow on her phone, and we listened to him croon "It's Just Another New Year's Eve."

At three in the morning, Ronnie brought out blankets and pillows and we all fell asleep in the living room. Ronnie led Vinnie to her bedroom, and the sounds of light moaning echoed from her door.

The next morning, I had a splitting headache as did Kenzie. Ronnie groaned and said that the wine was having its revenge. Rory, Sheila, and Jeanie even looked the worse for wear. I'd seen them drunk but never hungover.

"There is a solution, gates. Ronnie, darling, might I have a look at your larder? If you have the right ingredients, I have a sure-fire remedy." Vinnie stood, and Ronnie showed him the way to the kitchen.

A half hour later Vinnie emerged with a tray and seven tall glasses of a concoction he swore would help. My belly was sour, and I was willing to try anything to get relief.

"The Ramos Gin Fizz is the hissing hair of dog to cure all your ills, gators," Vinnie said, passing them around. "A friend in Florida taught me about these. His name was Cíké. This has lemon juice, egg whites, powdered sugar, cream, orange extract, and gin with a dash of soda water. Lines the guts and sends pixilated juniper to the brain. After having one, I suggest a hot shower with plenty of steam."

We all drank. It was tasty and did the job. My stomach thanked me. Rory, Sheila, and Jeanie headed to the bathroom in the master bedroom, Ronnie and Vinnie used the downstairs bathroom, while Kenzie and I used one on the third floor.

As we sat waiting for breakfast, Jeanie glanced over at me and Kenzie from the recliner. "Even if we move to the southwest, I'll stay in touch. Rory, Sheila, and I are a committed triad, but I really enjoy being there for you. I never had siblings."

Ronnie prepared ham and scrambled eggs with toast and guava jelly. Vinnie made coffee. Once breakfast had been consumed, Rory, Sheila and Jeanie drove home.

Vinnie looked in the paper and found a classic movie festival at a nearby theater. We decided to attend. After stopping by our hotel to grab snacks and sodas, we took the subway to Midtown. I hadn't brought my guitar, but I sang Manilow's "It's Just Another New Year's Eve" and "Auld Lang Syne." Several people approached and handed me dollar bills. I put them in my pocket as we exited.

On the walk to the theater, we passed a Puerto Rican man dressed in a shiny purple suit and an electric blue shirt. His hair was parted in the middle and slicked back with at least a pint of Vitalis. He had set up a folding table upon which sat three cards, face down, and was sing-songing while moving the cards in rapid circular motions under his hands. "Move 'em around. Move 'em around. Three queens go for a ride. Can you detect where the black queen hides?"

Vinnie walked by, put down a fifty, flipped the black queen and collected one hundred dollars without breaking stride. The dealer looked dazed at how fast that had occurred.

There were four movies showing: Bonnie and Clyde, The Getaway, Dog Day Afternoon, and Going in Style. Kenzie and I held hands, sharing our popcorn. Afterwards, we walked to a deli for sandwiches and coffee.

"A lot of street kids have nicknames. We should call you two Bonnie and Clyde," Kenzie said. "They were out to protect the little guy from the rich bastards, same as you."

"Actually, that isn't so." Vinnie said before sipping his coffee. "Beatty and Dunaway were a fine casting choice, albeit in both cases too slick and polished of appearance. But let me hep you to some reality, straight from the fridge. The longevity of their story is more of a testament to the power of mythos and media than any actual attributes." He bit into his corned beef on black bread. "You should check out some books and research the subject."

"Going in Style was hilarious." Ronnie snuggled into Vinnie. "There's a lot behind that movie, too. Both of you girls should research the oil crises and inflation in the seventies. The effects of that on the poor and the elderly is the serious undercurrent behind the humor."

My eyes burned and itched. I couldn't stifle my yawns. "We'll research tomorrow."

Kenzie leaned her head against me. "You research the oil thing. I'll research the inflation thing. We can swap information."

"Were you cognizant of the fact that George Burns grew up near here. And Lee Strasburg had an acting school in this city. I'll show you some places next week." Vinnie paid the check, and we headed back to our hotel.

After New Year's, life fell back into a groove. Kenzie was picking up her math lessons, and Ronnie helped her catch up to me. It still wasn't her best subject, but she worked even harder to compensate. We studied every day and played music. Vinnie would meet us in the park, and we'd have dinner at either a fast-food restaurant or a pizza parlor before heading back to our room to sleep. Some nights, we ordered Chinese takeout. Kenzie was drinking more often, now that we were settled; but there was little I could do, despite my concerns. She and Vinnie both drank far more than I or Ronnie.

Two months after our New Year's party on a Sunday after church, Vinnie, Kenzie, and I took a walk on Van Cortland Avenue to enjoy the spring weather. Ronnie had business at home. The three of us headed toward the subway station.

Ahead of us, a group of African-American youths were strutting along looking fierce and proud. They were dressed in electric-blue dress shirts, gray slacks, and shiny dress shoes. On their heads they wore matching gray, wide-brimmed hats. Their rich black skin glistened in the sunlight, and they exuded an air of superiority. A young, buxom brunette stood in their path holding a package containing a laptop. As the group approached, she clutched her box. I shook my head in disgust. "Give me a break!" I thought to myself. The group of teens sidestepped the lady and tipped their hats. They were a tough bunch, but not threatening unless first threatened.

Across the street, a basement door opened. A group of Puerto Ricans emerged. They all wore silver windbreakers with purple trim. An old, reconverted hearse with a psychedelic paint job sat on the corner. The Puerto Rican boys climbed inside and roared off. Kenzie smiled at them, and we kept ambling along. Los Enterradors were a classy clique. Dangerous, but classy.

As we approached the station, I saw a group of Caucasian teens with shaved heads approaching. They were dressed in brown t-shirts, jeans with suspenders, and combat boots. The group of African-Americans was still in front of us. By that time, I had come to understand what the skinheads stood for. It turned my stomach.

Vinnie took off on a lope and swept us along, running with the instincts born of survival. Dashing down the subway stairs, we stopped for a split-second to swipe our cards. Clicking through the turnstile, simultaneously waiting for a train and keeping our eyes on the stairway, I unsnapped the sheath on my left inner calf in case I needed my stiletto. Kenzie took a collapsible steel baton from her purse. Vinnie held up a hand, motioning us to stay cool.

Ten minutes later, the black youth descended. Some of them had fresh marks on their faces and hands. There were some tears in their shirts. Clearly they had won the skirmish, as much as anyone could ever win that sort of fight. I nodded to each of them as they clicked through and stood near us. Kenzie put her weapon away, and I closed my sheath.

"Hey, man. Thanks for staying and helping out," one of the youths shouted at Vinnie.

He replied with cold menace, "Like I told you before, Trey, I was born with a crack in my ass. I do not—absolutely do not— need you or those Nazi bastards finishing the job of breaking it. If they start trouble with me or my chicks on a personal level, it'll make national news. They know it. You know it."

"Yeah, maybe. Or, maybe you're chicken shit." Trey laughed.

Vinnie smiled and stepped into a t-stance with fists raised. "Want to test that out? You and me, one on one. The boys hang back and do nothing. Same for my girls."

The rest of the group moved into positions to attack. I grabbed my stiletto, and Kenzie popped open the baton. Trey held up a hand.

"Like hell if this needs to turn into a massacre. I saw what you three did the other night to that old dude who was hassling your chicks. You a'ight for being white. And watch who you calling boys." Trey smiled as everyone relaxed. The rest of Trey's family started laughing as they sensed the tension ease.

We boarded the train one car ahead of Trey and his crew. At one end of the subway car, a radio blasted ACDC's "Wild Child." I leaned on Vinnie, and he ruffled my hair. Kenzie kept her eyes on the connecting doors, but no one came through.

The following Saturday after Kenzie and I returned from the art museum, Vinnie was arriving home from work. "Feel like pizza, chicks?"

"Sure. Sounds good."

He sat on a bench, dialed, and put his phone on speaker.

"Gino's Pizzeria. Is this delivery or carry out?"

Vinnie affected a southern accent. "Howdy... My name is Dwight and it would be delivery, but I really need to speak with a manager first."

"This is. What can I do for you?"

"Well, you see buddy, I was in a few days ago and I got two large pies with mushrooms and pepperoni. But the person making them only gave me pepperoni. I just got back to town from visiting my sick aunt so I wanted to call. Never had this happen before." He sounded confused and a bit slow.

"Sorry to hear that, Mr. Dwight. Do you have your receipt?"

"Well, golly. I reckon I threw it away. Is it necessary?"

"Oh, it's ok this time. In the future, we require a receipt to replace food."

"Thank you kindly. Yeah, I'll keep the receipt next time."

Vinnie gave an address a block away from our hotel. He told us to go up, and he'd join us. We went upstairs to change into our pajamas. Kenzie took three bottles of Shock Top out of the mini-fridge as Vinnie came through the door with the pizza. We watched some action movies on TV before going to bed.

The next day, Ronnie wasn't at church. Her family was attending a function in Long Island, and she texted that she couldn't get out of going. As Vinnie, Kenzie, and I exited the church, a pack of dark clouds moved in. We caught a bus toward Queens before rain deluged the city.

We sat on a row of seats, and Vinnie smiled at three girls sitting across from us as torrents of rain spattered the bus. The girls wore army surplus jackets, ankle-length black skirts, and red lace-ups. They had pale skin, multiple piercings, and long hair dyed in various shades. One sported purple, another aquamarine, and the third an orange-red blend that went well with her freckles.

Vinnie affected a British accent "I'm a bit lost, ladies. Is Rockaway hard and far to reach? Can I catch a ride on this bus to Rockaway Beach?"

The girls stood up without a word and moved toward the back. Kenzie and I looked at each other, trying not to giggle. We failed, and our laughter pierced the silence of the afternoon. Vinnie reached for his sack and took out a twenty-ounce bottle of Coke. He sipped some and passed it to Kenzie. Kenzie had a swig and passed it to me. The Coke had bourbon in it.

A boy boarded with an iPod. Oblivious to us, he sat singing "Goodnight Saigon."

"Hey, Vinnie, you know everything about everything. Was Billy Joel having a gang bang in Vietnam?" Kenzie's eyes crinkled.

Vinnie shook his head, laughing. "No. And that's not what he meant about going down together."

It was times like that when Vinnie was relaxed and happy. We felt like a real family. I wish we'd had more of those moments.

Chapter 20

Three weeks later, Kenzie turned fifteen. The weather that Sunday was a mild fifty-two degrees with a slight cloud cover. I woke up early, dressing and slipping out the door while Vinnie and Kenzie slept. The previous night, we had stayed up late watching some old movie musicals. I had managed one martini with my corned beef on rye. Vinnie had consumed three and Kenzie, four. They would be asleep for a couple more hours.

I took the elevator to the first floor and walked through the cheaply decorated lobby, ignoring the ancient men reading their racing forms and newspapers, before exiting onto the sidewalk. I no longer panicked at being alone in the city. I enjoyed having Kenzie with me, but her constant presence was no longer essential to my mental well-being. Two blocks away, there was an Italian bakery. I purchased six bombolone and a box of birthday candles.

After returning to the room, I slid the keycard and opened the door. Vinnie sat up with a blade in his hand, ready to defend himself. Seeing me, he relaxed and climbed out of bed. We hugged, then prepared the breakfast and coffee. Vinnie and I stood at the foot of the bed, watching Kenzie sleep. We smiled at each other and began to sing.

"Happy Birthday to you. Happy Birthday to you. Happy Birthday, sweet Kenzie. Happy Birthday to you."

Kenzie opened her eyes and groaned with a smile. "Oh man! You two! Geez!" She climbed out of bed in her t-shirt and panties, giving us both hugs and kisses.

I lit the candle in the center of one of her donuts, and she blew it out. Tears dribbled down her cheeks when I handed her a wrapped copy of Black Robes, White Justice by Bruce Wright.

"Thank you," she said, giving me an enthusiastic kiss.

After a church service, followed by a sheet-cake for Kenzie at the potluck, we walked through Central Park. Many trees were blossoming, and the air was fragrant. The weather was perfect. Vinnie appeared preoccupied, but Kenzie and I were so wrapped up in each other that we barely noticed.

That evening, Vinnie sat across from us at a bar and grill. He knew the bouncer, Eric, and the bartender, Mac. We were shown a table in the far back where the light was dim, and we were less likely to be noticed. We each had a ribeye steak with fries and a cold martini.

Vinnie presented Kenzie with a birthday card. Inside were two authentic New York State ID cards. One had my name and picture, the other had Kenzie's. We were both eighteen years old according to the birthdates. I was going on nineteen if the card was taken at face value.

"My oldest sister, Gina, sent me those. Her boyfriend works in an office next to a DMV down south, and he knows a guy. They have access to a computer system and can get these from any state. There's another way, but it's complicated," he said, eating a bite of steak.

Kenzie squealed in delight, drinking her martini. "Thank you! This is so cool! Now we can get our GED certificates."

Vinnie winked. "Don't dive into the deep-end, but yes, you sure can. Just be careful. Don't use those for anything too nefarious."

I sipped my drink then asked, "In my parent's church, the men offered a girl special words of wisdom on her eighteenth birthday. You have any?"

Vinnie reflected for a moment as he chewed on a steak fry. He thumbed his chin and nodded. "You've got to love living, chicks, because dying is a pain in the ass. They say you only live once, but the way that we've lived these past few months...man, once is enough. We're not like those philosophical cats always looking for answers to the secrets of life. We just go on living, day to day, taking what comes. I mean, you both struggle with your pasts and those creeps who hurt you. In the end, though, we just take forever a minute at a time.

"If you want some sage advice to survive in this big bad world, chicks, I'd have to hep you to what my father always told me and my sisters. You have to play everything big, wide, expansively. The more open you are, the more you take in. Your dimensions deepen, you grow, you become more of what you are."

"That's how I want to be. Like you. I want to help everyone around me, and always look out for the underdog. I want to do it with style, like you." Kenzie finished her martini and was brought another. "I want to be a lawyer like Jack McCoy so that I can help others."

"That's the only way to do anything in life, doll. Do it with style, or it just isn't worth doing. Look at Frank Abagnale, or Richard Marcus—they managed to be the best because they had savoir faire. It set them apart. As for being a lawyer, why not be a lawyer like Mackenzie Guevara? You have a lot to offer just being yourself." Vinnie pushed his plate away and checked his phone. "Hey, we have to meet Ronnie at the hotel for cake."

We boarded an F Train and rode to our stop. After taking the elevator up and letting ourselves in, Ronnie grabbed Kenzie. She sat on the end of the bed and pulled Kenzie over her lap before delivering fifteen feather-soft swats to her butt.

"Happy Birthday, my sweet daughter!" She hugged Kenzie, kissing her on both cheeks. "Open your presents."

Kenzie unwrapped a calendar with a new vocabulary word for each day of the year. She also received True Stories of Law & Order, a book that detailed the actual cases used in the show. Her final gift from Ronnie was a DVD of Gideon's Trumpet. She hugged Ronnie and couldn't speak for a moment.

Kenzie gave Ronnie a broad smile. Tears trickled down her cheeks. "I never really had a birthday before. I mean, not a real celebration. Today sure as hell made up for that."

I handed Kenzie an envelope. I had purchased tickets to a Robin Williams movie festival. She squeezed me tight. Words couldn't get through the smiling tears, but her face said it all. We had chocolate torte with coffee and, after wrapping the leftovers, the four of us caught the subway to midtown where the festival was showing.

Kenzie and I sat holding hands and kissing as we watched the movies. Sneaking peeks at Ronnie and Vinnie, I saw that they were doing the same. My heart beat a bit faster for that. I wanted them to be together. After all that they had done for me and Kenzie, they deserved a happy relationship.

At four in the morning, we sat in a small café drinking espresso. Vinnie leaned back in the booth sideways, and Ronnie lay against him. He stroked her hair.

"Seriously, chicks, Popeye underplays its over-acting. There's too much going on at the same time. The writers took an already rough-and-tumble cartoon and made it even grittier. It takes the likes of Robin Williams for that to play. Like with Adrian's first radio broadcast in Good Morning, Vietnam, the best Robin Williams is when he goes full-on manic."

Kenzie yawned. "He's a riot. But, he's great at being serious, too. In Good Will Hunting, that climatic scene between Sean and Will, I could so relate to that."

"Yeah, me too. It's nice to realize that we aren't to blame for all the bad stuff in our lives," I added.

Ronnie nodded, blinking through her fatigue. "No, you're not. None of us are. We don't have to be victims, though. We're survivors." She yawned until I thought her jaws might detach.

The following day, we slept in. Vinnie had a day off. We found a bench in the park, sat, and enjoyed the day. For all its openness, the park might as well have been a cage. The benches acted as perches upon which elderly, drunken denizens of the urban zoo had been rotting away since long before Kenzie, Vinnie, or I had been born. I strummed my guitar, trying out the blues riffs I had learned from a book, and watching the people walk by.

Nearby, several old men played checkers. Kenzie fed the pigeons with a hunk of moldy bread she'd found atop a trash can. Vinnie read Busting Vegas by Ben Mezrich. Behind us, children laughed and screamed as they ran through the shower of a water sprinkler. Young mothers rocked their infants in strollers, prattling about the price of groceries, their husband's attempts to find work, or their kids.

It was six in the evening. We had already been sitting on the benches for four hours. I had collected about seventy-five dollars in throw money. The park in the afternoon wasn't as lucrative as the Theater District at night.

Vinnie lowered his book and watched Kenzie dispense small chunks of bread to the pigeons. "You like feeding those birds, huh?"

Kenzie shrugged. "I suppose. They're here, anyway. It's almost like having a pet. I know it'd be unfair to a dog to make it live our life. Those homeless kids with their dogs bug the hell out of me. This is sort of like I have pet birds."

I smiled a moment, then gave Kenzie a deadpan look. "You know, they say those birds carry disease."

"What disease?" She scowled.

"I'm not sure, I read it somewhere." I shrugged, giving Vinnie a well-timed wink.

"Never brought me any disease." Kenzie sounded miffed.

"Look, don't get me wrong. I'm not one of those chicks that has it in for birds. I agree it's kind of like having a pet." I was teasing her, trying to get a rise. She caught on, gave me the finger, and I laughed.

Suddenly an obese boy who looked about four came running toward us, waving his pudgy arms and screaming. He thundered right into the flock of pigeons Kenzie had herded together. The birds flapped in all directions. We covered our faces and I shielded my guitar as the cloud of crazed birds rose in the air, leaving behind dust, bird shit, and feathers. From the look on Kenzie's face, I thought I was about to see the kid go airborne.

The porcine boy stood in front of the park bench where we

sat. It was as if he had jumped into a pool and all the water splashed out over the sides. He had a round, florid face and a short crewcut. There was not a single aspect of his appearance that could've been considered cute or endearing. I eyed the landscape for a parent to remove him.

"What in the hell's the matter with this kid?" Vinnie grouched.

The boy kept up his steady gaze. It was apparent from the way his thick lips pinched together that he found our presence in the park distasteful. I tried smiling, but the butterball failed to respond. Purple and red food stains covered his mouth and poured onto his collar and shirt.

"This is what happens when parents use food as a reward, chicks. Straight from the fridge, gate. He shoves anymore snack cakes in his maw they'll have to haul his ass to nursery school in a dump truck." Vinnie grumbled. "For crying out loud, look at that mug. He could be a model for the Hotai statue at a Chinese buffet."

The boy's eyes narrowed.

"You believe the nerve of this lump of dough?" Vinnie scowled. "Scram!"

With surprising speed, the boy scurried away. Vinnie shook his head. "Little bastard."

"Kind of hard on the little puke weren't you?" Kenzie looked puzzled.

"Hey, I don't like being ogled like one of Barnum's exhibits. If he wants to stare, let him go hang out in Times Square or have his parents take him to a museum."

Kenzie and I side-hugged Vinnie, and he returned to his book. He calmed down some as he read. I kept strumming my guitar. A group of teens passed by, hanging on each other while kissing, groping, and goosing. I watched them pass.

"Sometimes while we sit in the parks watching the world pass, I get a real sense of coital sonder." I sighed.

"Sounds good to me. I could go for some dinner. I'm not sure where there's a KFC around here, though." Kenzie giggled.

I bopped her on the head. "You goof!"

An hour later, we were preparing to leave when another group of teens approached. I froze a moment when I recognized Valiant and his street family. They glared at us.

Kenzie turned to face them. "Well, shit. Destiny, it's that douchebag and his gang of pansies. Vinnie, this asshole is the one who got us arrested."

Valiant sneered. "We got eighty-sixed from our park because of you bitches. We owe you an ass kicking!"

Vinnie pushed us behind him. "Slow your roll, gate." He put his hands up in a gesture of surrender. "We're just cutting out."

Valiant snarled. "Don't think so, faggot. You can leave, but they can't."

Vinnie barely moved a muscle, but the right-hand slap rocked Valiant's head. A side kick dropped one of the boys, and a front snap-kick to the knee brought Valiant crashing down. Vinnie waited for more, but no one else approached.

He gave the group his best Charles Manson grin. "I'm their street dad, cats. You come near them, and they'll find pieces of you from here to Oyster Bay. You goons from Saskatoon catching my signal?"

Kenzie and I backed away, but Valiant's crew was already moving in the opposite direction. Valiant hobbled after them, leaning on his girlfriend. The boy who'd been kicked in the crotch staggered in another direction, stopping periodically to throw up.

We scurried away, caught a subway to Little Italy, and ordered a large anchovy and mushroom pizza. It took the entire subway ride before my adrenaline stopped pumping. As we ate, Vinnie received a text message. His brow knitted together, and he pursed his lips.

Kenzie paused mid-bite. "Something wrong?"

Vinnie looked shaken up, something I had never seen from him. "I'm not certain, doll. There might be a big problem. It doesn't concern you two, however."

I reached across the table and held Vinnie's free hand.

"We're FEBU family, remember? If it's a problem for you, it concerns us."

"I've schooled you chicks well but, in this case, I can't involve you. It's just..." he paused, searching for words. "I can't discuss my job. But, as with my parents, I may have gotten in over my head. Stupid on my part, but so far I'm safe. Thing of it is, dolls, if there's even a chance I could get jammed up, I'll have to clear out fast. Should anyone ask, you don't know me."

I stared at Kenzie, and she stared back. We waited, and then she looked over to Vinnie. "What's that all about? You kill someone? Knock over a bank?"

My temples throbbed. "We don't need details. If we have to run, then let's run. You name the destination, we'll get Ronnie, and go with you."

Vinnie sighed "No, you won't. Ronnie needs to stay out of this, too. Look, I care about you both, but I told you from jump street that I'm better off alone. I took a job because the bread was sweet, and I figured it wasn't hurting anyone who wasn't willing to get hurt. Now, that might be over."

Kenzie finished her last slice and another glass of beer. "If you leave, I'd suggest finding that girl you told us about. Call your sister, get a new name, and go find your soulmate."

Vinnie settled up on the check, and we walked outside. He hugged us both. We caught a subway and took in an AA meeting. Vinnie traded in his last bogus twenty and collected twenty-five in change. The sour tightness in my stomach refused to go away. Something bad was about to happen, and I couldn't protect one of the best friends I'd ever had.

Chapter 21

The peripeteia of life is rarely gentle. When fortunes commenced their reversal for Kenzie and me, fate ran a train on us like nothing we had ever experienced. It was all I could do to stay sane.

Two months after Vinnie's problems at his job began, I turned sixteen. I had been away from home for a year. I woke up on my birthday and slipped out of bed. Vinnie was already at work. I stood in front of the window naked, ignoring any neighbors, and thought about the year that had passed. I began to weep as I thought about how blessed I had been. I had a real family that was teaching me about the true meaning of love. I was gaining a proper education, for once. My music and singing was improving. Even my religious understanding had changed.

Strong, thin arms encircling my body interrupted my thoughts. Kenzie kissed my back. She turned me around and hugged me. "Happy Birthday." She led me back to bed and snuggled beside me. We spent two hours making love.

As Kenzie rested against me, she murmured, "Is there anything you've wanted to do or see, that we haven't had time for?"

I stroked her belly. "Well, there's the Statue of Liberty, the Empire State Building, the Brooklyn Botanical Garden, the Bronx Zoo..."

She interrupted me, giggling. "The tourist stuff? Hell yeah. We'll do some of that today. We have enough money to see some sights."

Two hours later, we were sipping coffee in Times Square and boarding the second level of an open-air tour bus. Our guide, Rocko, amazed us regarding his knowledge about the history of New York. He was animated while pointing out sights and places where we often busked. Albeit, some sights weren't new to us, but the historical information was fascinating.

The busses were set up so that we could hop off at any stop and catch the next one. We climbed off the bus at Fifth Avenue and took an elevator to the 102nd-floor observation deck of the Empire State Building. The views from there were exquisite! After looking through binoculars, we caught another bus and squeezed in the ferry ride to the Statue of Liberty and Ellis Island before it was time to meet Ronnie and Vinnie.

The four of us had dinner at a soul food restaurant in Harlem before attending a play called Harvey. Vinnie and Ronnie had fried whiting with collard greens, steamed okra, and red beans with rice. Kenzie and I opted for beef ribs, greens, mashed potatoes, and corn. The food was excellent, and Vinnie spiked our Kool-Aid with vodka.

Harvey was bittersweet, but funny. The story resonated with me as it dealt, in a sideways manner, with faith. After the play, we returned to our room. I was getting my pajamas out of the dresser and, while bending over, Vinnie grabbed me. Ronnie delivered my birthday swats and gave me a book of sheet music to Bob Dylan's greatest hits. Vinnie gave me a gold wristwatch with diamond chips in the bezel. I hugged them both. As I was about to thank them, Ronnie cleared her throat.

"Guys, I have something to tell you." She looked around the room as if trying to find the words she needed. "In July, I'm moving. I was accepted to Urbana. My mom isn't happy with that choice, and neither is my step-father. I'm going, anyway, and paying for it myself. I'm majoring in education."

My mouth opened and snapped shut, then I hugged Ronnie as hard as I could. Kenzie stared at us, turned, and walked to the window. She focused the apartments across the way. Vinnie walked over, embracing her from behind. She shook as tears flooded from her eyes.

I moved to one side and poked her. "What's wrong with you? I thought you'd be excited for her. Mom's finally free!"

Kenzie grabbed me in an embrace and bawled. "She's abandoning us. We need her, and she's leaving. She's dumping us."

Ronnie sat on the bed and pulled Kenzie into her lap, rocking her like a small child. "I have to go to college, baby girl. I have to live my life. You know that. You and Destiny are almost ready for your tests. I'll help you get that set up, and you'll both have your certificates before I leave."

Kenzie sniffled and blew her nose. "I'm sorry. I know it isn't fair of me, but everyone who's supposed to love me leaves."

Vinnie took out four glasses from the refrigerator. He filled them each with ice, a splash of club soda, and scotch. "To new beginnings." He toasted.

Kenzie gulped her drink and poured another. "I hope you enjoy college, Mom. I'll miss you."

"We can text and email. And by the time you're sixteen, you'll be in college too," Ronnie said, always sweet and encouraging. "I love you, Kenzie, but I've been trapped for years, and you know it. I have a chance now to escape the grand dysfunctionality I call a home."

Kenzie held her giant teddy bear. I wanted to comfort her, but I didn't know how. I was sad to lose Ronnie, but I was also glad that she was free to attend college and have her dreams.

Ronnie and Vinnie left together after finishing their scotch. Kenzie had a third drink and curled up in the bed, crying herself to sleep. All I could do was cuddle against her. I prayed for my new family and held Kenzie while she slept. Vinnie returned an hour later and tucked me in. He fell asleep between us.

The next morning, we received a text from Rory that he and Sheila were definitely moving to New Mexico in July. They were attending graduate school, and Jeanie was finishing up her BS degree there. Kenzie read the message, shrugged, and poured herself a glass of Jack Daniels.

She lifted the glass. "Here's to everyone leaving this city but us." She gulped the drink, and I scowled at her.

"You need to quit drinking so much. Especially this early."

Kenzie growled at me. "Who the hell are you? My mother?"

I growled back. "Don't even go there. I will put you across my knee, so help me! Fine!" I threw my hands up. "To hell with it. Drink, for all I care! What do I know?"

"I'm not a drunk. Dammit, I just feel sad and a drink helps. There's no crime in that."

We left and headed to the library to study. From that point on, each day was a concerted effort to prepare for our exams. Kenzie and I found we were too exhausted to busk or even go out to eat. We'd order in Chinese food, eat, and sleep for a few hours. Kenzie's alcohol consumption increased. At night, she'd have three or four drinks before bed; in the morning, she'd have a screwdriver to settle her hangover.

Vinnie returned every afternoon to read, but he didn't say much. He was moody and tense. I tried to talk to him about it, but he refused. Whatever was eating at him settled in deep. I began to have stomach cramps and flu-like symptoms. I slept more and woke up exhausted.

After two weeks, Ronnie insisted that Kenzie and I take a Saturday off and rest. We decided to catch the subway to Rockaway and spend a day sitting on the shore. Vinnie had a late-night meeting and agreed to meet us at the station at eleven.

We spent the day sitting on our beach blanket, soaking up the sun, and holding each other. For a short while, our worries and stress disappeared. We ate hot dogs and drank Cokes for lunch. I drank Cokes, anyway. Kenzie had stashed a six pack of Budweiser in her backpack.

That night, as the waves lapped the shore of Rockaway Beach, I felt connected to the universe. I had Kenzie in my arms, my corporeal love. I had the triune Spirit above, allowing me to experience agape love. I was still upset, and I had a deep sense of foreboding; but, for a moment, none of that mattered.

Vinnie met us at the station, and we rode back to the hotel. As usual, he had Sunday off. We ordered a late dinner of beef and broccoli, chicken fried rice, and steamed dumplings. I had one martini while Vinnie and Kenzie had three. We watched an old western on TV while we ate.

The next morning, we attended church. The service was excellent, as always, but, afterward, it began to rain. Ronnie had to go home, so Vinnie, Kenzie, and I attended a comedy movie marathon at a nearby theater. Kenzie and Vinnie sat drinking bourbon-laced Cokes while I drank my Coke straight. After the movies, we headed back to our room, ate dinner, and fell asleep early.

The next day Kenzie and I took practice tests. We both passed. Ronnie graded the papers after joining us at the library.

She gave us a gentle look. "You did OK. But OK isn't the best you can do. I think if we push for another week, you can really kick some butt."

Kenzie looked out a window. "Does it matter? Passing is passing. It's not like we're going to need perfect scores. We're going to be busking and living on the streets the rest of our lives."

Ronnie whipped Kenzie around. "Bullshit! You want to go to law school. That's your dream. So quit feeling sorry for yourself!"

I shrank into a corner of our study room. It was Kenzie and Ronnie in front of me, but I was seeing one of my sisters and my father. My heart raced, and I collapsed on the floor. Five minutes later, I came to with Ronnie and Kenzie holding me.

Kenzie had a look of horror on her face. "Jesus, Destiny! What happened? You fainted or something and kept saying something about 'Faith, just do what father says.'"

Ronnie held me in her arms. "You alright? You need a doctor?"

I stood up feeling shaky. "I'm fine. I don't know what happened. I had a vision or something."

Kenzie took a bottle of Coke out of her backpack and offered me a drink, but I refused it. She took a swig. "Who's Faith?"

I sighed, replying, "My youngest sister. One time she didn't want to do her chores. Father threatened to take off his belt. Sometimes I remember that it wasn't just me going through it."

Ronnie squeezed me. "I wasn't going to beat Kenzie's ass, much as she asks for it sometimes. I just won't have either of you giving up out of fear. I know damned well you can both pass."

Kenzie pouted. "I'm sorry. I'm scared. I can't explain it in words. Not words you'd accept, anyway." She took another slug of spiked soda.

The following day, I made an appointment for myself with Pastor Affenhoden. Kenzie stayed in the room studying. He poured us each some coffee. "From knowing you this past year, your life has not been an easy one. I am glad to see you attend church frequently, but I must ask, do you still believe in The Word?"

I sat thinking while the pastor patiently waited. "I still believe in The Bible. That's unshakeable. I guess I never allowed my parents, or their church, to affect that. I believe in the love and tolerance Jesus preached." Tears formed. "I worry for my siblings. I worry a lot. I wonder if I should have given in to protect them. Now, all I can do is pray for them."

Pastor Affenhoden nodded. "Don't discount prayer, sister. Also, denying your sexuality would have hurt you. I sincerely doubt it would have helped your siblings. The only way that could have happened is if you had stood up for them, and that might well have had the same result of you being thrown out." He paused, taking a sip of coffee. "Is anything else wrong?"

I thought about Kenzie's drinking. "No, sir. Nothing I can't handle."

"Well, if there is ever anything you need help with, my door is always open."

I returned to the hotel and studied with Kenzie. She took a practice math test and scored an eighty-nine. I applauded and kissed her. "That's fantastic for you! I'm so proud of you!"

Kenzie beamed and kissed me back. We climbed onto the bed and were necking when Vinnie came in, looking panicked. He began packing his books and clothing into his backpack.

"I've got a major hitch in the get-along, and we need to talk. As soon as possible."

We sat up, pulling ourselves together. I asked, "What's wrong? What can we do to help?"

Vinnie's eyes registered fear. "There's nothing you can do. I just got word that someone I know in the Bronx was arrested. Before they toss his computer, I have to get out of here. If anyone asks, you don't know me. No matter what."

Kenzie's eyes widened as she frowned. "Of course we won't dime you out, but it's a huge city. Why don't we just change hotels?"

Vinnie sighed. "It isn't the hotel. I can't tell you what this is about, but I have to get moving. You both have another three weeks paid for here. I'm leaving you three grand, as well. You can get another place next month."

We hugged Vinnie, and tears filled my eyes. "If you have to leave, go find that girl you lost. You taught us so much. You deserve happiness."

Vinnie walked with us out the door. "Then my work here is done. Let's go tell Ronnie."

Chapter 22

The conversation between Vinnie and Ronnie had been rough, to say the least, as we sat drinking coffee laced with Bailey's Irish Cream. My head hurt, my chest hurt, and I precariously balanced between screaming in rage and bawling like a three year old.

Vinnie held his cup, gazing to a spot a thousand yards away. "I'm sorry, doll. I wish circumstances were different. This is the tune the fiddler played, and we must needs jig to it."

Ronnie blinked back tears. "Can't you just hang on for a bit longer? The girls are almost ready to take the tests, and they'll pass. I'm sure of that. I'm almost ready to head to college. Shit, you three could likely get accepted there, too. We can all live together. Let's get married."

His expression softened. "Would that it could work that way. I can't do it. I have to cut and run—quick, fast, and in a hurry. I should already be gone now. One day, maybe, I'll find you chicks again. We'll stay in touch, anyway. For a while."

Kenzie and I looked out the window as the two of them shared a long kiss. I stood and walked to the bathroom. The tears pouring from my eyes were blinding. As I re-entered the living room, Vinnie was adjusting his pack. Ronnie hugged him and tried to smile.

"You going to be alright, Daddy-O? Because we can help. I'd do anything, and you know our girls here would."

He hugged us, giving us each a smack on the ass. "I'm not flushed out, chicks, but wrap your ass in a sling and bet it that I'll be a'ight."

Vinnie walked out the door, and that's the last we saw of him in person—so far. We did hear plenty—or rather, read texts.

We also weren't in the dark about his circumstances for long. What I found out left me conflicted.

Kenzie and I returned to our hotel room and made love all afternoon. We fell asleep early, and the next morning received a text from Ronnie. OMG! Get a copy of The Daily News and read page three. Then get to the Museum of Natural History. Fast! I have stuff for you.

Kenzie and I threw some clothes on and headed to the corner newsstand to buy the paper. I turned to page three and read.

Police made two arrests in the Hunts Point area. Giuseppe 'Joey Pipes' Cantare was arrested for possession of controlled substances, dealing in controlled substances, and running a prostitution ring. Also arrested was Daquan Faruq Mfume. Mfume is alleged to be a lead middle-man in Cantare's operation. The police are using computer files found at the Cantare residence to track down others implicated in the various illegal operations.

Her eyes grew wider as I read. "Holy shit! That crazy son of a bitch! He was working for gangsters!"

My head was spinning, and my breaths were uneven. I sat heavily on a bench. "It makes sense. Not prostitution, Vinnie wouldn't do that. So, it has to be drugs. Let me think. He said that he didn't believe he was hurting anyone who didn't choose to be hurt. So, that would be people who willingly use drugs. At five hundred or more dollars every day, and he only worked in the mornings mostly..."

Kenzie interrupted me. "He was meeting someone and picking up drugs in that satchel he carried. He delivered them and brought back money. Then, he got paid."

I laughed. I couldn't help it, nor stop. "Damn! That's why he never discussed his job." I screeched loud enough to be heard in Florida, "Run, Vinnie! We got your six!"

Kenzie held me and laughed. "We better go see Mom. We need to figure out when our tests are, too. I can't believe that badass son of a bitch!"

While riding the F Train, my chest was tight. My mind was a

whirling kaleidoscope of emotions. I had spent more than a year seeing what hard drugs did to people. I'd witnessed the devastation drugs caused and the shells of humanity left in their wake. Had it been anyone else, I would have found the running of drugs inexcusable. This was Vinnie, though. FEBU meant something. Loyalty only counted when it was severely tested. Even so, this wasn't some petty hustle. Vinnie had run drugs for major suppliers. That stung.

We bought bottles of ginger ale before heading to the museum. My stomach settled a bit, but Kenzie's face was taut. Her lips pressed together, and her eyes flicked back and forth. I kept looking behind us to see if we were being followed.

When we reached the museum, Ronnie walked toward us. Her face said it all. An overstuffed backpack strained her shoulders, but she hugged us and led us down the avenue. We entered a pizza parlor and took a table in the rear.

"I gather you read the article? He texted me this morning, very early. I was told to read the paper and contact a gentleman in Midtown. I did that." Ronnie paused as a waiter approached. "We'll take a large mushroom and sausage pie, the large antipasto, and a pitcher of root beer."

Kenzie looked around furtively. "What was he doing in Midtown?"

Ronnie gave us a gentle look. "I don't think you need to worry about people following us. They don't know we exist. Anyway, he gave me twenty burner phones. Ten for me and ten for you. I pre-programmed them with a number before you arrived. If you need him, use one to text. Then remove the sim card and crack it in two. Toss the pieces in a sewer, toss the front of the phone in a subway garbage can, and toss the back elsewhere."

I held my temples with my index fingers and rubbed in circles. "He's smart, but I'm confused. Is he coming back later? How could anyone even trace him in this city?"

Ronnie shook her head as our food arrived. "He's gone for good. The phones will work for two weeks. He texted that he's in a truck heading to Chicago. You each get five phones. One use only." She stopped and took a bite of pizza. "There's more. He left you three thousand dollars in hundred-dollar bills. That needs to last. He left us the name of a guy in the Garment District. If we need clothes, new backpacks—anything—we can talk to the guy and get good deals."

Kenzie popped a bocconcini in her mouth and chewed. "I'm worried."

Ronnie patted Kenzie's hand. "I know. So, here's the plan. I'm taking my daughters on the town. We're going shopping, hitting the sauna, getting ice cream, whatever. Tomorrow, we need to make sure you're both ready to test. Next week, you have your exams."

I excused myself and ran to the ladies room. I thought I was about to vomit, but I didn't. After returning, I had some root beer and tried to breathe. Kenzie gave me a look, then wrapped an arm around my waist.

There was little conversation after that, and we ate in silence—alone, with our thoughts. I was desperate to hold on to my emotions but, as we exited, I couldn't keep from crying. I leaned against a wall and slumped to the ground. The tears flooded out and my shoulders shook. Ronnie sat beside me and Kenzie stood lookout, waiting.

Ronnie kissed me on the cheek. "Hey. Hey, my little girl, I know. I understand. Vinnie had to do what he had to do. None of this makes sense. Just have faith that it'll all work out. It will."

I hugged Ronnie tight and sniffled. "Sorry. I should be tougher. Can we go to the beach?"

Kenzie hugged me, and we kissed. "Let's go ride the Wonder Wheel. We can come back this way, use the sauna, then catch a movie."

Ronnie smiled at us both. "Sounds like a plan."

Kenzie looked up at Ronnie. "I need something, though. Just like a pint of Beam, or something."

We found an old lady in the park who agreed to buy the pint if we bought her some wine. Kenzie poured the bourbon into a two liter of Coke. For once, I didn't care. I took sips, as well. It was that kind of afternoon.

Wonder Wheel in Coney Island is a giant eccentric Ferris wheel. Unlike a standard wheel with the seats attached to the rim, an eccentric wheel allowed certain seats to move between the rim and the hub. The giddy effects of the ride were indescribable. We rode three times.

After, Ronnie bought us ice cream. We wandered around the boardwalk, leaning on each other. There was a palpable depression in the air, and we couldn't shake it. I finally took one of my burner phones out and texted Vinnie.

I love you. You changed our lives. Please stay safe. I'll never forgive you. Love, Destiny. After hitting send I realized my Freudian slip. I sighed and texted again. I mean, I'll never forget you.

The phone pinged. I think you were right the first time, doll. I'm sorry. I wish things had been different. But, hey, if my grandmother had balls she'd be my grandfather.

I laughed at that last line. I broke open the phone and threw it away in several locations.

Afterward I hugged Ronnie and Kenzie. "I mistyped something. I meant to say I'd never forget him, but instead I said I'd never forgive him."

Ronnie gave me a sad, soft look. "It'll take time, for sure. He hurt us, even if he didn't mean to."

Kenzie finished the last of the spiked Coke. "Let's go back to the room. Maybe there's a decent movie on TV."

We caught the subway back and curled up together on the bed. A movie called No Highways to Heaven was just starting. It had Marlene Dietrich and James Stewart. We watched together as we sat on the bed. Ronnie sat between us, and we snuggled close. My mind kept drifting as the movie played. The feel of Ronnie stroking my hair, the warmth of her love, it helped; but, I couldn't shake the soul-wrenching sadness I felt about Vinnie.

After the movie, Ronnie returned home. Kenzie and I packed some gear and headed out to busk. On the way, Kenzie talked a lady into buying us a pint of Old Crow which we poured into a two-liter of Coke. She drank and watched me; I stuck to soft, sad songs and ballads which fit my mood. We still cleared $80.

Kenzie and I walked the avenues that night, stopping for burgers and fries twice. As the sun was coming up, we returned to the hotel and fell asleep holding each other. That afternoon, both of us woke up still feeling depressed. Kenzie looked across the way and saw one of the teenaged boys in his kitchen. She flashed her boobs at him, and he waved. Normally I would have been laughing, but I could only manage a half-hearted chuckle.

As I undressed, Kenzie found the last part of a bottle of gin in the mini-fridge and mixed it with some orange juice. I watched her, but bit my tongue. There was no need to make a big scene. We showered, had pastrami sandwiches at a deli, and caught the subway to meet Ronnie at the library.

Ronnie looked worn out. Her eyes were red and puffy, her hair held in a loose ponytail, and her clothes looked slept in. She had several stacks of paper and some booklets spread out on a table. She tried to give us a hearty smile, but her eyes betrayed her.

"Hey, girls. Good afternoon. I have everything ready for you to sign in order to take your tests next week. I had a friend of mine sign the parental release, just in case. But, they shouldn't ask for that because your ID's show that you're of age."

Kenzie didn't say a word; instead, she walked over and hugged Ronnie. I followed suit. We stood there together for ten minutes, just hugging. Ronnie's body shook, but she said nothing.

Finally, I broke the silence. "So we sign these papers and show up at the testing place?"

Ronnie nodded. "Exactly. I'll be there, too, but I'm not allowed to go in with either of you. You complete your tests in sections with a break between them."

Kenzie looked up at Ronnie. "I'm scared, Mom. What if we fail?"

Ronnie hugged her again. "Nothing to be scared of. You

know this stuff. You'll do fine. I promise."

And we did. After all the months of hard work and studying, the actual event was anticlimactic. The following week, we arrived at a public school at eight in the morning. The hallways reeked of dirty socks, cleaning solution, and something else I couldn't describe. It was like someone was cooking canned stew in a cheap shoe store after cleaning the place with Pine-Sol. I couldn't imagine dealing with that smell every day.

Ronnie had reviewed with us all week. In between sessions, I busked and slept. Kenzie drank. I was growing irritated, and my temper wanted to flare up; but, with the exams approaching, I felt like the timing was wrong for a discussion about Kenzie's behavior.

The classroom where the testing took place was full of cubicles. There was no sound except the scratching of pencils. I knew the material but, even so, my eyes burned after a while. There was a lot of writing and repetition. Kenzie had stuck to straight Coke, same as me, the night before and the effect was evident. During the breaks, she appeared pale and drawn. She barely spoke to me, and her hands shook.

Once we finished, Ronnie took us out for a late lunch. On the way, I stopped in a corner store. I had observed Vinnie removing items from grocery stores before, but I'd never done so myself. My very first time, I walked out with two cans of Steel Reserve down my pants. I handed them to Kenzie as we walked.

"Thank you!" Kenzie popped and chugged the first. "Damn, do I need this!"

I shook my head. "Unfortunately. Now you can act human again."

Kenzie scowled. "What the hell does that mean? Please don't start this shit with me."

Ronnie grabbed us both as we passed by a corner park. "Both of you, knock it off. Destiny Marie Wilbury, don't ever let me catch you shoplifting again. I didn't like Vinnie doing it, and I won't stand for you doing it. Mackenzie Elizabeth Guevara, you drink too much. I haven't said a lot about it, but it's true."

Kenzie and I looked at our feet and muttered apologies. After hugging us, Ronnie gave us each a sharp crack across the rear. For only being part of our life a short time, Vinnie left a massive void when he departed. The stress of the exams had been difficult, and Vinnie's absence hurt like a gut punch. That void would only grow worse as time went by.

Chapter 23

Two weeks after taking the exams, we received our results. Ronnie texted me and Kenzie to meet at the library. Kenzie was hungover. Her drinking had increased now that we had copious amounts of free time. I helped her sit up. "Hey, you need to take some aspirin and a cold shower. Mom wants us at the library. The results of our tests came."

Kenzie groaned. "I need a drink." She got undressed and walked into the bathroom. I sat to pray, hoping she'd ease up on her drinking now that we were officially done with our GEDs.

After she dressed, we caught the subway. On the way, we found someone and bought her a pint of beer to ease her nerves. As we approached the library, my heart jumped into my throat. Not only was Ronnie waiting, but so were Rory, Sheila, Jeanie, and Rainbow. That could only mean one thing.

Ronnie beamed. "Ladies and gentlemen, may I present the new high school graduates."

Kenzie and I shrieked loudly enough to be heard in Niagara Falls. "We did it! We made it! Woohoo! Yes! We kicked ass!"

Everyone hugged us, and we walked to an Italian restaurant for lunch. My mood was ebullient for the first time in weeks. Kenzie was positively beaming. For the first time since Vinnie had abandoned us, we were bouncing around, poking each other, and cracking jokes.

As the salads were served, Rory cleared his throat. "I'm proud of you both. I hope this means that college is your next stop. Our plans got pushed forward. We're heading to New Mexico in ten days. If you feel like trying for college there, we'd be happy to let you stay with us until you get settled."

Kenzie took a drink of San Benedetto water. "I'll think about it. I guess I'm happy for you guys, but I feel sad, too. I mean, Vinnie abandoned us, and now you guys are leaving."

Sheila shook her head and fed Rainbow some applesauce. "We heard about that. I'm sorry he took off, honey. But I don't condone his behavior. You both could have gotten in big time trouble. Ronnie, too."

Jeanie cut in. "He was a sweet guy, in his way. But, he was a hustler. You girls aren't stupid. You knew what he did was wrong, even if you didn't know about the drugs and white slavery."

I took a big gulp of water to keep myself from crying. I wound up belching loudly. "Excuse me." I giggled at the sound, even as my eyes burned with tears. "It hurts. I'm conflicted. I think we all are. But, dammit, FEBU means something. If it was anyone else—anyone other than us—I'd say fine. Throw the book at him. But, Vinnie protected me. He protected Kenzie. He'd have given up his life for any of us. Dammit, loyalty is only real when it gets tested."

Ronnie nodded at me. Kenzie raised her water. "Damn straight!"

Rory sighed. "I thought you were more intelligent, baby sister. I understand your point, and it might even be valid to a certain degree. I don't talk about it much, but I lost a few friends in Florida to opiates. They OD'd. I respect your feelings, but if Il-Cazzo was involved with dealing drugs or selling prostitutes, then he can go to hell."

Kenzie blanched and then took a deep breath. "We don't think he was dealing with the hookers. The drugs, OK, but only muling them. He was too classy to be dealing."

Sheila finished her salad as the waiter brought in manicotti, fresh bread, and more mineral water. "I agree that he had flair and charm. I liked him a lot. You and Destiny are our look-out, however. He put you at a serious risk, and that's not OK. I don't care how you justify it. Yes, FEBU means something, but loyalty cuts both ways. You can't put the people you love at risk and claim to be loyal to them."

I poked at my manicotti. "Can we drop this? Dammit, I love him. I love him no matter what. OK?"

Kenzie side hugged me. "So, should we apply to Harvard first or Yale?"

Everyone laughed and the mood lightened considerably. After lunch, we all strolled through the park. I whispered something to Kenzie.

She nodded and turned to Rory. "Hey, we have to clear out of our hotel in three days. Most of what we own we can carry or donate, but there are two giant teddy bears that Vinnie gave us for Christmas. Could you fit them into your van for Rainbow?"

Jeanie gave us an enormous grin. "Of course we can. We'll take you guys home. If you have any clothes we can stash, I have suitcase space."

We finished our stroll near a garage, and the seven of us squeezed into the van for a ride to Brooklyn. Kenzie and I sorted our gear and ended up packing three pairs of shoes and a bunch of clothes into two suitcases. We put them in the van with the teddy bears.

Jeanie hugged me and gave me a kiss. Kenzie was next. "You have a support system now. Don't forget that. You've survived situations that would make most people piss their jeans. There is no limit to what you both can do. Decide, and then go for it. You don't have to do it all alone, though."

Rory and Sheila hugged us and climbed into the van. As they drove away, Ronnie slung her arms around Kenzie and me. She took out one of her burner phones, and read aloud as she texted Daddy-O, our girls passed. We had a fancy lunch, and you were missed. No matter what, FEBU.

Her phone pinged three minutes later, and she read aloud, "Straight from the fridge. Of course, they passed. In Chicago with some new friends. Casino near here, and cards falling our way. Dice rolling the big scores. Heading west soon. V."

Kenzie and I sobbed, clinging as Ronnie continued to hold us. We stood on the sidewalk as waves of emotion crashed over us. We had won so much, lost so much, and none of it made sense to me. I was a jumble of anger, joy, and depression.

Ronnie spent the night with us. We rode to Rockaway beach and sat in the surf until the sun came up. After a pancake breakfast, she returned home and I took Kenzie to our room to sleep.

Chapter 24

Three days later, Kenzie and I checked out of the hotel by calling the front desk. Living once more on the streets and the subways was rough, and Kenzie's drinking increased. We had been spoiled by having a warm bed, regular access to a bathroom, and the other niceties of a home.

A month later, Ronnie left for college. Our send-off gathering was bittersweet. We'd known she was leaving and damned if she didn't deserve to go. She'd earned her freedom, and then some. The fact remained that she was our street-mom; no matter how you sliced it, we felt abandoned. Kenzie drank, and I grew increasingly irritated.

The final straw came the day after Ronnie left. Kenzie and I were sitting near Times Square. I was playing guitar and singing while Kenzie pulled on a spiked bottle of Dr. Pepper. I took a break and counted our earnings. "Kenzie, I love you. But, I can't keep doing this. All you do is stay drunk. I'm tired of it."

She glared at me. "So, what's your point? Everyone else in my shitty life abandoned me and hurt me, you may as well, too. You don't like being with me, then fuck you! Get lost! Go back to your fucking family. Just give me half the money, bitch!"

I stood and threw a wad of bills at her. "Fine. I'm gone. I can take care of myself. You can drink yourself to death and wallow in self-pity. You know what, you can go to hell, too."

As I stormed off, tears blinding me, I heard a wailing sob split the air. Kenzie rushed after, then grabbed my arm. "No! I'm sorry. Don't leave. I'll quit. I swear, I'll stop for you." She fell on the ground hugging my ankles, begging me.

I pulled her to her feet and let her sob on me. We collapsed against a wall and cried until we were hoarse. We threw away the rest of her booze and went see a movie, but I can't even recall what it was. We fell asleep in the dark, holding each other; we woke up as the credits rolled.

I'd hoped that by stopping drinking, our life would improve. Instead, we had a crisis on our hands that was out of control. The first day without alcohol, Kenzie was irritable. No matter what we did or where we went, she was on edge. By the second morning, she was vomiting up everything she ate and dry heaving afterwards. She had the hot and cold sweats and was twitching like Tigger on amphetamines. I couldn't watch her going through that, but I also refused to buy her liquor to stop it.

With no other choices that I could see, I walked Kenzie into the ER. We approached the admittance desk and a lady handed us a clipboard of papers. With her pinched face and severe bun, she looked as if she needed more fiber in her diet.

I tried to breathe and not sound frantic. I failed. "I'll fill these papers out, but my girlfriend needs help. She's really sick." Hot tears trickled own my face. "Please, help her."

And they helped her. I wasn't allowed to go back with her, at first. Instead, I filled out forms, praying desperately. At three in the afternoon—six hours after we arrived—a doctor approached me. He had a calming smile. "Destiny Wilbury?"

"Yes?"

"My name is Dr. Bromowitz. Mackenzie will be fine. However, we feel that it is imperative for her to be placed in a detox facility. If you wish to see her first, follow me."

I followed him through a set of double doors and down several hallways. Kenzie dozed on an examining table. She looked pale and drawn.

I leaned down and kissed her. "You're getting the help you need. I'll stay outside the building all week and wait for you."

Dr. Bromowitz chimed in. "I'm not certain you understand, miss. After detox, Ms. Guevara will need to be placed in a rehabilitation facility for ninety days."

My temples throbbed. "On whose dime? We can't afford that."

"There are scholarship programs and charities. We'll make it happen. I need you to fill out some more forms." Dr. Bromowitz handed me a thick stack of paper.

Kenzie moaned. "Destiny. Come here." I approached. "I love you. I don't tell you enough. You take care of you, now. I'm sorry. You saved my ass. FEBU."

I stroked her face as tears dribbled down my cheeks. "I won't leave you. I'll be waiting. You get better, and we'll be fine."

I left the room and found the cafeteria. Three hours, eight cups of coffee, and four bowls of tapioca later, I finished filling out forms. Most of the information was lies. The financial section was the only complete truth. We were broke. After turning in the forms and receiving the location of the detox, I exited the hospital and caught a D Train.

The sun was going down, but the weather was hot. I approached a building and sat against the exterior brick wall. I had my backpack and Kenzie's. I'd transferred her clothes—well, most of them—to a plastic bag at the hospital. I took my guitar from its case and tuned up. As I played "Always On My Mind," my chest heaved. The sobs I'd held in for hours exploded. I sang and wailed.

A few people walked by and put money in my case, but the area was empty compared to other sections of Manhattan. Sleep began to invade my mind, but I forced myself to remain awake. I played every sad song I knew. I sat alone for the first time.

Even after being kicked out, I'd met Rory, Sheila, and Jeanie. Then, I'd met Kenzie. I hadn't been completely on my own at any point. I was now and, as unsettling as that was, another feeling was interfering. I stood up fifteen hours later and packed my gear. None of this was fair. Not one damned thing. I wanted someone to pay for my pain.

I rode to Tompkins Houses in Brooklyn. The people sitting on the benches looked worn down and shabby. The entire area was seedy. I looked for any street family that might want a fight, but nothing appeared. I rode the A Train to Rockaway. I searched all day, but didn't find Contagion or his group. Nowhere allowed me the opportunity to fight, and I wanted to hurt someone. Sleep came in spurts, and nightmares woke me again.

Three days later, I caught a subway and walked twenty blocks to ACP and 127th. I spotted someone I vaguely recognized. I wasn't sure at first, but it was one of the girls who belonged to Valiant's street family. She was pregnant with stringy, matted, red hair, and deadened eyes. I approached her.

My shoulders squared and my mouth tightened as I set my gear against a wall and clenched my fists. "Pixie. That's what they call you, isn't it? Where's the rest of them?" I sneered.

She looked up, a small scar creasing the bridge of her nose where it had been broken and reset. "Ah, shit. Go away, bitch. Just keep walking, I don't need this."

"Valiant around? I figured I'd give him a chance to settle the score." A sense of calm came over me. I wanted a fight and finally might get one.

Pixie looked up at me from where she sat against an apartment building. "I don't know. They courted me out. Weed wants to kill me." Her face was a stone mask, but the words were soft and resigned.

I scowled. "Hold up. When was this?"

Pixie shrugged. "Clay got me pregnant. That's Valiant's real name. Wanda, Weed, wasn't available, and that asshole wanted some. So he picked me. She says I was stupid to get knocked up."

I tried to process the information. Was this a set up? Pixie was a mile away from their turf, and how could they know I'd be at this spot. I'd chosen the neighborhood at random. So it was straight. Inside my head, I heard Vinnie's voice. You always help the underdog, always. Make your enemy a friend.

I made a decision. "Just forget the past. You need help. I'm heading to my gym and they have showers there. I'll buy you breakfast." I put my hand out and helped her stand. "I have a spare pair of jeans and a sweatshirt you can have after your shower."

Pixie's eyes traveled down my body and then back again. "Why are you doing this? I don't need your pity."

Sure she did. "Fine. Stay here. I don't care." I started walking, and she followed me.

We walked down the staircase of a station, and I purchased our cards. After a short ride on the D Train, we exited and climbed back to the street. I was adjusting my gear when Valiant and his crew approached.

Valiant stepped up. "Well, look who it is. Where's your army, bitch?"

I set my gear behind me. "It's just me. Me and my new street-daughter. Your brood of excremental mutts kicked her to the curb, so I'm taking her."

Weed approached. "Over my dead body. I have business with her."

I smiled. "It will be over your dead body this time, Wanda! On the other hand, if Clay here wants to slap a leash on you I have a better idea. Spare yourself the embarrassment and lose one member. You don't want her, anyway. I do."

Valiant nodded. "Deal. But stay off of our street. Both of you. Or I swear I'll kill you." He shoved Weed toward the rest of his family.

"You'll try." I took Pixie by the arm and we walked two blocks before catching a cab that dropped off near another station. We caught the subway and walked three blocks to the fitness center.

"So you own me now?" Pixie looked uncertain.

"You own yourself. I'm just helping you out. Now get undressed and have a shower, you stink. I need to text some people."

While Pixie cleaned up, I used my last burner phone to text Vinnie. Then I used my regular phone to text Ronnie, Rory, Sheila, and Jeanie. I was in the middle of that when Pixie emerged, naked and dripping.

I pointed at the shower. "Back in and rewash your hair. Then scrub up again."

Pixie looked at me. "What for? I'm clean."

I stood and glared. "I said so. Do it."

Pixie's eyes widened and her mouth opened. "Fine. No need to get pissed."

I finished texting and handed Pixie some towels. She put on her panties and tried on my extra jeans and a t-shirt. It was a near perfect fit. I put an arm around Pixie's shoulder. "We need lunch, and then we have an appointment."

Pixie shrugged away. "An appointment? Where we going?"

"You're going over my knee if you don't listen up. No questions. You do as I say. Got it?"

Pixie nodded. "Yes, Mom. You sure are different than Weed. How many kids you got?"

"Just you." I led her out, and we caught a subway to a corner cafe.

After a lunch of cheeseburgers, fries, soda, milkshakes, and more fries, we caught the F Train to Brooklyn. I hadn't been to church in two weeks. Pixie and I entered the building and walked to the pastor's office.

Pastor Affenhoden gave me a hug. "Sister Destiny. Long time no see. I was sorry to hear about Sister Mackenzie. Who is your friend?"

Pixie turned and replied, "They call me Pixie. My real name's Lynette. What's this about?"

Pastor Affenhoden motioned us to chairs. "Sister Destiny texted that you are in the family way, Lynette. I know a female congregant who assists young ladies such as yourself. Either in returning home, or in finding resources. She has a large house, and you are welcome to stay with her while you figure out your situation. You would be safe from those wishing to hurt you."

Pixie looked at me. "You're something else. I tried to kill you twice and you buy me lunch and set me up with a place to stay? I don't get you."

I laughed. "One day you might understand if you stick around this church and read the Gospels."

An older lady entered, dressed in a light blue pants suit and flats. She had bluish-silver hair, and I recognized her from the choir. She asked Pixie to join her in another room.

After they left, Pastor Affenhoden looked at me for a long while. Finally, he spoke. "I appreciate you bringing her in. I truly am sorry about Sister Mackenzie. Had I known sooner, I could have helped. I suspect you didn't know either."

I shook my head. "I assumed she could stop if she wanted to. I tried to stop her. I mean, I really tried. But, I couldn't. Dammit to Hell, I swear I tried!" I began sobbing.

Pastor Affenhoden passed me a box of tissues and poured me some water from a pitcher. "Have I helped you and Sister Mackenzie enough to ask a favor of you?"

I sipped water and composed myself. "Sure you have. Ronnie too. Even Vinnie, although that's another crazy situation."

The pastor paused before speaking again. "I want to ask you to attend a recovery meeting tonight at another church. Just introduce yourself and listen. Only share if you feel led to do so."

"A meeting? I'm not the one with a drinking problem." I finished my water.

"No, you aren't," Pastor Affenhoden said, refilling my glass. "This is Al-Anon. For family and friends of alcoholics."

I agreed to attend. After checking on Pixie, I left the church. I took the subway to the Theater District and played guitar. I made $60 before heading to the meeting.

Chapter 25

I hadn't been at a recovery meeting since the ones I attended with Vinnie. This meeting was different, smaller, and with less palpable angst. That was fine by me; I had angst enough for all twenty-three attendees.

The other difference was the meeting format and attendees. I hadn't known that meetings like that had a variety of formats. Speaker meetings draw the largest crowds and, for that reason, Vinnie had preferred those. Furthermore, he had chosen meetings where those attending had plenty of wealth. In this current meeting, the attendees were dressed nicely enough, but no one looked extremely well-to-do.

I filled a Styrofoam coffee cup from the urn, grabbed a plate of cookies, and sat down at a large table, just as a gray-haired lady in elastic-waistband jeans and a yellow t-shirt rang a bell. "Hello, my name is Farina. We welcome you to the 'Not All There' Al-Anon Group."

She made some announcements about not smoking and read from some group literature. The main theme of the reading was that newcomers were not alone in their struggles. My stomach tightened as I listened. Tears fell down my cheeks, and someone handed me some Kleenex.

"Do we have any newcomers with us who wish to be recognized?"

I raised my hand. "My name's Destiny. I'm new. My pastor suggested this meeting."

The group clapped. "Welcome, Destiny. You're in the right place."

Farina continued her spiel. "As a newcomer you may feel that you are here tonight for the alcoholic, that your presence here may teach you how to stop his or her drinking. The truth is, you are here because of the alcoholic. You will soon learn you did not cause the alcoholic to drink, you cannot control the drinking, nor can you cure the alcoholic. You are here for yourself. You, and you alone, are responsible for dealing with your own pain. This is your program. It is your recovery from the effects of the disease of alcoholism.

"You will find love, understanding, and a lot of hope from this and other groups. The people around you tonight are experiencing the same varying degrees of hurt, anger, and anxiety that you are experiencing. We in Al-Anon share our experiences because it helps us to focus on ourselves and our recovery."

The tears began anew. I tried to stop crying, but the more I tried the less I succeeded. A younger lady raised her hand.

"My name is Ellen, and I'd like to welcome Destiny. It's normal and natural to cry and feel your emotions. We've all been there. I'm just realizing how necessary tears are. My alcoholic took three years last night, and I take three next week." The group applauded. "It wasn't easy in the beginning. I was used to controlling everything. I had been in charge for years because he couldn't be. It took time and effort to change. But, it is possible."

For the next hour, other members shared their experiences. I began to see a pattern; moreover, I noticed a direct connection between my life before I was kicked out and the new life I'd built. At the end of the meeting, Farina closed with another spiel. The group recited The Lord's Prayer, and the meeting concluded. I was leaning against a wall, nibbling cookies, when Ellen approached me.

"Hi, welcome. I don't mean to be forward, but if you want to get some coffee or some dinner, perhaps we can talk awhile."

I blushed. Ellen was about my height, with long black hair and a hook nose. She wore jeans and a tank top. Her arms were well-defined and muscular. "Sure. But, I'm spoken for."

Ellen threw back her head and laughed heartily. "I'm not asking you on a date."

We walked to a deli and ordered coffee and club sandwiches. Ellen looked at me long enough that I felt uncomfortable.

I shivered. "Yes? You keep staring at me."

Ellen shook her head. "Sorry, I'm trying to decide how to start. In both AA and Al-Anon, it's recommended to find a sponsor to walk you through the steps. I'm offering to do that for you, if you'd like."

I chewed, considering her offer. I sent up a silent prayer. "OK. I guess."

"Also, where do you live around here?"

I paused. "I don't. I'm homeless. I play music and get a room sometimes."

Ellen smiled. "I thought I recognized you from somewhere. Two months ago you were playing guitar on Broadway when my husband and I went to see The Lion King."

"Small world. The other chick you saw is in detox. She's my girlfriend."

She nodded. "You blame yourself for not stopping her before it got that bad?"

I sighed. "Yeah. I mean, I could have done something. I love her. I should have..."

Ellen cut me off. "No! Let's start right there. You couldn't do anything. That's not in your control and never will be. It's conceited to think that we can cure others or stop their behavior, conceited and self-important. That's not your job."

I blinked back tears. "Sorry. I love Kenzie, and I'd do anything for her."

Ellen looked at me for a while. "I totally understand. It doesn't change the fact that we're humans and that isn't in our control."

We ordered pie and talked until ten that night. Ellen texted her husband and offered me a couch to sleep on. I accepted.

The following morning, we continued talking. The more I talked to Ellen, the more I saw that not only did I blame myself for Kenzie, I blamed myself for not helping Vinnie; for not doing more for Pixie and the other street kids I'd met. I expected myself to save the world. The reasons were complicated, but my feelings of guilt remained.

As we ate croissant and drank coffee, Ellen talked with me. "Girl, you're tough. From everything you describe, both you and your girlfriend are extremely tough. Do you know what mental toughness really is, though?"

"It's about surviving no matter what. It's about not letting others beat you."

"That's true, but mental toughness is also the ability to accept the fact that you're human, and that you will make mistakes." She paused to sip her coffee. "You'll make lots of them. Some of them will hurt the people that you love. You should have the guts to accept the fact that you aren't perfect. Knowing that, you don't let your mistakes crush you and keep you from doing the very best that you can."

"I don't care if I'm perfect, Ellen. I just want Kenzie to be all better."

She shook her head. "Tough shit. She won't be. If she puts in the effort, she can have a happy life. She won't be all better. That's not how this disease works. You can accept that or not, but it's a fact."

Over the next three months, I attended three or four Al-Anon meetings a day. In between I met with Ellen, read in the library, and played guitar. The money I made added up, and most meetings had food and coffee. I slept on the subways, cat-napped in the back of speakers' meetings, and couch-surfed when given the chance. Every day, I used the showers and steam room at the fitness center, and from time to time switched out clothes or bought some FOT items.

As October approached, I made plans for Kenzie's return. I was scared, but I had hope that we might find a path forward that was healthy. At least, I needed to try.

Sitting on the sand of Rockaway Beach in the dank night air, a week before Kenzie's return date, I tried to formulate a plan. I wondered how Vinnie would've handled such matters. Damn him, anyway! He always knew what to do. I had such affection for him, but such anger.

Chapter 26

I paid three hundred dollars for a hotel room in Brooklyn. The hotel was plush, the room upscale. I sent the location to Kenzie at her rehab. The day of her release I stood in the lobby, pacing while looking at my watch every three minutes. After a while, a van pulled up from the rehab center.

The woman who stepped out wasn't a little girl anymore. She had grown two inches and bulked up—not fat, but she was solid. Kenzie now had hair hanging to her shoulders and pulled back in a sloppy ponytail. She stopped short for a moment, ran over, and grabbed me. We kissed and hugged, trying to speak through the tears. Words didn't come, but the hugging spoke volumes. I led her to the elevator, and we rode to the eighth floor. We hugged some more and gazed at each other. I had a six pack of ginger ale and filled two glasses with ice.

"I've missed you." Tears filled my eyes.

"I missed you so much. Here," Kenzie handed me a stack of folded paper. "I wrote you love letters every day."

I sat in the corner chair and Kenzie sat on my lap. I grunted. "You gained weight, sweetie."

"Sorry, I wasn't thinking." She moved and sat on the bed. I moved to sit beside her. "Pretty much all there was to do the last twelve weeks was eat, attend meetings, eat, work out in a gym, eat, talk to a therapist, eat, sleep—oh yeah, and eat."

I giggled. "I'm glad you did all that eating, you look outstanding. You're not rail-thin anymore."

She pouted. "You didn't think I was pretty before?"

I giggled more. "Sure you were, but what could I compare it to? You look better."

Kenzie kissed me and ran a hand over my belly and breasts. "You've been eating too, apparently. You look bothered. Everything OK?"

I lifted Kenzie's arms and took off her t-shirt. "I'm good. I've been going to meetings, myself. Four a day, most days. There's usually food at them, and I eat my fill. So much has happened."

Kenzie helped me take off my t-shirt. "You attend meetings? Like Vinnie did?"

We took off our pants and snuggled. "No, not like that. Pastor Affenhoden suggested I try Al-Anon. I like it. I took this girl, Pixie, to see him and afterward he suggested the meetings."

Kenzie kissed my neck. "Pixie? Like, that little skank who hangs out with that douchebag Valiant?"

I returned the kiss. "Same girl, but not quite how you remember her." I filled her in on the details.

Kenzie's mouth turned up at the edges, but her eyes looked sad. "So, like Vinnie always told us, make your enemy a friend. Damn, I miss him."

We laid there snuggling for a while. I looked over at her. "So you're cured now?"

"No. I won't ever be cured. I'm good for today. One day at a time. There's a lot more I need, too. You can't help with that."

I smiled. "Glad to hear you say that. I agree, we both need help, and we're too close to the problems to help each other. Plus, we aren't doctors."

She paused and looked out the window. I waited. "There's two things I have to tell you. Well, one to tell and one to ask."

I nodded. "Go on."

"My roommate in rehab was this girl who was our age named Caterina LaFica. We talked a lot, and she helped me realize some things." Kenzie stood and moved closer to the window.

I stood beside her. "What sort of things?"

She sighed. "Vinnie, for all I love his grifting ass, wasn't good for us. Ronnie was, but she needs freedom from responsibilities. Asking her to be our mom again isn't fair. It isn't what we need, either. We don't need a mom or a dad. We need something more...well, more adult."

A thought dawned on me. "So what are you saying?"

Kenzie smiled at me. "Do we have enough money to get to New Mexico? I was thinking we could visit. You know, see what's what."

I hugged her until she squeaked. "More than enough. I'll tuck you in for a nap and be back in about six hours. Here's forty in case you need a pizza or something."

I tucked her in and rode to Hell's Kitchen. After making contact with a guy that Vinnie knew, I sold my guitar. I could buy another one. I also purchased jeans, shirts, new backpacks, new boots, and—as a tribute to Vinnie—mirrored sunglasses for me and Kenzie. Following that, I purchased Greyhound tickets for a four in the morning departure. I used a bundle of coupons and stocked up on soda, cookies, snack foods, and toiletries.

When I returned, Kenzie was still asleep. I woke her and held her. It felt terrific with her head resting against me once more.

We left the next morning and headed south by southwest. The trip itself could've been a story, and one day we'll tell it. A week later, the news reported that a Hurricane named Sandy was ravaging New York City. I looked toward Heaven and smiled softly.

* * *

What? You were expecting a happily-ever-after ending? Kenzie and I are still alive, so that hasn't happened yet. Life doesn't work that way.

Ronnie texted us the other day that she was accepted to a master's program in California for teaching English literature. It isn't so far that we can't drive there to visit.

Rory and Sheila are married, and Rainbow is in first grade. Jeanie is with them still and—although it's financially complicated—they make things work. One day, I hope our nation will accept plural relationships among consenting adults.

As for Vinnie, he sent us a letter after tracking me down through Pastor Affenhoden. We text now every few days. He's living in Nebraska—ranching sheep, of all things. He found his long-lost love in Washington, and they moved. He's sober and on probation for assault. He was caught up in a rally, protesting the current occupant of the White House. Some white-power creep took a swing, and Vinnie fought back. I'm not shocked. A bit sad, but not shocked. He has his own story to write, and it's a doozy.

Kenzie and I used what we learned about survival to get through school. It took extra time due to a need for remedial classes, but we graduated from college with honors. I'm still busking and studying music. Kenzie and I manage a crowdfunding site that helps homeless kids stay afloat while they figure out the future. As Vinnie always said, pass along the help and largesse to others.

One more thing, I sent a postcard to my parents. It read, I love you. Whatever your beliefs, I love you, and I wish you all the best. Your daughter, Destiny.

Kenzie just finished filling out her intake forms for law school. We're heading to my slide-guitar lesson. After that is a meeting and dinner. Life goes on, after all.

Branca was right, the writing helped.

Printed in Great Britain
by Amazon